SEASON
of SNOWS
and SINS

THE HENRY TIBBETT MYSTERIES
BY PATRICIA MOYES

A Six-Letter Word for Death
Angel Death
Who Is Simon Warwick? ✓
The Coconut Killings ✓
Black Widower ✓
The Curious Affair of the Third Dog ✓
Season of Snows and Sins ✓
Many Deadly Returns
Death and the Dutch Uncle ✓
Murder Fantastical
Johnny Underground ✓
Murder by 3's (including *Down Among the Dead Men,*
Dead Men Don't Ski, and *Falling Star*) ✓
Falling Star ✓
Murder à la Mode ✓
Death on the Agenda ✓
Down Among the Dead Men
Dead Men Don't Ski ✓

SEASON
of SNOWS
and SINS

Patricia Moyes

An Owl Book

HOLT, RINEHART and WINSTON
New York

Published by Holt, Rinehart and Winston,
383 Madison Avenue, New York, New York 10017.

Library of Congress Cataloging in Publication Data
Moyes, Patricia.
Season of snows and sins.
(An Inspector Henry Tibbett mystery)
"An Owl book."
I. Title.   II. Series: Moyes, Patricia.   Inspector
Henry Tibbett mystery.
[PR6063.09S35   1983]   823'.914   82-23258
ISBN 0-03-063542-X (pbk.)

First published in hardcover by Holt, Rinehart and Winston in 1971
First Owl Book Edition—1983
Designer: Nancy Tausek
Printed in the United States of America
1 3 5 7 9 10 8 6 4 2

ISBN 0-03-063542-X

For winter's rains and ruins are over,
And all the season of snows and sins;
The days dividing lover from lover,
The light that loses, the night that wins;
And time remembered is grief forgotten,
And frosts are slain and flowers begotten,
And in green underwood and cover
Blossom by blossom the spring begins.

—A. C. Swinburne. *Atalanta in Calydon*

JANE

1

Though I say it myself, it was the wedding of the year in Montarraz. Robert Drivaz's wedding to Anne-Marie Durey, I mean. This may seem rather strange to you, if you happen to remember all that fuss in the papers in January when Giselle Arnay, the French film star, celebrated her runaway marriage to the pop singer Michel Veron, in her "Swiss mountain hideout." So secret were the preparations for Mlle. Arnay's third excursion into matrimony that, several days ahead of the event, Montarraz was invaded by a small army of journalists, television interviewers, gossip writers, show-biz columnists, fashion experts, and all the rest of the circus—all fighting for rooms in the already full hotels, swarming over the *après-ski* cafés and nightclubs, and generally making life hideous. But that was different. That was during the season. Arnay and Veron were visitors. The world might make a nine-day wonder of their nuptials, but Montarraz did not.

By contrast, Robert Drivaz—son of the widow Drivaz from the grocery—married Anne-Marie Durey at the end of April, when the last of the visitors had departed, and the people of Montarraz were settling down thankfully to count their takings from a bumper winter season and to resume their own private lives for a while.

Giselle Arnay was married in the *hôtel de ville*, wearing an ankle-length ermine coat, black patent-leather thigh boots, huge dark

3

glasses, and a diamond ring the size of a walnut. Anne-Marie was married in the little Roman Catholic chapel on the mountainside, wearing a white cotton dress which she had made herself, and a veil held in place by a circlet of artificial orange blossoms. She carried a small bouquet of gentian which Robert himself had gathered that morning from the meadows below the village.

Robert Drivaz looked bronzed and improbably handsome, if a little awkward, in his best blue suit—which was rather too small for him—and when he led Anne-Marie down the aisle from the altar, everybody cried. Michel Veron at his wedding looked haggard and pale—what you could see of him, that is, behind dark glasses even larger than his bride's—his shoulder-length hair sprawled untidily over the collar of his fringed suede topcoat, and nobody cried. The only thing which the two weddings had in common was that both were well-attended, and large quantities of alcohol were consumed afterward.

At this stage, I should perhaps explain how it came about that I, Jane Weston, was the only foreigner present at Anne-Marie's wedding—and, indeed, what I was doing at all in the village of Montarraz, high up in the mountains in the Swiss canton of Valais. In fact, I had better introduce myself. I'll be as brief as I can.

I am English, and at the time when this story begins I was forty-seven years old, and had been a widow for six months. My husband had left me a modest but adequate income, which I supplemented when I could by selling my work, being a sculptor by profession.

Left alone, I had no desire to stay in England. On the contrary, I longed to cut the ties which had now become painful—the lopsided friendships with other couples, the consciousness of the empty place at the dinner table, the unspoken "poor Jane" in other people's eyes. I wanted to make a new life and new friends, to turn the page definitively, not to live in the past. I also loved high places and spoke good French; so I did not hesitate when Meriel Blunt, the portrait painter, offered me the indefinite use of a small chalet in Montarraz.

"It sounds marvelous," I said.

Meriel made a face. "It's not," she said. "It's pure hell, and I don't want you to be under any illusions about it. It's utterly primi-

4

tive—one cold tap and a coke stove. Charlie inherited it from an obscure uncle who used to spend his time climbing mountains and collecting alpine flora. In his day, it must have been picturesque, even if uncomfortable—Montarraz was just a tiny village, with a few cows and a church. Now . . ." She shrugged expressively. "At the latest count, there were thirty hotels, three télécabines, six nightclubs, and about a hundred apartment blocks of varying hideousness. One is actually being built right in front of the chalet, which will completely block the view which was the one compensation. The only reason we haven't sold the place is that Charlie says land values are rocketing, and he's determined to hang on until some millionaire pays him a fortune in Swiss francs for the privilege of knocking down the horrid little house and building an even more horrid concrete box on the site. So sordid." Charlie, Meriel's husband, was a successful businessman.

"I don't care what it's like," I said. "I shall love it."

"I think you're mad," said Meriel, "but if you're determined to move to Switzerland, at least it'll be a roof over your head until you find somewhere better."

And so, after many formalities, I established myself as an official resident of the Valais, and moved to Montarraz—the only non-Swiss, as far as I could make out, who proposed to live all the year round in the village. Every winter, just before Christmas, the polyglot avalanche of winter sportsmen began to arrive. Until the end of March, the village glittered and quivered and burst at the seams under the relentless pressure of a lot of money chasing a good time. Then, in April, the tide retreated just as abruptly, and sweet peace flowed back up the valley. Hotels shut their doors while the proprietors took a well-earned holiday, and only a few *pensions* remained open to accommodate the handful of earnest middle-aged Germans and English who tramped the mountains in leather shorts or sensible tweeds in search of wildflowers.

In August a brief, strange summer season burst into bloom. Cut-price-tour operators propelled a spate of cut-price tourists into the "special-summer-rate" hotel rooms (for all but the most eccentric of wealthy holiday-makers head for the sea in summer). Many of these

5

visitors were English, and the terrace cafés, which abounded in sables and vicuña in February, now found themselves entertaining braces, shirt sleeves, floral cottons, and useful cardigans. Whereas winter visitors tended to come back to Montarraz year after year, we seldom saw the same faces two summers running.

"We'll save up for Spain next year, Arthur. I mean, there's nothing to *do* here, is there? Just walk, I mean. See this card Mabel and Ron sent from Majorca? Now, *that*'s more my idea of a holiday."

"At least it's cheap here, Doris."

"Cheap, is it? Oh, the inclusive is cheap, that I do grant you. But do you know what they charged me for a small gin and orange in that bar up the mountain? Robbery, I call it, *and* I told them so. Mabel says drinks are ever so cheap in Majorca. . . ."

So September comes, the summer migrants fly away home, grumbling, and the best time of the year begins. The deciduous trees turn the mountainsides into blazing gold, the sun shines in a fresh blue sky, the first new snow falls on the high peaks, and the village becomes a village again, for those short months until the Christmas invasion.

I moved into the tiny chalet called Les Sapins at the end of September, and this in itself was enough to make me an object of extreme curiosity. Curiosity—but not, at first, friendliness. The Valaisans are a small, dark, secret people. There is no malice in them, but they do not squander their precious friendship. The quick-smiling enthusiasm with which they greet winter tourists is deceptive. It is a form of extreme good manners, which should not be mistaken for an invitation to intimacy.

I was not a winter visitor. I had arrived, apparently on a permanent footing, just as the village was gathering itself to itself for its annual spell of privacy. It was silly of me to feel depressed and lonely, because everybody was kind and correct, and I had no right to expect any more of them. And yet . . .

For a start, Meriel had been quite right about Les Sapins. From the outside, as I drove up in my ancient little car, it looked enchanting—an illustration from a Christmas calendar. Built of dark wood on little stilts, beneath which winter firewood was neatly stacked, its small windows peeped out from under steep, carved eaves, and the front door was flanked by two small wooden balconies. Inside, however, things were undeniably bleak.

There were four tiny rooms opening onto a narrow hall, in which a large black stove glared at me in cold menace. One of the rooms contained the single cold tap, and this was the combined kitchen-bathroom—that is to say, there was a sink under the tap, and a tin bath with an outlet pipe. My old cooking stove, connected to a bottle of liquid gas, completed the modern conveniences. The lavatory was of the kind known as a chemical closet, and stood in a lean-to shed outside the back door. All the rooms were very dark, and oil lamps provided the only artificial light. The sole concession to modernity was the telephone.

My first, horrified thought was, "Where am I going to work?" Meriel had talked gaily of a studio in the garden, but the inside of the house had lowered my spirits to such an extent that I could not believe the *dépendance* would be anything but a windowless hovel. Fortunately, I was wrong.

Les Sapins stood in its own half-acre of land—the plot from which Meriel's Charlie hoped to reap such rich rewards. The pine trees which had given the chalet its name had now disappeared, and—as I had been warned—a breeze-block construction was rising to a height of four stories right opposite the front door, on the downhill side of the private track which led down from the main road. The superb view over the Rhône valley, which Les Sapins had once enjoyed, was now the prerogative of the south-facing windows of this new block, while all I could look forward to was a panorama of the building's north-facing main entrance and car park. Farther along the track, on the same level as Les Sapins, was another chalet of about the same size, but in rather better repair. What I had not realized at first sight was that the steep meadow between the two chalets was all part of my domain, and only when I explored it did I see the long, low building standing among the apple and cherry trees, nearer to the other chalet than to mine.

By the look of it, it had once been a stone-built cowshed, but Charlie's uncle had renovated it, presumably for use as a garage. He

7

had concreted the floor, reglazed the windows, and installed a stove similar to the one in the house. Most important of all, he had fitted a big pair of stable doors on the southern side, through which, when I dragged them open, the bright mountain sunshine flooded; and, as an additional bonus, the view from here was not blocked by the new building. So I had space to work, with light and heat. I was overjoyed. It even made up for the lavatory.

As I said, the going was fairly sticky at first. I made the acquaintance of Mme. Drivaz, with her plump friendly smile and calculating little eyes, who presided over the grocery in the main street; of Mlle. Simonet, the stout, monosyllabic spinster who ran the bakery; of M. Frey from the dairy. M. Monnet, the wizened little carpenter, came to make me a workbench for the studio, and M. Brasseur delivered a load of coal for the winter. But wherever I went, I seemed always to be giving out information, never receiving it. Always answering questions, never asking them. Very soon, everyone in the village must have known all about me, but I felt that I knew nothing about them. I was an outsider, isolated. The breakthrough began with Anne-Marie.

As soon as I had settled into Les Sapins, I decided to get down to some work. I was lucky in that I had a definite commission to work on—oh, nothing very grand, but a good incentive. A wealthy stockbroker friend of my late husband's had asked me to do a small sculpture to put in his Chelsea garden. Neither he nor his wife was particularly artistic, as they cheerfully admitted, and they gave me a free hand. Just something about three feet high that would look good on the pedestal under the trellis arch which mercifully obscured their view of Lot's Road power station.

I had intended to do them one of the abstract forms with which I had been experimenting; but somehow it would not come right. I made sketches and models, and only succeeded in producing lifeless shapes, like exercises in proportion. It took quite some time to dawn on me that what I was really hankering for was to step backward to the realism which I thought I had left behind forever. In my isolation, I longed to create a human form, to people my small world. Well, the stockbroker and his wife would probably prefer a conventional nymph in their garden to an elongated sphere with a hole in it. The only trouble was that I would need a model.

The Café de la Source was just about the only restaurant which stayed open all the year round, and so, inevitably, it was there that I went on the rare occasions when I treated myself to a break from my own cooking. It was small, unpretentious, and scrupulously clean, with a typically alpine paneled interior and red gingham tablecloths, and it was much patronized by the local people. It was owned by a large, genial man by the name of Bertrand, who presided over the bar, and his small, energetic wife, who was a good plain cook. I must have been aware of the fact that they also had a young girl to help them, but quite honestly I had never noticed her —until that particular October evening when I finally tore up my last sketch for an abstract form and decided to go down to the Source for steak and fried potatoes.

It so happened that the café was busier than usual. M. Bienne, the local house agent, was entertaining a couple who were obviously important clients—a big, smooth, smiling man in a beautifully cut suit, and a small, gently pretty woman in cashmere and mink. From their accents, I guessed that they came from Paris, and were almost certainly negotiating to buy one of the new chalets or apartments which were mushrooming all over the village.

There was also a large party of soldiers—or rather, of young men temporarily in uniform, doing their annual military service in the region—as well as the usual smattering of local people. The Bertrands had their hands full, and so, for once, it was not Mme. Bertrand who bustled up to take my order, but the young servant girl. And so I took a proper look at Anne-Marie for the first time.

She was shy and awkward, and obviously overawed at her promotion from washing-up and clearing-away to actually waiting at table. Her golden hair was drawn harshly away from her face and screwed into an ugly bun on the crown of her head, her hands were large and reddened by hot water, and her nose was shining with sweat. Nevertheless, she was unquenchably lovely. Nothing could spoil the perfect line of her jaw, her wide cheekbones and pointed chin, her little straight nose and long, slender neck. She wiped her hands on her apron, thrust the well-worn menu card under my nose, and said, *"Madame désire?"*

I ordered my steak and chips, and then said, "What's your name?"

She blushed violently. "Anne-Marie, madame."

"Have you been working here long?"

"Six months, madame."

"Do you enjoy it?"

She said nothing, tongue-tied with embarrassment. Then Mme. Bertrand called her sharply, and the girl turned and ran clumsily around the bar and through the swing door that led to the kitchen.

The next day I went back to the Café de la Source at eleven o'clock in the morning, when I knew things would be quiet. As I had hoped, there was no sign of the Bertrands—only Anne-Marie polishing glasses behind the bar. I sat down on a bar stool and ordered a coffee. Then I said, "Do you know who I am, Anne-Marie?"

She reddened, and shook her head.

"I'm sure you do," I said. "I'm the Englishwoman who lives at Les Sapins."

Anne-Marie nodded silently.

"I don't just live there," I went on. "I work there, too."

"Work?" She looked up, surprised.

"Yes. Making statues. I'm a sculptor, you see."

"Oh." She looked disappointed. "I thought you meant *work*."

"I'm making a statue of a girl just now," I said, undeterred by this snub. "I'm doing it specially for a lady and gentleman in London."

"Yes, madame." Anne-Marie's interest had reached vanishing point.

I said, "The trouble is, I need a model."

"A model, madame?"

"A real girl for me to copy. A girl like you."

"Like me?" She sounded intrigued.

"Yes," I said. "I was wondering if you would come and sit for me sometimes, when you're off duty. I'd pay you, of course."

"Pay me?" No doubt about the interest now. "How much?"

How much? I had no idea of the going rate, but neither had Anne-Marie. "Three francs an hour," I said.

"When can I come?"

"Now, look," I said, "I think you should ask your parents first. I wouldn't want to—"

"When can I come?"

"How old are you, Anne-Marie?"

"Eighteen. When can I come?"

"Not until you've spoken to your mother."

"I haven't got a mother." She turned away, bitterly disappointed. "Why do I need a mother to get three francs an hour for sitting down?"

"Well, you must have some family . . . someone who looks after you."

She shrugged. "Only Mme. Bertrand. I live here, in the café. I have a little room right up at the top of the house. I've lived here ever since I came from the orphanage."

In the end, I insisted on consulting Mme. Bertrand, much against Anne-Marie's will. She was evidently terrified that her employer would somehow contrive to prevent her from laying hands on what she considered a small fortune. However, she need not have worried. Mme. Bertrand was supremely uninterested in what Anne-Marie did, so long as she did it in her own time. The girl had been sent to her, she said, by the good Sisters who ran the orphanage in the valley. The child had been found abandoned as a baby, and the Sisters had picked her a name—Durey—at random from the telephone book. Mme. Bertrand had given her a job and a roof over her head, purely out of kindness. The girl was willing enough, but quite untrained in café work. She (Mme. Bertrand) hoped I would not spoil her. She had one afternoon off a week, and two hours each day, either midmorning or midafternoon, and I was welcome to her, so long as she was not late back for work.

And so, that afternoon, Anne-Marie turned up at Les Sapins, and together we lit the stove in the studio and set to work. I persuaded her to unpin her hair and let me comb it so that it fell in a soft, golden bell around her face, and to exchange her unbecoming blouse and skirt for an old blue silk sari—a faithful "prop" of mine —which I managed to coax into some interesting folds. Then she perched happily on a wooden stool, and chattered like a little bird while I modeled her head in clay.

I am almost sure—although now I cannot be quite certain—that it was on that first afternoon that I noticed M. Bienne, the house agent, picking his way gingerly among the planks and bricks and cement bags which littered the new building, accompanied by the couple with whom he had been dining at the Source. They were carrying colored brochures and architect's plans, and it was clear that they were prospecting the site with the possible idea of buying one of the apartments. Anne-Marie recognized them at once.

"Oh, look," she said. I was taking a short rest and a cigarette, so I looked. "There's the lady and gentleman who were in the café with M. Bienne. Mme. Bertrand was talking about them. She says he's a very important gentleman from Paris—something to do with the government, Mme. Bertrand says. D'you think they're going to come and live here, madame?"

I said I had no idea, and set to work again; but the couple from Paris came back to the building site again the next day, with lists and measuring tapes, and soon it was all over the village that Pierre Claudet, a junior minister in the French government, had bought one of the apartments in the new block, Panoralpes. It meant little to me, one way or another, who was going to live in Panoralpes— although I did rather grudge them the view that should have been mine.

It was on the Friday, when Anne-Marie had her half-day off and was therefore able to give me more of her time, that the young man from the building site came up to the studio on the pretext of asking whether I could spare some milk for the boys' afternoon coffee. Even in his dusty overalls and workman's cap, I could see that he was astonishingly good-looking—and I also saw the way he looked at Anne-Marie. That was when it all started. I did not even know at the time that he was Robert Drivaz, the son of the widow from the grocery. I couldn't help noticing, however, that henceforward he made some excuse to come up to the studio at least once during each of Anne-Marie's sittings.

By the time the little figure for the Chelsea garden was finished, Robert had taken to hanging about at Panoralpes after his workmates had gone home, so that he could walk back down to the village with Anne-Marie; and this arrangement continued later on when Anne-Marie—at her own earnest request and to my delight—continued to come and clean my little house for me during her free time from the café.

It was in November, when Panoralpes was almost finished, that Anne-Marie arrived one day in floods of tears and poured out her story to me.

She and Robert, she confided, were in love. This came as no news to me. However, the course of their true love was running according to form. Robert had told his mother that they wished to marry, and the widow Drivaz had exploded like an outraged volcano. Out of the question! Unthinkable! Her only son, Robert, to marry a penniless orphan! Never! Where would they live, and what would they use for money, she would like to know? Robert certainly wasn't going to bring a girl of *that* sort into the cozy apartment above the grocer's shop. Oh, the shame of it! What his poor, dear father would have said . . . !

"But, Anne-Marie," I said, "Robert's over twenty-one, isn't he?"

She stopped sniveling for long enough to confirm that he was twenty-two.

"Well, then, why not go ahead and get married? Mme. Drivaz will come around in the end, especially if you present her with a grandson—you'll see."

"But, madame," wailed Anne-Marie, "what she says is true. How could we live without her help? Robert has been making good money on the building site for the summer, but what is he to do in the winter?"

"I thought he was training to be a ski instructor."

"Oh, yes—yes, he is. But he still has to take the examination, and it is very difficult. In any case, even if he passes, he will not earn much at first. And where are we to live? We have no house, and Mme. Bertrand will sack me, and I shall not even have my little room at the café. . . ."

"Now, do pull yourself together, Anne-Marie," I said. "I'm sure we'll be able to work something out."

Anne-Marie flung her arms around my neck. "Oh, madame," she sobbed. "I knew you would help us. I said to Robert, Mme. Veston will find the way for us . . . oh, thank you, madame. . . ."

And so I became involved.

I first braved the grocery for a talk with Mme. Drivaz, and found her every bit as intractable as Anne-Marie had said. They were a respectable family, she kept repeating. Her husband and her husband's father had owned one of the largest farms in the district. Her son, Robert, was good enough for the finest lady in the land.

In vain I extolled Anne-Marie's virtues. Certainly, Mme. Drivaz conceded grudgingly, she was a pretty girl, and the good Sisters had brought her up to be a hard worker. That didn't alter the fact that she was an orphan, almost certainly illegitimate, and quite without a dowry. She had a right to expect that her son's bride would bring a marriage portion with her.

"What do you mean by a marriage portion, Mme. Drivaz?"

Well, now, that would depend, wouldn't it? In the old days, sons and daughters of farmers had married each other, and so land was amassed into the family. The very least she would expect from Anne-Marie was a house for the young couple to live in, and a steady income—not the sort of pittance she made now, working all hours at the Café de la Source. She certainly wouldn't allow any daughter-in-law of hers to slave away as a skivvy for that old dragon Bertrand. . . .

Mme. Bertrand was no help either. She took the view that she was doing a charitable, Christian duty by employing Anne-Marie at all. She'd only taken the girl on as a favor to the good Sisters. Heaven knew, she'd lavished money and training on the girl, and this was how she was to be repaid, was it? Waltzing off to marry above her station, neglecting her work, painting her face and doing her hair in that fancy style. Well, Anne-Marie needn't think that

Mme. Bertrand would have any more use for her once she got married—no, thank you very much. She could pack her bags and get out, and good luck to her. The room in the attic would come in handy for the Italian girl Mme. Bertrand hoped to get as a replacement. Italian girls were hard-working and didn't ask much in the way of wages. Not like some. As for Anne-Marie, Mme. Bertrand was reduced to near-tears of self-pity at her wanton ingratitude for all that had been done for her. How disappointed the good Sisters must be. . . .

Anne-Marie brought Robert to see me, and he sat in my tiny drawing room, handsome and tongue-tied and seeming too large for his chair, while his fiancée explained to me earnestly that his work on Panoralpes would soon be finished, and that even if he passed his ski instructor's examination this year, he could only be a junior instructor for the first season, which didn't mean much money; and if he failed, he'd have to go back to working the ski lift, and his mother would never help them, even though she was terribly rich, having sold the family farm to the company who had built the Hotel Carlton. . . .

It all seemed rather hopeless, and I was embarrassed that these two likable young people had apparently adopted me as honorary fairy godmother. At the end of the interview, Robert—who had hardly opened his mouth till then—surprised me by asking me if I would like to have a look at the Panoralpes building. As is usual in the mountains, the builders had planned their schedule to finish the outside of the building before the cold weather started; in that way, work on the interior could continue through the winter months. The doors were going to be fitted the next day, Robert said, and after that nobody would be able to get in except the workmen or prospective buyers brought by M. Bienne. This struck me as a welcome diversion from the young couple's troubles, and I agreed gratefully.

Even in its half-completed state, Panoralpes was an impressive building. It was not large—it contained only eight apartments, two to each of the four floors—but one could see already that *grand luxe* just about described them. Each flat had two bedrooms, two bathrooms, a huge double living room, big balconies, and a super-modern kitchen. Parquet and marble abounded, and huge double-glazed windows commanded the magnificent view which had once been enjoyed by Les Sapins.

Robert showed us around with a rather touching pride in the fact that he had helped to create all this splendor, and, unlike me, appeared not at all abashed when the door of one of the top-floor flats opened while we were admiring the enormous *salon,* to admit M. and Mme. Claudet with M. Bienne.

"But naturally, madame," Bienne was saying in his Genevese accent, "naturally there will be a *concierge.* She will live in the small chalet opposite, and be responsible for all the cleaning and . . ." He broke off in surprise at the sight of Anne-Marie, Robert, and myself.

"So sorry," I mumbled. "Just looking around. . . ."

"Good afternoon, Mme. Weston," said M. Bienne coldly. "Were you interested in buying an apartment? I'm afraid this one is already sold, but if you would call at my office, I can arrange to show you some of the others."

"No . . . no," I said. "That is . . . I mean, yes. I'll call at your office." And I fled back to Les Sapins, bubbling with my new idea.

The next day I called on M. Bienne. He was a plump, fair, soft-faced man—a stranger from Geneva, not mountain-bred. He sat in a small, crowded office, surrounded by brochures and blueprints, quietly amassing a fortune by acting as middleman between rich property dealers and rich pleasure seekers. He was not, I admit, my favorite person, but for Anne-Marie's sake I turned on what charm I could muster.

M. Bienne greeted me with a warmth which cooled perceptibly when it became clear that I was not a prospective purchaser. He admitted, however, that no arrangements had yet been made about appointing a *concierge* for Panoralpes.

"We are looking for a young couple, not a single woman," he said severely. It occurred to me, hilariously, that perhaps he thought I was after the job myself. "Elderly *concierges* are no use—none at all. I want a good, strong, hard-working girl who will keep the building clean, see the snow is swept from the driveway, and so on. She will be able to make a nice little bit on the side, doing private cleaning jobs for the tenants. Her husband should have an independent job, but he would be expected to help with heavy work like digging snow, fetching firewood, and so on."

"And they would live in the little chalet next to mine?" I asked.

"That is correct. A very nice little house—in rather better shape than yours, if I may say so, madame, *and* with central heating."

"The house would be free, and the *concierge* would get a salary?"

"Of course." M. Bienne was sounding definitely puzzled by now. "But I did explain that I am looking for a married couple, and young—"

"Exactly!" I said triumphantly. "Robert Drivaz and Anne-Marie. The very people for you!"

Well, it took a bit of a struggle, but I won in the end. M. Bienne interviewed both Robert and Anne-Marie, and even he could find no fault with them. He knew that Robert was a good worker, for he had been employed on the building of Panoralpes—which meant, incidentally, that he knew about the hot-water and central-heating systems and other such mysteries. Bienne knew Anne-Marie from the Café de la Source, and even Mme. Bertrand had to admit that the good Sisters had given her a thorough training in housework. The couple were both young, strong, honest, and hard-working. What more could M. Bienne ask?

And so it was arranged. Mme. Drivaz was forced to admit that Anne-Marie was contributing a free house and a steady income, together with a job which would not prevent her from looking after her home and husband. In any case, in this new situation, she knew very well that the couple could defy her and get married anyhow. Graciously accepting defeat, she withdrew her opposition to the match.

And so the winter passed, in its usual winter-sports whirl. Robert took his ski instructor's examination in January, on the very day that Giselle Arnay married Michel Veron, and he passed it. In the spring, Panoralpes was finally finished down to the last brass door handle and crystal chandelier, and the little chalet next to my studio was scrubbed and furbished by Anne-Marie. So in April, as I have said, when the tourists had gone and the cherry blossom was coming out in the valley, Robert Drivaz married Anne-Marie Durey, and I was the only foreigner present, and everybody cried.

The only other noteworthy thing that happened to me that winter was that I invited Henry and Emmy Tibbett to spend Christmas with me at Les Sapins.

2

After I had made such a point of cutting myself off from England, I suppose it may sound odd that I should have invited friends out to stay that very first winter. I told myself that I was just doing a good turn to the Tibbetts, who adored skiing and would probably not have been able to afford a winter holiday; but if I am to be honest, I have to admit that I dreaded the prospect of Christmas alone.

The snow came late that year, I remember. Right up to the second week in December, the sky remained obstinately blue and the mountains green. And then, one morning, the village woke up to find itself swaddled in a soft cloud of white snowflakes, and when the sun came out again, two days later, the transformation scene was complete. Everywhere, diamond points of light dazzled off the snow, the pine trees were outlined in frosty white like decorations on an iced cake, and the snow plows flung great fountains of snow into the air as they cleared the village street for traffic before the Christmas rush. The whole place throbbed with the anticipation of gaiety and good cheer, and I felt miserable. So I put through a telephone call to Emmy Tibbett in London.

The Tibbetts are, I think, very special people. They had been neighbors of mine in London in the old days, when we all lived near the World's End, and called it Fulham and not Chelsea. In those days Henry Tibbett was a detective inspector of the C.I.D. at

19

Scotland Yard, and although I knew that he had now risen to the rank of Chief Superintendent, I did not imagine that this would have had any marked effect on him. He was unspectacular to meet —a smallish man in middle age, with sandy hair and blue eyes—but the criminal fraternity had a healthy respect for him, just the same. Emmy was plump and dark-haired, with a very fair skin and a bubbling laugh—an immediately attractive person. Of all my friends, I knew I could rely on the Tibbetts not to "poor Jane" me, to cope cheerfully with the coke stove which I had christened Herbert, not to upset the tin bath, and to appreciate the scenery. I was only afraid that I might have left it too late, and that they would already be booked up for Christmas.

My fears were ill-founded. "Jane, darling, how absolutely wonderful. Of course, we'd *love* to. What? No hot water? But you've got a stove, haven't you? Well, then, what are you worrying about? . . . Just one thing, love—be an angel and reserve some skis and boots for us to hire from a reliable local shop. . . . I know what it's like over Christmas. . . . I'll drop you a line to say exactly when we'll be arriving. . . . Oh, Jane, what fun it's going to be!"

And so it was. I bought a small Christmas tree from the newly opened co-op store in the village, and Anne-Marie helped me to decorate it. I bought boxes of red candles and reels of silver tinsel, so that the little chalet glowed and sparkled. Even Herbert seemed to put on a cheerful face as he roared comfortingly away through the wintry evenings.

The Tibbetts arrived on the Friday before Christmas, on the indomitable bus which climbed ponderously up the winding road from the valley, come rain, hail, or snow. They were in high spirits, and obviously delighted to be back in Switzerland. They had spent a couple of days in Geneva en route, they told me, meeting old friends—including an Inspector Colliet of the Geneva police, with whom Henry had been concerned on a case a few years ago.

"You mean, you were working with him? I thought only Interpol—"

Henry laughed. "No, my dear Jane, I was not working with him. Very much the reverse. Actually, I was the chief suspect."

"What?"

"Oh, it's a long story. Anyhow, we ended up the best of friends, and it was good to see him again."

The Tibbetts settled in at once to Les Sapins, miraculously transforming all its discomforts into a delightful sort of game. What was more, they even persuaded me to go skiing.

When Emmy first broached the subject, I simply roared with laughter. "No, no," I said. "Not me, darling. Far too old."

"You're no older than we are," said Emmy.

"But you've been doing it for ages."

"No, we haven't—we only started a few years ago, and we haven't been able to keep it up. You can learn at *any* age, so long as you're reasonably fit and you take proper lessons. Come on, Jane. You *can't* live in a place like this and not ski."

There was a lot in what she said, of course. It was sad and silly to have to watch the chattering, laughing groups of skiers every morning, climbing the hill outside the chalet with their skis on their shoulders, and never to be able to join them. It was just one more thing to cut me off from the mainstream of life in Montarraz, and when it came to waving good-bye to Henry and Emmy—my contemporaries—and going back to the studio and kitchen while they headed for the high slopes, it was the last straw. My resistance to Emmy's idea was halfhearted, and the very next day I agreed to hire the necessary equipment and join the beginners' class. Although I did not realize it at the time, this was to prove a fateful step.

It did not start very fatefully. Henry and Emmy escorted me to the ski-school assembly point and left me standing beside a blue-and-white notice board marked "Classe 1." I was feeling idiotic in my red trousers and white anorak, trying to remember how the man in the shop had told me to put on my skis, and wishing heartily that I had never come. The Tibbetts went off to join the lordly characters of Class 4, and for an awful moment I thought that I was to be the only beginner of the day. Then I saw another woman approaching, looking uncertainly from notice to notice, and finally hurrying toward the spot where I stood.

"Excuse me, madame," she said in French. "Is this the assembly point for beginners?" And I saw that it was Mme. Claudet.

Unlike me, Sylvie Claudet looked exquisite. We must have been about the same age, but whereas I am tall and somewhat angular, she was petite, with a pocket-Venus figure and beautifully set fair hair with artificially silvered streaks sparkling in it. She was all in beige—impeccably cut trousers flaring over beige ski boots, and a little mink-fringed battle-dress jacket. One thing we did have in common, however—we were both patently scared.

I reassured her that this was, indeed, Class 1; and by the time the other pupils arrived, we had exchanged names and were chattering away, our friendship blossoming in the hothouse of shared apprehension.

As a matter of fact, the morning's lesson turned out to be great fun and not at all frightening, and both Sylvie and I were complimented by the instructor—unjustifiably, perhaps, but it made us feel we hadn't done too badly in comparison with the rest of the class, who were all youngsters. When it was all over, it was only natural that I should invite Mme. Claudet to come with me to the café, where I had arranged to meet Henry and Emmy for a pre-lunch drink.

Class 4 had gone off on some great excursion to the top of the mountain, and the Tibbetts had warned me that they might be a bit late, so Sylvie and I (we were on "Sylvie" and "Jane" terms by then) were on our own for some time. I reminded her that we had, in fact, met briefly once before—in the unfinished apartment at Panoralpes.

"But, my dear Jane, of course!" She was speaking English now, with a deliciously fractured accent. "All morning, I have asked myself where it is that I see your face before!"

"You saw more of my seat than my face this morning," I remarked.

"No, no, you were so good. You English are all *sportif*. I would not come to ski, but Pierre insist. He say that now we have this apartment—you have seen it, the apartment at Panoralpes?"

"Only that once," I said.

"Oh, when it is all ready, you must come often and visit us. How nice that we shall have a good friend so near." Sylvie was like a kitten, for all her forty-plus years. I couldn't help smiling at being called a good friend after a two-hour acquaintanceship—but that was Sylvie all over. She went on, "Bienne tells us the building will be quite ready in the spring, and then we shall move in. After that, we shall be busy in Paris, but next winter we will spend all the time we can here. Oh, I do so *like* Montarraz. I think I shall stay all this winter, with you and my darling Giselle, and if Pierre has to go to his silly old office in Paris, that is—how do you say?—his bad chance!"

"Does . . . does your husband ski?" I asked. My hesitation was due to the fact that I hardly liked to refer to a minister of the French government by his Christian name.

"Pierre? Oh, yes, he is the great expert—or so he says. That is why he insist for me to learn, so that when he come here I shall not be so *maladroite*."

"He's not with you now, then?"

"No, no. He is at this boring conference in Brussels."

I blushed. I had quite forgotten about the Common Market Christmas summit, as the papers called it. I should have known where Pierre Claudet was.

"And so I stay until Christmas with my darling Giselle, but then I go back to Paris to Pierre. Or so he think. Me, I think I shall stay here in the sun." And Sylvie stretched her arms luxuriously toward the blue sky.

Then the Tibbetts arrived, more drinks were ordered, and before we knew where we were, the whole party from Les Sapins had been invited for drinks that evening to darling Giselle's chalet, to meet darling Giselle. I felt a bit dubious; after all, Sylvie was apparently a house guest at this Chalet Perce-neige, and I wondered what her hostess would think of such an invasion. However, Sylvie was adamant, and so we accepted.

The Chalet Perce-neige, or Snowdrop, was as different from Les Sapins as was possible for two dwellings which could both be described as chalets. Wood as a basic building material and a faintly alpine flavor in the design were all that they had in common. Perce-neige was in the most fashionable part of Montarraz—far enough outside the village to make it extremely inconvenient to reach without a car, as we discovered to our cost. It stood in a couple of acres of ground, protected from any prying eyes which might be lurking even on that small country road by a dense plantation of fir trees, as well as a stout wire fence. If you were not keeping a sharp lookout for the discreet signboard beside the formidable iron gate, you could easily miss it altogether.

Emmy, Henry, and I arrived on foot that evening—by bad luck, my little car was temporarily out of action. We had not realized just how isolated the chalet was, and consequently we were very late, footsore, and irritated. As I rang the bell, we all agreed that we would stay for just one drink, and then telephone for a taxi to drive us home.

In fact, we wondered whether we would get as much as one drink, because the place seemed to be deserted and in total darkness. However, the chime of the bell had hardly died away before a light came on in the little porch under which we were standing, illuminating us prettily. At the same moment, a faint clicking sound came from behind the little iron-barred window in the front door. We were being inspected from the inside.

There was a tiny pause, and then a light went on in the hallway inside, and the door was opened by an excessively handsome young man—dark-haired and sunburned—wearing very tight white trousers and a purple silk shirt.

"Come in," he said in French, but with a strong Italian accent. "Sylvie is expecting you."

I think this is the moment to describe the Chalet Perce-neige, even though, of course, we were able to explore its exterior only later on. The house was modern, but genuflecting toward a traditional alpine design, and had been built on a manmade plateau on a steep, south-facing slope. The plateau had been carefully landscaped to include a tennis court, a reconstruction of an old Valaisan stone well, complete with wrought-iron superstructure and bucket-lowering gear, and an elaborate dovecote. The gardens, at the time of our first visit, were covered in snow, but the swimming pool had cleverly been incorporated into the house. That is to say, an enormous sort of lean-to structure made of plate glass jutted out from the west wall to enclose the pool and its adjacent fountains, so that swimming could be enjoyed at tropical temperatures even when the snow was drifting outside. I remembered my chemical water closet and couldn't help smiling. The principle was the same.

For the moment, however, we saw none of this. We found ourselves in a warm, pine-scented hallway paneled in light-colored wax wood, where the young man divested us rather brusquely of our anoraks and then flung open a huge frosted-glass door.

"They're here," he said, and propelled us into the main living area of the Chalet Perce-neige.

I say "living area," because the word "room" really does not apply to such an enormous space. Designed on several levels, it included a cocktail bar, a dining recess, a music area (complete with grand piano, drums, and several guitars, electric and hand-operated), and a vast open fireplace from which a log fire sent flames leaping up into a rough stone funnel, as well as a sizable drawing room furnished with elegantly opulent leather-covered furniture. In this part of the room, obliquely lit by flickering flames and lamplight, were two women. Sylvie Claudet, wearing a leopard-printed trouser suit, was lying full length on her back on a sofa, smoking a black Russian cigarette; and crouched on a sheepskin rug in front of the fire was a tiny figure, like an orphan child sheltering from a blizzard.

"Darlings!" said Sylvie, not moving from her horizontal position. She waved her cigarette vaguely in our direction. "Come in. Have a drink. Mario!"

"Yes, Sylvie?" The young man reappeared at the door.

"Bring some booze for these people, darling Mario." Suddenly she sat up straight. "Jane, Henry, Emmy. Forgive me. I am so stiff after the ski lesson this morning, I can hardly move." But she jumped to her feet lithely enough, and stretched out both hands in a warm, simple gesture of welcome. Then she said gently, "Giselle, darling."

The small figure in front of the fire did not move. She was sitting crouched, her knees drawn up under her chin, her head down, and her long black hair falling around her like a mourning veil. My first thought had been to compare her with an orphan of the storm; now, all at once, she looked like a witch. Then she raised her head, pushed back her trailing hair with long, white fingers, and smiled at us—and I saw that it was Giselle Arnay.

I suppose it always comes as a shock to meet face to face someone whom you know from their screen performances. The meeting is so very lopsided. To me, Giselle Arnay was somebody I felt I knew very well. I had laughed with her in *Vacances à Paris,* I had cried with her in *Le Diable de la Nuit,* and in that extraordinary modern film version of *Oedipus à Colonus* we had shared—or so it seemed to me—a deep spiritual experience. To her I was a total and perhaps not very welcome stranger. Then, there is the question of dimension. The exquisite face which had filled a wide screen in close-up now shrank to a tiny, pale triangle; the body—well, of course, the camera is a notorious liar, making the skeletal look normal, and the normal elephantine. Still, I had not been prepared for how minuscule she was. I felt that I could pick her up in one hand, like a baby bird.

"Hello, Sylvie's friends," she said in barely understandable English. The smile said the rest; but after the first dazzlement, I realized that it was a press-conference smile. It meant nothing.

We accepted drinks and made a few foolish and stilted remarks about the house and the snow conditions, and tried not to gawk too obviously. I felt a little annoyed at having been taken off my guard. Sylvie might have warned me who "darling Giselle" actually was.

Mlle. Arnay herself said very little, retreating under her curtain of hair again, and staring at the fire. After ten minutes or so she suddenly stood up and said, "Excuse me. I go to bed now."

Like a well-mannered child, she solemnly shook hands with each of us in turn, and then—again like a child—ran out of the room. It was just half-past six. I saw Mario and Sylvie exchange a brief glance. Then Mario poured another round of drinks, and unobtrusively slipped out of the room. It was all a little odd, but soon forgotten.

Sylvie slid easily into the role of hostess, and soon we were joined by other guests—mostly young, mostly from Paris. I never gathered half their names, but I know that one of the girls was a fashion model, one of the older men a film producer, and at least four of the young men were a pop group, who quickly took over the guitars and drums. Mario reappeared with a big tureen of onion soup, which he served with hot, garlicky bread and jugs of red wine. We all sat on the floor.

Before long Henry was deep in conversation with the model girl —who, it appeared, knew a niece of his in the same profession in London; Emmy was explaining to a long-haired young guitarist how to make a Christmas pudding; and I found myself expounding the joys of skiing to the film producer, who knew even less about it than I did—that is to say, nothing at all. It was a gratifying experience.

When the group struck up for the second session of the evening, it seemed to me that it was time we went home. We had been asked only for drinks, after all, and it was already past ten. Henry and Emmy agreed, and the film producer volunteered to drive us back— an offer which we accepted gratefully. We withdrew quietly, leaving Sylvie and the young people to enjoy themselves.

It was only when I was tucked snugly up in bed at Les Sapins, listening to the infinite silence of the alpine night outside the windows and the quiet roar of the stove, Herbert, in the hall, that it struck me just how strange the evening had been.

For a start, none of the guests had even mentioned Giselle Arnay, and she had not reappeared; and yet, it was her house. Perhaps, I thought, I understand the young even less than I thought I did. Then, there was Mario. What was his position at Perce-neige? A servant? A friend? It was none of my business, of course . . . but it was puzzling, and I don't like puzzles. Anyhow, I thought sleepily, I'll see Sylvie at ski school tomorrow. I'll keep in touch. The real interest that I had in the Chalet Perce-neige was a purely professional one. I was absolutely determined, somehow, someday, to get Giselle Arnay to sit for me.

As it was, I was doomed to disappointment. Sylvie Claudet did not appear at ski school on the following day. The day after, she turned up in a stunning lilac velvet outfit, and remarked casually that Giselle had gone back to Paris. Somehow, I was not surprised. The image of Giselle Arnay lingered in my mind as an insubstantial shadow, a tiny, dark presence, not quite a real person.

Sylvie Claudet, however, was very much flesh and blood. She had another two days in Montarraz before rejoining her husband in Paris on Christmas Eve, and most unusually she found herself alone at the Chalet Perce-neige. I don't want to sound cynical; I think that Sylvie had genuinely taken a fancy to me and to the Tibbetts. All the same, I don't believe she would have embraced us with quite such fervor if she had not felt somewhat deserted. In any case, for whatever reason, the Chalet Perce-neige became our headquarters for the next few days.

Mario had departed with Giselle, leaving Sylvie in the care of Mme. Brizet, the cook, and her elderly husband, who tended the garden. The Brizets did not live in, but made their way up from the village each day, from eight in the morning until six in the evening. Mme. Brizet busied herself in the kitchen, producing delicious meals, while we swam in the heated indoor pool in the daytime and sipped hot wine around the fire in the evenings. It was delightful and luxurious, and Sylvie was gay and friendly, and yet . . . and yet, I never felt entirely at home in the Chalet Perce-neige. I was not really sorry when Christmas Eve came.

We all went to the station to see Sylvie into her first-class compartment on the Paris train, and with a distinct sense of relief we went back to Les Sapins. Herbert was roaring cheerfully in the hall, the Christmas tree sparkled in a corner of the tiny living room, and Anne-Marie was singing to herself as she scrubbed the kitchen floor. I think we were all glad to be home.

It was a quiet, happy Christmas, up there in the snows. We skied in the daytime—I was promoted to Class 2, to my great pride. In the evenings, we relaxed over good food and drink. On Christmas Day Emmy and I cooked a frozen American turkey and opened a tin of English Christmas pudding. Anne-Marie and Robert came in for a glass of wine, and we all exchanged small presents. And then, the holiday was over. Henry and Emmy went back to London, and I resumed my tranquil life, feeling every day more at home in my new place—Montarraz.

Then January came, and with it, as I have said, Giselle Arnay's runaway wedding to Michel Veron. In April, the snow melted, and the tourists with it, and Robert Drivaz married Anne-Marie. Panoralpes was finished, and Sylvie arrived to supervise the lorry loads of expensive furniture that rolled up the hill from Geneva.

I must say, the Claudets' apartment was beautiful, and I spent a lot of time there, helping Sylvie to move in. Anne-Marie, happy as a bird with her new husband and her new home, was a tower of strength, and Sylvie—to my delight—made a point of congratulating M. Bienne on finding such an ideal *concierge*. She also left a spare set of keys with Anne-Marie, and concluded a satisfactory bargain by which Anne-Marie would clean the apartment whenever required.

Then Sylvie went back to Paris, and the beautiful summer began. Life seemed very good and very tranquil. There was no hint in the clear blue mountain skies of the clouds which hung over our future.

3

The clouds made no sudden or dramatic appearance. In fact, they seemed at first to be not clouds at all, but silver flecks in a blue sky. What I mean is that, after a serene summer and an autumn of gentle green and gold, the prickling excitements of the new winter were welcome—stimulating rather than menacing.

For instance, I was as delighted as Anne-Marie at Robert's success as a ski instructor. Never before, Anne-Marie told me proudly, had a new instructor received so many bookings for private lessons in his first season. Robert was working hard and earning good money—and so was Anne-Marie, with Panoralpes filling up and so many apartments to keep clean. Oh, but she loved it, she was so happy, and all due to you, Mme. Veston. And Anne-Marie laughed, and went waltzing around the studio, embracing her broom like a dancing partner, while I continued to chip away at the white marble form on which I was working. After my excursion into representationalism with Anne-Marie's figure, I had gone back to abstract work. If Giselle Arnay would sit for me, I would return to portraiture. Not otherwise.

My second Christmas at Montarraz was very different from my first. I was skiing regularly now, and had recently been promoted to Class 4, which is a big step for a middle-aged beginner. So my days were busy, and I made plenty of transitory friends among the visitors. In fact, I found that if I was to get any work done at all, I had to impose a strict timetable on myself. This consisted of ski school in the morning, followed by the usual after-class coffee and drinks with friends. Then a few practice runs on my own, and home to a late lunch, after which I made it a rigid rule to work in the studio from half-past two until half-past four, by which time it was too dark to see properly. Later in the year, as the days grew longer, I increased my working hours to five o'clock.

This timetable I maintained even during Christmas week, and in spite of the fact that Pierre and Sylvie Claudet arrived from Paris. They invited me over on their very first evening, and so I made the acquaintance of Pierre Claudet.

I must admit he was rather frightening. In contrast to Sylvie's warm, kittenish friendliness, Pierre was grave and aloof, a tall man like a rock, the very epitome of a minister of the Republic. It took me some time to discern that beneath the correct public image was a much more human personality.

That first evening, I was overawed—as much by the apartment as by Pierre Claudet. True, I had helped Sylvie with moving in, but I had not seen the flat in all its glory—if that is the right word. It was not the decor that I would have chosen for the mountains, I must say, although it would have been fine for a fashionable penthouse in Paris. Everything was exquisite: Louis Quinze furniture, delicate and ornate, upholstered in silk brocade; engraved crystal glasses and Sèvres porcelain; Aubusson carpets wreathed in roses; fine silver tableware; lace and silk and ivory and eggshell china. The irresistible first impression was a dazed mental calculation—*what* must it all have cost? The second impression was one of acute embarrassment, as heavy, snow-packed ski boots trampled the woven garlands underfoot, and cold, clumsy hands fumbled with a thin-stemmed crystal champagne glass.

Pierre Claudet was pretty hard going, too. He inquired politely about my progress on skis and thanked me for the help I had given Sylvie in fixing the apartment. After that, conversation languished, and I was relieved when a diversion arrived in the form of Chantal Villeneuve—a blond, willowy girl of about twenty, whom Sylvie introduced as her goddaughter who was spending Christmas with them. Even then, however, the talk was hardly sparkling, for Chantal confined herself to whispered monosyllables and heroine-worshiping glances at Sylvie, whom she obviously idolized. It was a relief when the champagne was finished, and Pierre proposed that we should all go out to dinner at the fashionable Hotel Mirabelle.

Things went much more easily over dinner, but afterward I was ready to go home to Les Sapins, and my heart sank when Claudet—now in thoroughly good form—insisted that we all go down the street to the little Farinet bar for a final drink. However, I didn't like to refuse.

The bar was small, dark, and smoky, crammed with people in ski clothes and overflowing with an ear-splitting tide of talk, laughter, and canned music. We forced our way to the bar, and were greeted loudly and joyfully by a couple of ski instructors who had had the dubious pleasure of steering Sylvie and myself down the mountain several times. Pierre, who seemed to my annoyance to be self-consciously slumming, insisted on buying drinks all around, and made a great fuss of the instructors, whose names were Jean and Henri. It was very noticeable, however, that Chantal cheered up at once in the company of people of her own age. I suddenly realized that she was a very pretty girl, and that she was enjoying herself for the first time that evening.

I suppose that it was because of Chantal and her newly found sparkle that I agreed to the next idiotic move. Pierre Claudet, playing the jolly uncle with an arm around the shoulders of each of the young instructors, boomed genially that we should all move on to Le Jockey Bar—the ridiculously named nightclub which was patronized by the smart set of Montarraz, and whose prices were rumored to be higher than those in Paris.

Chantal cried, "Oh, *yes,* Uncle Pierre!"—and kissed him on the nose. Sylvie, amid much laughter, volunteered to teach Henri something called *le thing,* and so take her revenge for his bullying on the ski slopes. I made an attempt to get away—but since I was dependent on the Claudets for transport, it was made clear that by doing so I should break up the party. I gave in. All six of us were crammed into Pierre's flashy Mercedes, and whirled away up the hill to Le Jockey Bar.

This proved to be every bit as dark as the Farinet, but larger and less crowded. In fact, it was most attractive. In the center of the wood-paneled room, a big open fire blazed under a central chimney. Around it was a small dance floor ringed by tables in inglenooks, each in darkness except for one big, wax-dripping candle. Soft piped music, discreet waiters, and the clinking of ice in champagne buckets completed the atmosphere. Several couples were dancing languidly, considerably intertwined and scarcely moving. The tables were in such deep shadow that it was hard to tell whether the place was full or empty.

We quickly found a table, and Chantal and Jean—young Bertrand from the Café de la Source—were on the dance floor before the first drink had been ordered. A moment later Sylvie was dragging a mock-reluctant Henri off to dance. Pierre Claudet ordered a bottle of whiskey and a soft drink for Chantal, and then leaned back, lit a cigar, and savored the scene. After a moment he said, "Sylvie enjoys herself here in Montarraz."

"I'm not surprised," I said. "So do I."

"I'm very grateful to you, Jane," he added, using my Christian name for the first time. "I know I said that earlier this evening, but you may have thought I was just being polite. I wasn't. I mean it." He paused. "I have to leave Sylvie on her own quite a lot, you see. Sometimes I worry about her. I like to think that she has you as a friend. She is lucky."

"And so am I," I said. I found myself warming to Pierre. "Sylvie's been wonderful to me."

As though he had not heard me, Claudet went on, "Some of the people that she . . . well, some of the people here are not . . ." His voice trailed into silence. He was watching the dance floor. I followed his gaze, but could see nothing exceptional. Sylvie and Henri were dancing energetically and laughing a lot. Chantal and Jean, in the modern manner, appeared to be ignoring each other's existence while performing complicated gyrations. A few other couples . . . And then I saw what had caught Claudet's attention.

33

Into the flickering illumination of the firelight moved a couple dancing so close that they appeared to be a single person, each lost in the other. But I would have recognized Robert Drivaz anywhere, and there was no mistaking, either, the long black hair and the tiny, supple body of his partner. So Giselle Arnay was back at the Chalet Perce-neige, and for the first time I was aware of a cloud.

Then the waiter arrived with our drinks, and by the time I was able to study the dance floor again there was no sign of either Robert or Giselle Arnay. I tried to put the whole thing out of my head, remembering how often and how innocently a ski lesson ended up in a party; but the uneasiness remained, and was not allayed when Pierre and Sylvie finally drove me home at three o'clock in the morning. For I could not help noticing that there was no sign of Robert Drivaz's little car outside his chalet, and that a light was still burning in Anne-Marie's bedroom. After that, I noticed that she no longer sang as she went about her work.

Of course, it was not long before rumors began to spread. They even reached me, which meant that nobody in Montarraz could have been ignorant of the scandal. Michel Veron was in Paris appearing in cabaret at various nightclubs—everybody knew that. Giselle Arnay, attended by the ambiguous Mario, remained at the Chalet Perce-neige. Every afternoon she skied with Robert Drivaz, and every evening she danced with him. Anne-Marie's lovely young face grew more and more unhappy, her gaiety quenched. I wondered if she would confide in me, but she did not. So, of course, I said nothing. At that point, she may even have imagined that I did not know.

It was in February, soon after Pierre and Sylvie Claudet had gone back to Paris, that the whole thing exploded into a public bombshell—an open and acrimonious row between Robert Drivaz and his second-cousin Lucien Simonet, who was the head of the Montarraz ski school.

The issue was very simple. Robert, as a newly qualified ski instructor, had naturally signed on with the ski school for this, his second winter season. This entailed his taking a regular class, as allotted to him, every weekday morning from half-past nine till half-past eleven. After that, he was free to accept bookings from private pupils, and it was an open secret that he had been engaged on a long-term basis by Giselle Arnay.

So far, so good; but in the middle of February Robert Drivaz submitted a formal request to his cousin Lucien, painstakingly written in a labored hand. In view of the fact, Robert wrote, that Mlle. Arnay proposed to engage him exclusively as a full-time ski instructor, he wished to cancel his contract with the ski school. Mlle. Arnay, he added somewhat naïvely, required his services in the morning as well as the afternoon. He hoped that his cousin Lucien and the other members of the school would agree to release him from his contract.

For several days the village talked of nothing else. Lucien received the letter on a Monday morning, and had called a meeting of all the instructors for Wednesday evening to consider the matter. Meanwhile, tongues wagged and gossip buzzed. Robert and Giselle Arnay not only skied and danced together, but walked defiantly and provocatively through the village street arm in arm at five o'clock in the evening—the great shopping and *après ski* hour, when a maximum number of people would be sure to see them. Since, as a rule, Giselle Arnay never appeared in the village at all, this gesture was unnecessarily blatant. The next day a couple of journalists from sensational French newspapers arrived at the Hotel Carlton.

Anne-Marie, her face pale and drawn, her lips set in a hard line, went doggedly about her work and spoke to nobody—not even to me. I abandoned work on my abstract form and—for no good reason—whiled away the time modeling the head of a baby in clay. When Anne-Marie came in to sweep out the studio, she took one look at it and burst into tears. But still she would not talk to me.

Of course, no outsiders were present at the meeting of the ski school on Wednesday evening, but the news leaked out that it had been bitter and unanimous. In any case, whatever was actually said, Robert received a formal letter from his second-cousin Lucien informing him that the director and members of the ski school of Montarraz had decided to refuse his request to be released from his contract, and that he was expected to report for duty as usual the following morning. Robert did not turn up, nor did he ever go near the ski school again. The breach was public and complete.

Village opinion was inevitably divided, but I think it is fair to say that all of it was basically anti-Robert. All, that is, except for the young man's mother—the widow Drivaz from the grocery. I suppose one could contend that it was right and proper for her to support her own son, but her manner of doing so was unfortunate. For a start, she had taken to flaunting a fur coat, and she made no secret of the fact that she had ordered a washing-up machine and a hi-fi stereo radio—and her neighbors were offering no prizes for guessing whose money would pay for them.

Then, when the row broke out between Robert and Lucien, Mme. Drivaz used it as an excuse for lashing out bitterly at poor, gentle Mlle. Simonet at the bakery—Lucien's aunt, who had cared for her orphaned nephew ever since he was six years old. Lucien's treatment of Robert, according to Mme. Drivaz, was provoked by jealousy, pure and simple. Aided and abetted, of course, by his aunt. None of the Simonets, Mme. Drivaz declared, could bear anybody else to be cleverer or more successful than they were—and Robert's spectacular rise to fame and fortune had naturally brought on this cheap and vicious attempt at revenge. Mme. Drivaz also took every opportunity of lamenting Robert's unfortunate marriage. Had she not said at the time that Anne-Marie was unworthy of her son? And had she not been proved right? It was a tragedy, no less, that Robert—with a glittering future in high society ahead of him—should be shackled to that little skivvy. And much more in the same vein.

Mme. Bertrand, from the Café de la Source, also lamented the marriage in hindsight—but from the opposing viewpoint. She, it now appeared, had always known that young Drivaz was unreliable —a playboy, or worse. If she had been consulted, she would never have allowed that poor girl to get involved with him.

"What will become of her now, Mme. Weston?" Mme. Bertrand demanded, glaring at me accusingly from behind the bar of the café.

Miserably, I replied that I hoped it would all blow over. Mme. Bertrand snorted. "That young man is rotten to the core, just like his mother. You mark my words."

Robert's former associates at the ski school, the young men of his own age, were divided between downright disapproval and a sneaking envy. Sly sniggers and blatant obscenities were exchanged in bars and cafés, together with overt speculation as to what actually went on behind the high fence of the Chalet Perce-neige. The same speculation, in a slightly more guarded form, was spun by the gossip writers from the Hotel Carlton into several sensational articles for the gutter press of Paris. It was all extremely unpleasant and distressing. As the days went by, tensions stretched until it became obvious that the breaking point could not be far away.

What happened next seemed curiously like an anticlimax. I heard of it from Mlle. Simonet, one morning in late February, when I went into her warm, sweet-smelling little shop to buy my usual *livre* of *mi-blanc*.

"Have you heard, Mme. Weston?" Mlle. Simonet's round, scrubbed face was alive with suppressed excitement, and two bright spots of color glowed in her chubby cheeks.

"Heard what, Mlle. Simonet?"

"Why, about Giselle Arnay. *That* will show Isabelle Drivaz just how high and mighty her precious son really is." Mlle. Simonet flicked a square of flimsy white paper out from below the counter to wrap my bread.

"What has Giselle Arnay done?" I asked.

"Why, gone back to Paris. That's all. Without a word to anybody. My cousin Louise Brizet, who obliges at the Chalet Perce-neige—you've heard me speak of her, madame—well, she arrived there this morning to find the place empty, if you please. Mlle. Arnay . . . *Mme. Veron, I should say*"—Mlle. Simonet corrected herself with great emphasis—"Mme. Veron and that Mario have gone back to Paris. They left a note for Louise. And more than a note, Louise says. The state of that house, madame! . . . Well, there you are, I suppose one can't expect film stars to behave like ordinary people, and Mlle.—Mme. Veron—is very generous, so Louise says. But it'll take her a good week to set the place to rights. She said to me herself, 'Annette,' she said, 'I don't know what goes on in that chalet, and that's the truth.' Of course, she's never there of an evening—"

"And what about Robert?" I asked.

"Him?" Mlle. Simonet snorted with satisfaction. "Well may you ask, Mme. Weston! Back home, with his tail between his legs, and looking very foolish. The ski school won't have him back, that's for sure. He can thank his lucky stars he has a roof over his head and a sensible young wife with a job of her own." Mlle. Simonet had always had a soft spot for Anne-Marie. "Yes—back to the ski lift for young Robert, back to being a builder's laborer in the summer, and serve him right. That'll be seventy-five centimes, Mme. Weston. Lovely weather, isn't it?"

That day I decided to buy my groceries from the cooperative store. I did not feel up to a confrontation with Mme. Drivaz, nor did I wish to appear to be gloating over her discomfiture.

Back at Panoralpes, life settled into a dull and dismal round, as far as the young Drivazes were concerned. Robert had indeed come home, but this seemed to bring no joy either to him or to Anne-Marie.

As Mlle. Simonet had prophesied, Robert did not go back to the ski school—but whether from his own choice, or because they would not have him, I never discovered. Neither did he go back to his old job on the ski lift. Instead, he sat around, sometimes at home, more often in one or other of the village bars, drinking too much and doing too little. I am congenitally averse to eavesdropping, but my studio was very close to the Drivaz chalet, and I could not help overhearing several bitter quarrels. Once I nearly went to intervene when it became obvious that Robert—who was more than half-drunk—was physically attacking his wife; but before I was out of the studio, Anne-Marie came running out in the blue overall she always wore for housework, and hurried over to Les Sapins, where I found her a few minutes later energetically polishing the sitting-room floor.

"Anne-Marie," I said, "what are you doing here? I wasn't expecting you until tomorrow morning."

"I didn't have time to do the floor last time," she said briefly, not lifting her eyes from her work. Her voice was quite steady.

"Well," I said, "now that you're here, come and have a cup of tea with me in the kitchen when you're through."

"Thank you, madame."

We both saw Robert making his slightly unsteady way, a few minutes later, past my chalet and up to the road leading to the village; but neither of us remarked on it. Anne-Marie, with chilling self-possession, made a good job of the floor, accepted a cup of tea and a cake, and went back to her own empty house. I longed to comfort her, but she was playing it her own way, and I had to respect her self-imposed privacy. I just wondered how much longer she would be able to stand it. The most distressing thing was to see how, in less than a year, all the youth and joy had been drained out of her. Even toward me she had grown cold and hard, and old before her time.

The only redeeming feature of that wretched spring was a short surprise visit by Sylvie to Panoralpes. Pierre was once more away at a conference, she told me, and Paris had become intolerably boring.

Indeed, Sylvie herself seemed depressed and in need of company, and I had to use considerable tact to continue my self-discipline of regular working hours. In the end, however, I think I did make her understand that without routine an artist cannot work, and she settled for my company before two and after five. I did not mention the scandal of Robert Drivaz and Giselle Arnay, and Sylvie certainly seemed unaware of it, for I heard her gently teasing Anne-Marie about her handsome husband. Poor Anne-Marie mumbled something and fled, but Sylvie did not appear to notice anything strange.

A few days after Sylvie had left, the village was swept by a new sensation. Robert Drivaz left home and went to Paris. Or said he did. After a particularly acrimonious wrangle with Anne-Marie, young Drivaz lurched into the Café de la Source one Wednesday evening and announced loudly and tipsily that he had had enough of this one-horse village and his common little slut of a wife—his very words, as reported by Henri, the ski instructor. He had friends in Paris. Friends in high society. Rich friends. He had an open invitation to Giselle Arnay's house. He didn't intend to stay in Montarraz to be insulted, when he could be living it up in Paris, with people who appreciated him. And much more.

The other lads in the bar—once again, Henri was my informant—took all this with a pinch of salt, teased Robert a bit, and expected that he would go home and sleep it off. Mme. Bertrand took a less lenient view. She told Robert point-blank that she would not have loudmouthed drunkards in her bar, and ordered him out.

"Go home to your poor wife, you miserable sot!" she yelled at him, while the other young men laughed awkwardly and tried to pass it off as a joke.

Robert went—but not home. The local bus driver—a grizzled and intrepid man—confirmed the next day that Robert had taken the last bus down into the valley that night, the half-past nine which connects with the ten-thirty-five train to Lausanne. He had left the bus at the railway station, and was last seen walking onto the platform. Later, the widow Drivaz and Anne-Marie both—but separately—made inquiries at the station. The ticket clerk did not know Robert personally, but confirmed that a young man answering his description had bought a single ticket right through to Paris that Wednesday night, after being assured that there was a connection with the Lausanne-Paris night train. He had paid in cash from a full wallet.

Anne-Marie came to me, white-faced, in the morning, and told me that Robert had not come home; together we traced his movements of the previous evening, from the café to the bus, from the bus to the train. All that Anne-Marie said was, "I am glad there was not an accident." Robert sent no word, and after a week or so the whole village assumed that he had gone for good.

As far as I was concerned, the next move came in the form of a visit from M. Bienne. Somehow, I seemed to have slipped into the role of foster mother to Anne-Marie—and of course I had been instrumental in getting her the job of *concierge* in the first place. M. Bienne was not an unkindly man, but he was in an awkward situation. So, as I said, he came to me.

"It's not that I want to turn the poor girl out, Mme. Weston," he said earnestly, sipping a glass of local wine in my tiny sitting room. "And she does the job well, I grant you. No complaints—all the tenants are full of praise. But, as I told you originally, this is a situation for a young couple. We must have a man to shovel the snow and cope with the boilers and so on. I'm not a monster, madame," he added, almost pleadingly, "but people will call me one if I dismiss Anne-Marie. And yet, she simply cannot do the job alone. What am I to do?"

Assuming a briskness which I was far from feeling, I said, "Now, look here, M. Bienne. It's March already; there won't be any more big snowfalls." I knew that this was not necessarily true, but Bienne was not a local man, and he nodded his assent. "Anne-Marie is perfectly capable of coping with the central heating and the cleaning on her own." Another nod. "Well, then," I went on, "give her a little longer. Personally, I am convinced that Robert will come back, and soon. He'll be out of his depth in Paris, poor boy—he's young and foolish, but he's learning the hard way. Things like this happen in any young *ménage*"—a preposterous statement, but kind M. Bienne nodded again—"so give them another month or so, please. I'll help all I can. I promise you that Panoralpes will be managed as well as ever, and that Robert will be back."

M. Bienne took my word for it. I had gained a reprieve for Anne-Marie, but I was desperately worried—especially when, contrary to my prediction, there was a heavy fall of new snow during the last week of March. Anne-Marie was hard-pressed to cope, even with my help, and I was far from being sure that Robert would ever come back.

But he did. On the last day of March, in a vile temper. He told nobody what had actually happened in the big city, but it was easy enough to guess. Giselle Arnay had undoubtedly invited her handsome ski instructor to visit her in Paris, anytime. Had Robert been more sophisticated, he might have recalled the apocryphal story of the Hollywood film star who was alleged to have displayed a suitably placed notice reading NOTHING I SAY IN BED CONSTITUTES A CONTRACT. Robert, however, had taken Giselle Arnay's invitation at its face value, and had burned his fingers as a consequence. So he came home.

Unfortunately, it was not the return of the prodigal. Anne-Marie produced the equivalent of the fatted calf, and I did my best to make young Drivaz feel welcome. His mother wept over him, and most of the villagers, with instinctive kindness, received him warmly. But in order to achieve the happy ending, the parable requires a repentant prodigal, and this Robert Drivaz was not. He made it only too clear that he disliked Montarraz and everything about it, including his wife, that he would never have come back if he had had any other place to go, and that he would be off again as soon as possible. He even put up a blustering story about being about to come into money, and then he would go back to Paris, and everybody would see. . . .

Meanwhile, he sat around—at home, or in the village bars—drinking and talking too loudly. M. Bienne came to see me again, even more distressed. This time he was threatening to find a new *concierge,* not because Robert was not there, but because he was. He was a useless layabout, said M. Bienne, and tenants were beginning to complain. The situation was explosive, and one evening in April it duly exploded.

At this stage, I shall do no more than set down the hard facts, as they happened. At five-forty P.M. on April 14, Anne-Marie Drivaz arrived at the local gendarmerie, hysterical and with blood on her clothes, screaming that her husband was dead. She had been driven to the police station by, of all people, Mario Agnelli—Giselle Arnay's manservant.

The explanation of this curious fact was that Mario, who had arrived at the Chalet Perce-neige that very day with Giselle, had driven down to Panoralpes to deliver a note for Sylvie Claudet, who was expected at the weekend. When he came out of the building, he said, he was met by Anne-Marie, who ran blindly out of her own chalet toward mine. She literally collided with Mario, and sobbed out her story to him. He at once took her to the police station in his car. I myself was quite unaware of all this, as I had finished work in my studio at five o'clock as usual, and was having a cup of tea in my kitchen at Les Sapins.

The police duly arrived at the Drivaz chalet, where they found Robert dead in the kitchen, stabbed with Anne-Marie's large carving knife. A postmortem examination showed that he had been drinking heavily. Anne-Marie's fingerprints were everywhere, including the knife handle—and there were no others, apart from Robert's own. The story of the disintegrating marriage, of Robert's affair with Giselle Arnay, of his flight to Paris and subsequent return, was well-known. It also transpired that Anne-Marie was four months pregnant. She was arrested and charged with the murder of her husband.

Had she admitted her guilt, pleading provocation and self-defense, the likelihood is that she would have got off without punishment. As it was, however, she stuck fiercely to the story that she was completely innocent. She had received a telephone call, she said, just after three-thirty from Madame Claudet in Paris, asking her to go over and clean up the apartment immediately. Sylvie denied making any such call, and Anne-Marie agreed that she had not spoken to Madame Claudet herself, but to a woman whose voice she did not know, who claimed to be Sylvie's maid.

Anne-Marie said that she had gone over to the apartment at about four o'clock, and I was able to confirm this, as I was working in the studio with the doors open, and had seen her go past toward Panoralpes. She had remained there, she swore it, until nearly half-past five. Then, satisfied that the apartment was clean, she had returned home—and found her husband lying dead. Horrified, she had panicked—she admitted picking up the bloodstained knife—and had rushed out in search of me, only to run full tilt into Mario's arms. Someone, she maintained, must have gone into the chalet and killed Robert while she was in the Claudets' apartment. If Mme. Claudet or her maid had not made the call, then it must have been designed deliberately to get her, Anne-Marie, out of the way.

Unfortunately for poor Anne-Marie, her account was discredited by that of an independent witness—myself. Of course, when the police came to ask me what I knew of the affair, I had no idea of the story which Anne-Marie had told, nor of how damning my evidence would be. I simply told them the truth.

This was that I had been working in my studio, as always, from half-past two until five. The big doors had been open, as it was a dull afternoon and I wanted to get the maximum of light; this gave me a clear view of the path which led from the Drivaz chalet, past Les Sapins, and down to Panoralpes, and anyone taking that path had to pass within a few feet of me.

I had seen Robert Drivaz returning home, somewhat unsteadily, at about three o'clock. An hour later Anne-Marie had gone past in the other direction, toward Panoralpes. So far, so good—I confirmed her story: the trouble was the next part. Because, in all innocence, I told the gendarmes that I had also noticed Anne-Marie returning from Panoralpes to her own house—not, as she claimed, at about half-past five, but shortly before five o'clock, just as I was packing things up in my studio. After that, I had gone back to Les Sapins to make tea. The point was that my evidence made it quite clear that Anne-Marie—far from rushing straight out of the chalet on discovering her husband's body—had in fact been indoors for half an hour before she came running out in hysterics.

The result of the trial was a foregone conclusion. Defense counsel tried to suggest that an intruder might have approached the chalet from some direction other than along the path, but the prosecution quickly disposed of that theory. The late snowfall that I mentioned—which was, incidentally, the reason why people like the Verons and Claudets were returning to Montarraz for some late skiing—had laid a carpet of unbroken whiteness all around the little chalet. The police had, of course, checked immediately for footprints in the new snow, and had found none. Unless the hypothetical murderer had dropped in by parachute and departed in the same way . . . Miserably, I had to confirm that, even though I was busy working, nobody could have passed my door without my seeing them. Anne-Marie was found guilty.

It was not as terrible as it might have been, I suppose. The judge was a sympathetic man, and the general climate of opinion was one of pity for the poor girl. She was given a sentence of three years' imprisonment, suspended on condition that she return to the good Sisters in the convent, where—after the birth of her child—she was to remain for at least three years, doing domestic work. This she agreed to do.

Before the trial, Anne-Marie had been held in custody. I had done all I could to get in touch with her and to help her. Under Swiss law, however, a suspect can be held incommunicado until the police have prepared their case, and I was not allowed to visit her. Once it was all over, I again tried to make contact with her at the convent—and this time I was roundly snubbed. Not surprising, I suppose, considering that it was my evidence which had convicted her.

A sweet-faced but iron-firm Sister informed me that Anne-Marie did not wish to see me. After what had happened, the girl very naturally wished to have nothing more to do with Montarraz or its inhabitants. The baby was to be adopted by its grandmother, the widow Drivaz, and Anne-Marie intended eventually to take her vows and enter the convent. The matter was closed.

M. Bienne found another young couple to fill the job of *concierges* —a gay, hard-working pair of Italians who seemed to have no qualms about living in the house where a man had been killed. Gradually, the ripples of sensation and scandal died down. Montarraz became engrossed in preparations for the summer season. Everything returned to normal; and so, in a way, did I. Except that I smashed the clay model of the baby's head which had made Anne-Marie cry. And I did not—could not—forget.

4 ✦

After the tragedy of Robert and Anne-Marie, my first instinct was to pack up and leave Montarraz forever. I had no special links with the place, and my one excursion into involvement with village life had ended in appalling disaster. I knew that, in one way, it was coward-ice to run away, but I felt too old to start making courageous ges-tures, and anyway, I could not imagine that anybody in Montarraz would care a rap whether I stayed or went.

But it seemed that I was wrong. Before my resolve to leave had had time to harden into action, I had become aware of a new and different attitude toward me among the villagers. Most of them, with the natural exception of the widow Drivaz, pitied Anne-Marie, although they accepted her guilt without question. The trial was, of course, a *cause célèbre* in the village, and the public benches in the courtroom had been packed with Drivazes, Bertrands, Simonets, and other Montarraz citizens. I suppose the word had got around that I was deeply distressed by the part which I had unwittingly played in the drama, and the village felt sorry for me. Also, in some strange way, it perhaps made me part of the place, one of them. I don't know. Anyhow, the result was that everybody became amazingly and touchingly friendly.

Mlle. Simonet sent her nephew Lucien around with the gift of a specially baked cake, because she had heard that it was my birthday (it wasn't); M. Bertrand at the Café de la Source insisted that I sample a bottle of his best wine with my meal, took a glass of it with me at my table, and did not put it on the bill; even M. Bienne came to visit me to tell me about the new Italian *concierge*. He brought with him a bunch of grapes which he said had been sent to him by a friend in Geneva, and as he was not fond of fruit, he hoped I would accept them. It was only by chance that I had noticed him buying them that morning in Montarraz's most expensive greengrocery. I was very touched, and my decision to leave began to waver.

It finally crumbled altogether when Sylvie Claudet arrived back at Panoralpes in June. She had appeared briefly at Anne-Marie's trial, in order to deny having made or instigated any phone call from Paris; as soon as she had given her evidence, she had hurried off to the car which was to whisk her to Geneva airport, as she and Pierre were due at an official function in Paris that evening. We had had no time to do more than exchange quick, sad smiles, and I had not seen her since.

It was a beautiful sunny afternoon in late June, I remember, and I was working in my studio as usual when a shadow fell across the doorway. I looked up, and there was Sylvie silhouetted against the sunshine, her blond hair lit up in a bright halo, and her arms full of ridiculously extravagant flowers.

Like a small tornado, she swept me along with her to the Panoralpes apartment, insisted on opening a bottle of champagne—which seemed specially and deliciously wicked in midafternoon—and then curled herself up like a little cat on the huge brocaded sofa and announced that we must have a lovely long talk about everything.

"I have *missed* you so much, Jane," she said. "In Paris there are people, people, people . . . but no real friends. Oh, I wish I could live here always, and talk to you and watch you work in your little studio. . . . How is poor sweet Anne-Marie?" she added suddenly, with a typical swerve of subject. I told her all I knew.

Sylvie nodded gravely. "One can understand how she feels," she said. "Do you think if I went to see her . . . ?"

"I wouldn't, on the whole," I said. "The Sister was probably right. The girl's been through a frightful time. She's best left alone."

Sylvie's brow wrinkled, then cleared. "I know," she said. "I'll . . . When is the baby due?"

I did a quick mental calculation. "Around the beginning of September, I suppose."

"Then I shall make a *big* gift for the baby—clothes, cradle, perambulator, everything, and send it to the convent. Anne-Marie need never know that it came from me." Sylvie smiled delightedly at the idea.

"The trouble is," I pointed out, "that Mme. Drivaz is going to adopt the child. I believe in such cases it's usually considered better if the mother never even sees the child herself."

"Oh." Sylvie made a *moue* of disappointment. "Then I must send a big present to Anne-Marie herself. To help her forget the little baby. Flowers. I shall send a whole roomful of flowers, and also champagne."

I couldn't help smiling. "I'd cut out the champagne, I think," I said. "The Mother Superior might not approve. But the flowers are a splendid idea. They'll make her feel she's not forgotten and unloved." I was intending to send flowers myself, though not by the roomful.

"Then that's settled." Sylvie sipped her champagne and twinkled at me over the rim of her glass, like a child with a delectable secret to impart. "And now, my Jane, I have plans for *you*."

"For me?"

"I should say . . . I have great favor to ask you. Will you help me?"

"If I possibly can—you know I will."

Sylvie set down her glass and looked straight at me. "Come and live in this apartment, Jane," she said.

I was so taken aback that I said nothing, but I could feel my eyes opening wide in astonishment. Sylvie laughed. "You are surprised."

"I'm . . . I don't understand what you mean, Sylvie."

"Oh, my Jane—you look so very *English* when you are surprised. Do you think I make a wicked proposition?"

"Of course not. I simply don't see what you're driving at."

"Forgive me." Impulsively, Sylvie put out her hand and touched mine. "I am naughty—I so like to see you *bouleversée.* It is charming. No, my Jane, it is very simple, my idea. Pierre is so busy, there is no chance for us to come again before Christmas. Any little holiday he may take in August, we must go on some yacht in the Mediterranean because of the important people. Important c-r-r-ashing bores," Sylvie added, rolling the R's around. She had picked up the English expression "crashing bore" from me, and for some reason found it exquisitely amusing. She went on, "Now, when Anne-Marie was here, it was different. She kept the place clean and looked after it well. But this new girl—who is she? You don't know her. I don't know her. Maybe she is all that Bienne says—maybe not. We have some good things here, and Pierre does not want the apartment to be empty for months, with the key in the pocket of some little Italian girl we don't know. Now do you see?"

"You mean, you want a caretaker?" I said.

"Oh, Jane—*you,* a caretaker? Don't be silly. But we would be so very grateful if, as a friend, you would move in here until December. You will still have your pretty little house and your studio for working," she added, almost wheedling. "And you could have your friends to stay—there is the guest room with its own bathroom, and you have so little space at Les Sapins. Would you do it for us, Jane?"

I laughed. "There's no need to persuade me," I said. "Living here would be sheer heaven after Les Sapins and Herbert. The only thing that frightens me is . . . well . . . all this beautiful stuff." I made a gesture, a rather despairing one. "Your china and glass, the carpets . . . I'd be terrified of wrecking the place for you."

Sylvie jumped to her feet. "If that is all that worries you, my Jane, we may say the bargain is fixed and drink to it with another glass of champagne." She flourished the bottle gaily. "What are *things*—they are just things, made to be broken, made to be used. You may break anything you like, my Jane—you may pour red wine over the carpets and stub out cigarettes on the parquet. You may set fire to the curtains and rip the chair covers! You are our friend!

What we do not want is to be robbed by some mean little stranger."

I could not help smiling at her Gallic logic—the beautiful, generous gesture coupled with the fact that I knew, and she knew I knew, that I had been carefully selected for the caretaking job. Sylvie knew me; she had seen how I kept my own house. She knew that if there were any breakages, they would be the result of bad luck and not of carelessness. Even as this thought flashed through my mind, I felt guilty and ungracious for quibbling at Sylvie's motives.

Sylvie handed me my refilled glass, raised hers to touch it briefly, and we both drank. Then she said, "And now comes the *bonne bouche*. The reward to my Jane for being so kind and saying yes."

"Don't be ridiculous, Sylvie," I said. "I don't want a reward. It'll be heaven for me, living here—"

"Ssh. Don't interrupt. It's very rude, and you English are so ver-r-y correct." Sylvie made a face, which was supposed to indicate Brittanic rectitude. Then she went on, "You said you wanted to make a head of Giselle, no?"

I could hardly believe my ears. I didn't dare jump to the beckoning conclusion. Trying to keep my voice offhand, I said, "You mean Giselle Arnay?"

"Who else?"

"And has she . . . ? Will she . . . ?"

"She and Michel," said Sylvie, "are planning to spend September in Montarraz. I've told her that you'll be living in my apartment, and she's agreed to sit for you. She's quite excited about the idea."

After that, the idea of leaving Montarraz never crossed my mind again.

I moved into the Claudet apartment the following week, and for a time I simply sat back and reveled in the sheer luxury of it. The contrast with Les Sapins could not have been greater. Instead of Herbert and his grinning, ever-open maw demanding offerings of wood and coal, there was discreetly concealed central heating which adjusted itself to keep a steadily delightful temperature. I had the choice of two bathrooms—pink or lilac—in both of which hot water gushed endlessly. The kitchen was a dream—a fully automatic electric oven topped by a battery of gleaming gas rings. There was a washing-up machine, of course; a huge refrigerator with a deep-freeze compartment; an electric mixer with attachments which took a whole cupboard to house them; twin stainless-steel sinks; in fact, every gadget that modern science could devise had been mustered to take the edge off the Claudets' "roughing-it," servantless holidays. I don't think I need dwell on the difference between the Claudets' sanitary arrangements and the lean-to chemical closet. I was very happy indeed.

I also remembered what Sylvie had said about having people to stay, and the idea was tempting. I knew enough about Montarraz by now to realize that August—the so-called "high season" of the summer—was a disastrous month, whereas September was entrancing. Consequently, I wrote to Emmy Tibbett and suggested that she and Henry might like to spend some time with me in September. I could promise them, I wrote, a rather more comfortable holiday than the previous one.

I would, I hoped, be busy on my head of Giselle Arnay at the time, but I knew that the Tibbetts would be able to amuse themselves. They were both keen walkers, for instance, and the mountains around Montarraz are famous for their *"excursions à pied,"* especially in the autumn. The Tibbetts accepted with enthusiasm, and so it was that, on a balmy evening at the end of August, I found myself once more at the post office, waiting to meet the gallant orange bus when it puffed its way up from the plain. Giselle Arnay was due to arrive in her private helicopter the next day.

Henry and Emmy were in great form, and regaled me with a blow-by-blow account of a mad twenties-style pajama party which they had attended earlier in the week—an aftermath, apparently, of the Balaclava case. I had been reading the trial reports in the English papers, knowing that Henry was involved. Even in the rather stilted press accounts of Chief Superintendent Tibbett's evidence, I could always detect the man himself, his dry wit and deceptive diffidence. I was glad that justice had been done, and I knew that Henry was, too.

My visitors were gratifyingly impressed by the Claudet apartment, and took an unaffected delight in its luxuries. Emmy and I had great fun experimenting with the various gadgets in the kitchen, and with their aid we produced a really splendid lunch of homemade cheesecake followed by *entrecôte beurre Café de Paris.* It was after we had eaten, and were sunning ourselves on the balcony with our coffee, that Henry said, rather sleepily, "By the way, Jane, we saw a thing of yours the other day."

"A thing? What sort of a thing?"

"That figure you did for the Bassingtons. They're neighbors of ours, you know. They gave a drinks party in the garden the other evening, and everybody was admiring it. We came in for quite a bit of reflected glory, since we not only knew the artist but had met the model. Nobody would believe that she was your char. How are Anne-Marie and Robert, by the way? They must have been married for over a year now. Any offspring?"

For a moment I couldn't say anything. Then I said, "Oh, dear. I'd forgotten you didn't know."

Quickly Emmy said, "Oh, Jane, I'm sorry. It's bad news, isn't it?"

I nodded. The bright sunshine suddenly seemed brash, the gaiety of the afternoon had evaporated. Far down in the valley below us I could just see the tall gray turrets of the convent where, in a few weeks, Anne-Marie would have her child. "I'd better tell you," I said. And I did.

When I had finished, there was a long silence. Then Emmy said, "That poor child. How terrible. And how awful for you, Jane. You had to give evidence against her."

"Not only that," I said. "It was my evidence that convicted her. You can imagine how I felt."

"I never did like the setup at the Chalet Perce-neige," said Emmy. "You remember that sinister party we all went to?"

"Don't be silly, Emmy," said Henry quite sharply. "You said afterward what fun it had been, and how charming they all were."

"Well, I didn't know then—"

I said, "You really can't blame Giselle Arnay. Lots of rich people make a great fuss of their ski instructors, and lots of instructors take it all with a pinch of salt, enjoy themselves, and forget the whole thing at the end of the winter season. I'm afraid the answer is that

Robert Drivaz was weak and vain and greedy, and hopelessly spoiled by his mother. I should have realized that before I encouraged Anne-Marie to marry him. If I'd been able to—"

"You wouldn't have been able to change anything that happened, Jane," said Henry. After a pause he added, "We have far less effect on people than we like to think—even people close to us." Emmy looked quickly at her husband, but he was frowning down at his coffee cup. "You say she denied killing him?"

"Yes. Right up to the end. That was what made it so awful, in a way. If she'd admitted it—well, it would have been a sort of catharsis. A cleansing, a relief. Do you see what I mean?"

"For her, or for you?" There was a dry edge to Henry's voice that I recognized.

I said, "All right. For me, I suppose. As it is, I'm left with more than sorrow. Doubt."

He looked at me then. "Real doubt?"

"I just don't know. I'd have staked my life on the fact that Anne-Marie would never tell a lie."

"But you say the evidence was conclusive?"

"Absolutely. Damn it."

"You think she would have been capable of killing Robert? Psychologically, I mean."

I considered. "In hot blood, yes. She's a passionate creature. But . . . all that time. What was she doing in there all that time, before she came rushing out and bumped into Mario? It's just not right. Not like her."

Henry said, "This has been worrying you badly, hasn't it, Jane?"

"Yes, it has."

"Then why not tell me about it properly—in detail, I mean. Everything you can remember."

I shrugged. "There doesn't seem much point, now. What's done is done. Heaven knows, I've done all I can to help, and so has Sylvie. If it wasn't for the baby—"

Henry said, "Yes. The baby. Who is going to be brought up by a grandmother who has already ruined his father, and who will undoubtedly tell him that his mother is a murderess."

"Oh, Henry—don't!"

"You see," Henry said gently, "it might just be worth telling me. You never know. There's always a chance."

So I told him everything I could remember, everything I have written in this account so far. When I had finished, he said, "And you are quite sure that you saw Anne-Marie going back to her chalet before five o'clock?"

I gave an exasperated sigh. "Good God, Henry, of course I'm sure. Don't you think I've been over and over it, with the police, with the lawyers, in my own head? There was no doubt at all. I was packing up my things a bit earlier than usual, because the light had gone. It had started to rain, and I couldn't see to work any longer. I was back inside Les Sapins by five, because I switched on the radio in the kitchen and listened to the five-o'clock news summary. I tell you, there's no doubt at all."

"H'm." Henry seemed lost in thought for a moment. Then he said, "You say she had good legal advice?"

"The best. She was represented by a famous advocate from Geneva. He did all he could—all that anybody could."

"Who paid him?"

The question was unexpected. "Paid him? I don't know."

"You don't get a legal celebrity for nothing. Someone footed the bill."

"I . . . I really don't know, Henry. I did inquire . . . that is, I offered to help with legal costs, but the police assured me that Anne-Marie was being adequately represented, and so she was. I never thought about who paid. Somebody who was sorry for her and wanted her cleared, I suppose."

"Or," said Henry, "somebody with a guilty conscience."

"What do you mean?"

"I don't really know," Henry admitted. "I'm just groping around a bit in the dark. Just thinking." He took a deep breath, and sat up straight in his chair. "And now that you've got that off your chest, my dear Jane, try to forget it, and let's enjoy our holiday. What about a walk to shake down our lunch?"

"Will you forget it?" I said.

Henry looked at me and grinned, but all he said was, "Where's that excursion map you were showing us? I'd suggest a walk of about an hour and a half, and *not* on one of the routes that are only for people who don't suffer from vertigo. . . ."

We picked a walk which took us up through meadows thick with autumn crocus, and brought us down through an aromatic pine forest. Nobody mentioned Anne-Marie, and gradually our mood of contentment came drifting back. Henry had been right, I thought. It had done me good to get the whole story off my chest. Besides, in an obscure way I felt that the whole matter was now in good hands.

5 ✦👑

The next day I arranged a raclette *picnic in the mountains. If you* know the Suisse Romande, you have probably eaten *raclette* in a café, for it is one of the specialties of the region; and I know that a good many foreigners find it a little disappointing. Briefly, the idea is to take a Bagnes cheese (no other will do), which roughly resembles a disk about the diameter and depth of a scooter tire, cut it in half, and apply the cut surface to the hot embers of a fire. As the cheese begins to melt and bubble under the heat, it is scraped off onto your plate, and eaten with small potatoes boiled in their skins, pickled onions, and gherkins. Each helping of melted cheese is quite small, and the idea is to see how many scrapings you can manage to eat. Seven or eight is about average, ten or twelve is good, and the record is alleged to be around forty.

As I say, in spite of the particularly delicious and delicate taste of the Bagnes, some people find *raclette* rather banal. This is because they have eaten it only in stuffy restaurants, prepared on electric grills. The proper way to eat *raclette* is as follows.

Take a large rucksack. Into it put half a Bagnes cheese; a kilo of raw potatoes; a jar of mixed onions and gherkins; a saucepan; a plate, glass, knife, and fork per person; a large knife for scraping the cheese; and a couple of liters of local white wine (don't forget the corkscrew). An old ski glove is also useful to prevent burned fingers.

Next, climb your mountain, with the rucksack on your back. As you go, look out for certain geographical features—a stream, a flat clearing with plenty of large gray stones to make a hearth, and pine trees for kindling and fuel. When you find your ideal site—remember, it should have a fantastic mountain view and be surrounded by flowering meadows—you pitch your camp.

Having constructed your hearth, you light your fire, fill the saucepan from the stream, and boil the potatoes. Open the first bottle of Fendant. By the time the potatoes are done, the embers of the fire will be red and glowing, and you can make your *raclette*. Each member of the party toasts his own cheese, holding the Bagnes in his ski-gloved hand against the red-hot wood ash. The second bottle of wine has, of course, been cooling in the ice-cold running water of the stream and is now ready to accompany your meal. The pines are green, the sky is deep blue to match the gentians, the distant peaks are capped with white. The smell of wood smoke and toasted cheese drifts deliciously upward through the crystal air; the stream burbles busily and the wine glows golden in the sunshine. Now you know what *raclette* is all about.

Henry, Emmy, and I climbed steadily for an hour through the woods and meadows above the village before we found the perfect spot. It was a little glade, sunny but surrounded by trees, and the stream tumbled and danced over dark, shiny stones toward the valley below. As the crow flies, we were not far out of Montarraz, but we were high above it, and only a corner of one house was visible, far below us.

We were soon busy with our fire and our cooking, and after that, eating and drinking took over. At first we were famished after our climb, and were queuing up for the ski glove to scrape ourselves another delectable dollop of cheese; but gradually we grew replete, the tempo slowed down, the last of the wine was poured, the neglected embers began to cool. And one by one, we stretched out luxuriously on the fragrant, springy turf and fell asleep.

I was woken abruptly by the sound of an engine. An insistent throbbing, somewhere near at hand. Sleepily I thought, A car? No. Not possible. We were far from any navigable road. An airplane? No. The steady, powerful drone was missing. I was still only half-awake, but the sound persisted, annoyingly, like the buzzing of a bluebottle. I heaved myself up onto my elbows and looked around to locate the source of the noise.

I saw it at once. Flying up the valley from the direction of Geneva came a jaunty, noisy little red helicopter, its blades spinning busily, its uplifted tail and clawlike undercarriage giving it the appearance of an aggressive insect.

I reached for the rucksack. As well as the picnic ingredients, I had put in my binoculars, knowing that the Tibbetts were keen birdwatchers; I pulled out the glasses and focused them on the little red flying machine.

Suddenly magnified, the helicopter looked less like an insect and more like a toy. In fact, I could distinctly see the heads of four people inside the cabin, as well as the pilot. The machine stopped in midair, hovering. Several hands waved from its open windows. Then it began to drop toward the ground. I followed it, fascinated, as it descended slowly and vertically, until its wheels touched the green grass. Then the whirring of the engine died away, the blur of the blades resolved itself into separate metal spokes, revolving ever more slowly. The pilot's door opened, and he jumped down and went to let out his passengers. As they emerged, I realized for the first time just what I was looking at.

The small visible portion of house was, in fact, a corner of the Chalet Perce-neige; the irregularly shaped piece of water beside it, which I had taken for a tiny mountain lake, was the swimming pool—now, of course, devoid of its protective glass; the area of green where the helicopter had landed was the chalet's private lawn; and the tiny, dark-haired figure scrambling down the ladder from the cabin was Giselle Arnay.

I suppose I should have felt like a Peeping Tom, but somehow I didn't. It did cross my mind, though, to wonder whether Arnay and Veron knew that their house could be so overlooked. They had taken elaborate precautions to keep the chalet secluded from prying passersby, but in a vertical landscape like this, it was virtually impossible to guard against a bird's-eye view. For their sakes, I hoped the journalists from Paris had not discovered our picnic glade. Meanwhile, I'm ashamed to confess that I watched the party with absorbed interest.

Giselle was followed out of the helicopter by her husband, Michel Veron. At least, I presumed it must be him, for I recognized the tall, skeletal figure, the long hair, and the huge dark glasses from the published wedding photographs. After him, Mario jumped lightly and athletically down to the grass, ignoring the ladder, and then turned to help the fourth passenger down. This was a girl in a highly unsuitable dress—a long, flowing affair in flowered chiffon, apparently inspired by Botticelli; with it she wore a pair of chubby-heeled leather knee-boots, as favored in the pioneer days of the Wild West, which must have been killing her in that heat. She had quite a bit of difficulty with her dress as she climbed down the ladder, and it was lucky that Mario was on hand to disentangle her from various parts of the machinery. At last she made it to the ground, and turned toward the house. And I saw that it was Sylvie's demure goddaughter, Chantal.

Another man had come out of the chalet to greet the party, and he and Mario now proceeded to unload suitcases from the helicopter, while the pilot shook hands with his distinguished clients. Then the last case was lifted out, the door of the helicopter slammed shut, the pilot jumped into the cockpit, and once again the noise of the motor sliced the quiet air, as the blades began to whirl. This time, they woke Henry.

"What on earth . . . ?" he muttered, heaving himself into a sitting position.

I handed him the binoculars. "Take a look," I said. "That's the Chalet Perce-neige down there. My model has arrived."

Henry gave me a sharpish look, and then took the glasses and directed them at the group in the garden below. I suppose he had detected a sour note in my voice; and no wonder. For I had recognized the man who had come out of the chalet, and who was now standing with the others, his arm around Chantal's shoulder. It was Jean Bertrand, the son of the Bertrands from the Café de la Source, the ski instructor with whom Chantal had danced that night at Le Jockey Bar.

Irrational anger flooded through me. First Robert Drivaz, now Jean Bertrand. What right had these rich, spoiled, selfish worldlings to come here to our village, to use our honest, simple people as playthings, to corrupt . . .

"What's the matter, Jane?" Henry had laid down the glasses and was looking at me.

I told him.

Henry said lightly, "Oh, come now, Jane. Surely you're exaggerating."

"I don't think so. Up until a few years ago most of these people had never even traveled outside their own valley. Life was simple and hard-working, and moral codes were strict. Now, suddenly, they're exposed to—"

Henry interrupted me. "You don't seem to think much of the moral fiber of your beloved mountain people," he said. "Ignoble savages, is that it?"

That stung me into anger, as he knew it would. "I think a great deal of them," I said hotly. "They are fine people, with integrity and courage and a sense of values."

"Then," said Henry, "they can surely stand up to the very superficial blandishments of a few trendy imbeciles with more money than sense?"

"Robert Drivaz—" I began.

"There you go again. Guilt complex. All right, Robert Drivaz was weak and foolish. There are individuals like that in any community, anywhere. It doesn't mean that the whole population of Montarraz is about to be corrupted." He smiled at me. "Be sensible, Jane."

I found myself smiling back, a little ruefully. "I'm sorry, Henry. I've been so distressed about Anne-Marie, I suppose I'm not thinking straight."

Henry didn't answer me. He had picked up the binoculars again and was training them on the garden of the Chalet Perce-neige, which was now—as far as I could see—empty. The party must have gone indoors.

"In any case," I added, "I can hardly wait to get going on Giselle Arnay's head. Those bones . . . I can feel them under my fingers. . . ."

"How very bloodthirsty that sounds," Henry remarked, without removing the binoculars from his eyes.

I laughed, delighted to find that the tension had been smoothed out of my thoughts. "Idiot . . . you know what I mean. . . ." I rolled over onto my face again, and before I knew it, I was asleep.

I woke an hour later, feeling stiff and a bit sunburned. The sun was already beginning to slide downhill toward the western mountains, and a fresh little breeze was taking the edge off the afternoon heat. The fire had died down to a mass of soft gray ash. Beside me, Emmy was stirring and stretching herself into wakefulness; Henry was kneeling a few yards away beside the stream, washing up the plates and glasses. Far below us, the Chalet Perce-neige appeared deserted. We packed up the rucksack and walked slowly back to Montarraz, down through the cool aisles of pine trees.

I must say that it was a delight to go back to the Claudets' elegant apartment and hot, scented baths, instead of having to hump up fuel for Herbert and fill the tin bathtub from kettles. All the same, I felt a remorseful pang as I walked past the shuttered windows of Les Sapins. It was, after all, my home. The sight of the padlocked double doors of the studio also caused me a stab of guilt, but I told myself firmly that I would be back at work tomorrow. All that was needed was to make an appointment with Giselle Arnay.

I bathed and changed, and came into the Louis Quinze living room to find Henry looking very spruce, and smelling of Pierre's expensive after-shave lotion. He was sitting on the sofa, riffling appreciatively through the pages of a beautifully illustrated book on Byzantine art. I fixed drinks for us both, and Henry explained that Emmy would join us shortly—he had left her up to her neck in the bath. Then, after a little silence, he said, "I think perhaps I owe you an apology, Jane."

"An apology? Whatever for?"

Henry answered with another question. "How well do you know these people—these Arnays or Verons or whatever their real name is?"

"Not at all. Well, no more than you do—you were there that evening. I haven't seen Giselle since, and I've never met Michel Veron. I . . ." I hesitated. "I *feel* that I know Giselle quite well, but that's only because I've seen all her films, and Sylvie talks so much about her. I'm hoping I'll really get to know her when she sits for me. You can't make a good head of somebody you don't know. The first few sessions are really more for talking than modeling. At least, that's the way I work."

"H'm," said Henry. He began to fill his pipe. "Rather a curious thing happened this afternoon, Jane."

"Curious? You mean the helicopter?"

"Later on. While you were asleep."

"I thought they'd all gone into the house," I said.

"Yes, they had," said Henry. "But later on, they came out again." He laughed, a little embarrassed. "This sounds very silly, put bluntly. The fact is, they were all naked."

"I don't blame them, frankly," I said. "It was terribly hot. The poor things couldn't know they had a Peeping Tom with binoculars sitting up the mountain spying on them."

Henry laughed. "I asked for that," he said. "You're perfectly right, of course. I had no business to be snooping, and heaven knows there's nothing wrong with a swim in the nude. No, it wasn't just that. The manservant, Mario, came out of the house after they'd had their swim. He was fully and rather elaborately dressed, which was a bit—well, it looked strange. He was carrying a tray."

"Honestly, Henry," I said. "I thought you lived in Chelsea. What's so very odd about having a dip and then a drink? I admit, some people might insist on the formality of a two-inch bikini, but thank God young people these days aren't ashamed of their bodies."

"That's just the point," said Henry.

"What is?"

"Your remark about having a drink. The tray which Mario passed around didn't have drinks on it."

"Then what did it have?"

"As far as I could see—cigarettes."

"Oh," I said. "I see what you mean. Reefers. Pot."

"I can't prove it, of course," said Henry, "but it looked very much like that to me. And your young ski-instructor friend didn't refuse one. Nor did that young girl—what did you say her name was?—Chantal. Then, after a while, they . . ." He broke off, and sat looking down into his glass, swilling the golden whiskey around and around.

"Oh, well," I said, "who are we to criticize? We drink alcohol, which is just another drug."

"It's not quite the same," said Henry with a sort of sad stubbornness. "I just don't like it, that's all. I think you may have been right when you said that these people are a bad influence on the village."

It's a funny thing, with me. I suppose I'm a natural arguer. Anyhow, as soon as somebody agrees with a point of view I've expressed, I immediately begin to see the flaws in my own argument; whereas if anybody disagrees with me, I get more and more convinced that I'm right. Be that as it may, I now found myself taking precisely the opposite line with Henry than the sanctimonious sentiments I had voiced earlier.

People like Giselle Arnay and Michel Veron, I heard myself saying, represented the new, exciting, talented generation. It was young people like them who gave one hope for the future. Here we were—I said "we," but I really meant "you, Henry Tibbett"—with our prudish Victorianism, our inherited and irrational prejudices, our essential small-mindedness. No wonder we had succeeded in getting the world into such a mess. The new generation had thrown off the whole shackling weight of traditional behavior. All right, maybe it meant smoking pot and sexual permissiveness. What was wrong with that? Pot was no worse than alcohol, and sex was nothing to be ashamed of—on the contrary. Young people now had a vision of a different world, of a wider, broader . . .

Henry said quietly, "And what about Anne-Marie?"

"That was below the belt," I said crossly. "Anne-Marie was . . . is a natural victim, poor child. Robert, as you said yourself, was weak and silly. It wasn't Giselle Arnay's fault—"

"Are you sure of that?"

"Of course I'm sure. It's people like you—"

It was at this moment that Emmy came in, looking fresh and attractive in blue silk trousers and a flowered shirt. She was not unnaturally surprised to find Henry and me glaring at each other from opposite ends of the sofa, obviously in the middle of an argument; but Emmy is tact personified. After a split-second reaction, she began talking naturally and pleasantly about our plans for the evening—I had suggested driving down to the valley for dinner at a restaurant famous for its excellent local wines. In a matter of moments the heat had gone out of the atmosphere, and I was feeling more than a little ashamed of my outburst, and of the way I had allowed my so-called opinions to swing from one extreme to another. I was reassured when Henry grinned at me in an almost conspiratorial way as we left the apartment; but all the same, I noticed that he was unusually quiet during the evening, and looked grave.

The next morning I telephoned the Chalet Perce-neige just before eleven o'clock. The number was not, of course, listed in the telephone directory, but Sylvie had written it down for me on a scrap of paper torn from her diary, with the words TOP SECRET scribbled beside it.

The phone was answered by Mario—I recognized his voice at once. He began by saying that Mlle. Arnay was not available to talk to anybody and would not be so all day. I told him who I was, threw in Sylvie's name, assured him that Mlle. Arnay was expecting me to call, and begged him at least to go and tell her that I was on the line. At last he agreed, and went away. I held on for what seemed an eternity, and was about to give up and try again later on when a new masculine voice came onto the line, speaking French and demanding to be told exactly who I was and what I wanted.

"Am I speaking to M. Veron?" I asked.

There was a little hesitation, and then he said, "Yes, madame.

Now, please explain what you want with . . . with my wife." He sounded cold and bored.

I explained the whole thing all over again. When I had finished, Michel Veron said, with an unamused little laugh, "I am sorry, madame. I realize it is not your fault. Sylvie Claudet is really quite irresponsible. If you know her, as you say you do, you will understand what I mean. She had no right to promise anything on Giselle's behalf. My wife would not dream of posing for you. We are here for a holiday, and a little privacy from people like you." You'd have thought I was a gossip columnist from the tone of his voice—although, on second thoughts, he might have dealt more politely with the press. After all, journalists are a necessary evil to entertainers, however famous. "I am sorry to disappoint you, madame, but it is out of the question. Good-bye." And he rang off before I could say a word.

I don't deny that I was bitterly disappointed, but I was not really very surprised. Michel Veron had been right about Sylvie, of course. Warm, impulsive, friendly as a kitten, Sylvie would make the most extravagant promises to her friends, just to see them happy. Where it was within her own powers to fulfill those promises, she would do so; but I could see only too well how she might blithely commit other people to courses of action on the strength of some chance remark made and forgotten. I had been a fool to believe that Giselle Arnay would sit for me. I decided to put the whole thing out of my head, and to concentrate on enjoying the company of the Tibbetts. When they went back to London, I told myself, I would open up the studio and start on a completely new project. A series of abstracts to be cast in bronze, perhaps.

Meanwhile, the sun was shining, and we decided to spend the morning climbing to a high mountain pasture which was renowned for its gentians and wild orchids. It was not a very arduous expedition, but a long one, and exhausting enough for a middle-aged trio like ourselves. We were all glad to stop for an *assiette Valaisanne*—a plate of local smoked and dried meats—and a flask of white wine at a mountain restaurant on the way down; and after this, we took things easy, getting back to the apartment about four o'clock.

It was the day when Lucia, the new Italian *concierge*, came in to clean the apartment. She was a big, strapping, black-haired girl who sang melancholy Neapolitan love songs in the most cheerful possible way as she worked. The Tibbetts had gone to their room for a rest and to change, and I was steeping myself in Sylvie's pink bathtub when I heard the front doorbell ring—a short, nervous buzz, quite unlike the postman's imperious peal or the baker's pert tattoo. I heard Lucia go to answer the door, and the sound of quiet voices. Then the clatter of Lucia's sandals on the parquet, and a rap on the bathroom door.

"Yes?" I called. "What is it?"

Lucia's voice came penetratingly from the corridor outside. "Pardon, *signora*. It is a girl, *signora*." She used the Italian word *ragazza*, which does not exactly imply respect. Some village schoolchild, I supposed.

"What does she want, Lucia?"

"She wants to see you, *signora*."

"Well, she can't. I'm in my bath. Go and ask her what it's all about, will you?"

Lucia clattered away again. A few moments later she was back at the bathroom door. "She asks if she may wait to see the *signora*."

By this time I was becoming a little irritated. I said, "Who is she, anyway, Lucia?"

"I don't know, *signora*. I asked her name, but she just said might she wait until the *signora* could see her."

"Tell her, if she won't leave a name or a message, I certainly won't see her," I said.

Once again Lucia departed, and again returned. "Please, *signora*, she says that it is about Anne-Marie."

Of course, this changed everything. It must mean that the baby was imminent, or had already arrived. I grabbed the hand rail and pulled myself to my feet, reaching for a towel. "All right," I called. "Take her into the kitchen and give her a biscuit, and I'll see her as soon as I'm dressed."

"Si, signora."

I dried myself quickly and put on a pair of slacks and a cotton shirt. Then I ran a comb through my hair, treated my face to a dab of powder and lipstick, and came out of Sylvie's beautiful bedroom, walked across the sitting room, and into the hallway. The kitchen door was open. In the kitchen, sitting on a stool and nibbling a ginger biscuit, was Giselle Arnay.

I couldn't blame Lucia for not recognizing our visitor. As I've said before, Giselle was tiny and could easily pass for a fourteen-year-old without the elaborate eye makeup which she usually wore. Today her face was scrubbed bare of any cosmetics whatsoever. Her long dark hair hung straight down to below her shoulders, falling over her peaky little face so as to half-hide its features. She wore a pair of faded blue jeans which had been hacked off carelessly just below the knee to make elongated shorts, and a shapeless navy-blue toweling T-shirt. Her feet were bare. She looked less like a film star than anybody I had ever seen. Lucia was sitting at the far side of the table, also munching a biscuit. The two of them were chatting as fluently as Lucia's halting French would allow.

Giselle saw me, looked up, and smiled. "What delicious biscuits, Mme. Weston," she said.

"Mlle. Arnay!" I exclaimed. "Oh, I am so sorry—"

"Why are you sorry? The biscuits are divine, and I have been having such a nice talk with Lucia."

Lucia, who had done a double-take of staggering proportions, now dropped her ginger nut as if it had bitten her, leaped to her feet, and clamped both hands to her mouth, giving a sort of whiffling scream, in which the words "Giselle Arnay!" were just audible.

Giselle smiled ravishingly at her. "You must come to my house one day, Lucia," she said, "and we will talk again."

Lucia, now entirely bereft of speech, turned crimson. I said, "Let's go into the sitting room, Mlle. Arnay."

"Oh, please call me 'Giselle.' And it is 'Jane,' is it not? I feel I know you very well, even though we have met only once. Sylvie has told me so much about you." She stood up—and somehow managed to make a movement of infinite grace out of it; then, like a naughty schoolgirl, her hand flickered to the biscuit tin to snatch another ginger nut. Leaving Lucia in a state of near-collapse, she led the way into the sitting room, followed by a trail of biscuit crumbs.

"I really must apologize," I said again. "Lucia simply told me there was a girl to see me. I had no idea—"

Ignoring me, Giselle said, "I must tell you why I have come here."

"Lucia said . . . Anne-Marie . . ."

"Ah, yes. Anne-Marie." Giselle nodded gravely, as if making a point in some inner conversation with herself. "Later, we can talk of Anne-Marie." She paused. Then she looked straight at me from under that curtain of silky hair. "Mme. Weston . . . Jane . . . I have come to ask a big favor of you. I know you are a famous sculptor. I have heard much of your work. Would you be willing to make a head of me in marble? The price would not matter. Anything you name."

I was so taken aback that I could only gape at her for several moments. Then I said, "Mlle. Arnay—"

"Giselle," she corrected me gently.

"Giselle, your husband must have told you that I telephoned this morning—"

She smiled, not to me but to herself. "Michel can be very stupid," she said. "I think he must have been rude to you. I have come to make amends, if I can. Michel is ignorant of such things, but I appreciate the honor you do me in wishing to make my head. I would like to accept your kind offer, and to pay a proper price for your work."

"I don't know what to say," I replied, truthfully enough. "Of course . . . naturally . . . I shall be delighted. . . ."

"That's good, then," she said, suddenly offhand. She began wandering around the room, inspecting the pictures, the furnishings, the curtains, like a little cat—and all the time nibbling her biscuit. I watched her, fascinated. Then she said, "That is settled, then. Come to the chalet this evening and bring your friends. Eight o'clock."

"But I can't work—" I began to protest.

"Not to work. To get to know. We will work in your studio tomorrow, I think."

"Yes," I said feebly.

"Good." Again the little nod, to herself. *"A bientôt."* And suddenly she wasn't in the room any longer. She had the facility of moving as fast and as unexpectedly as a small wild animal. I heard her for a brief moment in the hall, saying, *"Au revoir,* Lucia." Then the front door clicked shut, and she had gone.

I ran to the bathroom window, which overlooks the car park. Outside the front door stood the most beautiful car I had ever seen. It was canary yellow, and I know now that it was a Monteverdi—probably the most expensive sports car in the world. A moment later it roared away up the drive, driven by Lucia's barefoot *ragazza.*

6 ♛

I enjoyed myself that evening. I suppose, to be truthful, that I was riding on a wave of euphoria. I like to think of myself as a reasonably mature and balanced personality—who doesn't?—but it's not every day that a middle-aged sculptress of modest talent finds herself so much in demand. I had been begging Giselle Arnay to do me a favor by sitting for me, and now she had turned the tables and was, to all appearances, flattered and honored that I wanted to sculpt her. Looking back now, I can see that perhaps I was foolish and gullible; I can only plead that the temptation was great.

In any case, the whole atmosphere of the Chalet Perce-neige quickly dispelled Henry's sinister suspicions. This evening, in contrast to our previous visit, a carriage lamp was burning over the front door, which was opened by Giselle herself while Henry's finger was still on the bell push. Michel Veron and Chantal were laughing together as they brewed aromatic *vin chaud* over the log fire—Chantal looking enchanting in a dark, silky cat-suit, Michel Veron looking surprisingly young and vulnerable without his dark glasses, like a handsome, well-mannered schoolboy. There was no sign of Mario, nor of Jean Bertrand.

It was soon made clear that the evening was to be do-it-yourself.

"It is Mario's evening off," Giselle confided to me—thereby, in one short sentence, relegating Mario to the servants' hall. "I think he has a girl friend in the village; when we are in Montarraz, he can never wait to get away. So now, I will show you that I can make the French kitchen myself." Her English was as attractive as Sylvie's. "Look, Jane. There is a special surprise for you."

Giselle grinned, like an urchin with a secret, and went over to the window, where she pressed an electric switch. At once the gardens beyond the big panes of plate glass leaped into life. Colored lamps had been set among the trees and shrubs, giving the whole place the air of an enchanted stage setting. The glass screens were in position again around the swimming pool, for the evening was chilly, but—high up—panes for ventilation were open; and the reason for these was obvious. Around the shimmering pool, barbecue equipment was ranged, joints of meat were already spitted, plates and bowls of salad were waiting on low ebony tables. As we went out through the French windows into the semigarden of the pool area, I could see and smell that the charcoal fires had been smoldering for some time. All that was needed was to stir aside the ash, revealing the burning heart of the embers, and to set the steak and lamb joints turning. Do-it-yourself, perhaps—but somebody else had already done a great deal.

Giselle, gay as a trivet, made a great joke about being *chef de cuisine,* putting on a tall white hat and a butler's apron. Chantal was appointed her kitchen maid. Michel Veron was to provide the cabaret. The Tibbetts and I were the honored guests.

So, in that dreamlike garden, we relaxed on cushioned swing chairs, while Chantal served us with wine, and Giselle Arnay bent her internationally famous profile over the glowing fires as she basted our meat, and Michel Veron strummed softly on his guitar for our amusement, and sang wistful songs in the voice which cost nightclub owners in Paris a thousand pounds an evening. By the time the meat had been cooked and carved and served, we were laughing and chattering away like old friends.

Giselle had acquired a black streak of charcoal down her flawless cheek, and when Michel drew attention to it, she grabbed a charred stick and proceeded to embellish all our faces with curly moustaches or Mephistophelian eyebrows. Veron turned out to have an unsuspected gift for comic mimicry, despite the fact that he made his name singing tender, bittersweet love songs. As the evening wore on, however, he treated us to hilarious parodies with voice and guitar—how Maurice Chevalier might interpret Alban Berg, how Mme. Callas would tackle a Beatles number, what Noël Coward might make of a Rossini aria. Not only the voices, but also the music was precisely caricatured, with a most lighthearted erudition. I remembered the wedding photographs of Michel and Giselle, and realized what a false impression a newspaper reportage could convey. Not only were these two brilliant, but they had a quality of innocence which was totally unexpected.

It was after two o'clock in the morning when we got back to Panoralpes, still slightly euphoric and simmering with laughter. Like a child on Christmas Eve, I felt that I wanted to get to sleep as soon as I could, to bring the morning closer; for Giselle was arriving at eleven o'clock for her first sitting.

I said good night to Henry and Emmy, and went into my bedroom. As I closed the door behind me, I was dimly aware of Henry's voice. He was talking to Emmy, in a tone quite as astringent as that of Michel imitating Coward, and he was saying, "What a *very* extraordinary performance." It didn't even occur to me to wonder what he meant. Within minutes I was in bed, and in a dreamless sleep.

The next morning I was in the studio by nine o'clock, getting everything ready. Moist clay was waiting in a bucket, covered by a damp cloth. A modeling board with a central spike stood ready to take the first tentative shaping of the head. I hauled a comfortable but straight-backed chair out from Les Sapins and placed it near the open stable doors so that the clear sunlight would catch and outline the lovely contours of Giselle's face. I also set out some large sheets of thick drawing paper and thin sticks of charcoal for making sketches. Lucia brought out a tray with glasses, soft drinks, beer, and a flask of wine in case Giselle wanted refreshment. By half-past ten everything was ready. I perched myself on the edge of my work bench, lit a cigarette, and waited.

It was only five minutes past eleven when I heard the sound of a car coming down the lane from the main road. I jumped up, stubbed out my cigarette, and came out into the sunshine—in time to see Giselle climbing out of the yellow Monteverdi. She was alone, barefoot, and wearing the same truncated blue jeans as the day before. She saw me, waved, and came running up to the studio.

Giselle was at her gayest and most charming. For a moment she reminded me of Anne-Marie, as she sat perched on the edge of the chair, chattering a lot of attractive nonsense about my work and the studio, asking me how she should pose, and moving from one position to another with such speed that she gave me no chance to reply. "Like this? Or so? Or is this better? My chin up, so? Or like that?"

I put the thought of Anne-Marie firmly out of my mind. I don't mean to sound callous, but to do good work, one must be entirely concentrated on the job in hand; if I had allowed myself to get emotionally upset by thinking about Anne-Marie's tragedy, and the parts that Giselle and I had both played in it, the result would have been disastrous.

I told Giselle that for the moment she should just sit comfortably and talk, moving her head and upper body as much as she wanted to. Then I picked up a sheet of paper and a stick of charcoal and began making sketches. I had warned her that I probably would not listen to what she was saying—and indeed, I quickly became so absorbed in work that her chatter passed right over my head.

Sheet after sheet of paper I covered with quick, bold outlines, and the more I drew, the more enchanted I became. Giselle's bone structure fascinated me, for a start—the wide, high cheekbones, the delicately pointed chin, the firm angles of the jaw. And then, she had such grace of movement, as if her muscles were a well-trained corps de ballet, executing each seemingly careless gesture with beautiful precision, gliding naturally from one lovely line to another. I had, in fact, been intending to ask Giselle why she had mentioned Anne-Marie the previous day, and whether she had any news of her; but everything was now forgotten in the delight of my work and the

73

problem of how to convert such mobile beauty into a static medium.

The time passed so quickly that I could hardly believe it when Lucia put her head shyly around the door to announce that it was half-past twelve and Mme. Tibbett had asked her to say that lunch was ready.

"Do forgive me," I said to Giselle. "I had no idea it was so late. You must be tired."

"Tired? What for? I do nothing—it is you who work."

"You're very kind," I said. I began to pack up my materials. "Are you going to be even kinder and sit for me again tomorrow? Then I can start on the actual modeling."

"Tomorrow?" There was obvious dismay in her voice.

"Or the day after," I amended hastily. "I realize you must be very busy—"

"Can I not come again this afternoon, then?" She was like a child begging for a sweet.

"But of course you can! I never thought you would want to."

"I do want to, Jane," she said seriously. "I think this is to be a good work, and I know that when a good work is started, it must continue until it is finished. In a little way, I am an artist too, you see."

All I could think of to say was, "Thank you." And then, as an afterthought, "Will you stay and have lunch with us?"

"Oh, I wish I could. But Michel will expect me." She stood up, stretched, and walked over to my work table. She picked up the top sketch from the pile, studied it gravely, and then said, "This is good. When all is finished, may I buy these drawings, too?"

"You won't be buying anything," I said. "Of course, you can have all the sketches, as well as the head, if you want them."

"As my model fee," she said pertly. "You will pay me in your own beautiful paper money!" She laughed, delighted at the conceit. Then she said, "I will be back at three," and before I knew it she had gone, running down the path to the car park, her bare feet twinkling through the grass. A moment later the Monteverdi roared into life and swung up the narrow driveway at dangerous speed.

Henry and Emmy were waiting for me in the drawing room of Sylvie's apartment, drinking white wine from a chilled bottle. As I poured myself a glass, I told them as well as I could about my excitement, the progress of the work, and Giselle's marvelous, unbelievable decision to come back in the afternoon.

"I'm ashamed of myself," I admitted. "I was thinking of her just as a beautiful object—I had forgotten that she is a very considerable actress. Even so, it shows extraordinary sensitivity."

"Extraordinary," said Henry a trifle dryly.

Emmy had prepared a delicious cold meal, but I hardly noticed what I was eating. My mind was entirely occupied with plans for the afternoon's sitting. I suddenly became aware that Emmy was saying, "Will they, Jane?"—with the sort of emphasis which indicated that she must be asking the question for the second time.

"Sorry," I said. "I was miles away. Will who what?"

"Will the nuns nurse Anne-Marie themselves during her confinement? Will she have her baby at the convent?"

"I shouldn't think so," I said. "They're not a nursing order. They run the orphanage, of course, but that's different. The actual convent, where Anne-Marie is, is supposed to be very enclosed, or pent-up, or whatever the technical term is. You know—they never go outside the convent, and only one Sister at a time is allowed to speak to visitors from outside."

There was a little silence, and then Emmy said, "Does that mean that they won't even visit her in the hospital?"

"I suppose so." I was thinking that, for the head, I would have Giselle's chin tilted just slightly upward, so that the muscles in her neck would be taut against the skin. Upward, and bent a little to the left.

"It's the Convent of the Holy Cross at Charonne, isn't it?" Emmy's voice was persistent, like an irritating insect.

"Yes," I said shortly and not very graciously.

After that, a welcome silence descended, and I returned to my own thoughts. It was the sight of Emmy bringing in coffee from the kitchen that roused me to a guilty sense of my duty as a hostess.

"It was a wonderful lunch, Emmy," I said. "You're an angel. I'm sorry to have to leave you to your own devices again this afternoon."

"Please don't worry about us," said Emmy, and there was an edge to her voice.

"I shall go for a walk up the mountain," Henry announced. "And then do some shopping—a few presents for people back home."

After a moment of silence Emmy said, "I thought I might go down to the valley. I believe there's an interesting church at Charonne, and a museum. It was a Roman settlement, wasn't it?"

"I think so," I said. "I'm afraid I've never really explored it. I'm like the Londoners who've never been to the Tower."

"Well, if you don't mind . . ." Another pause. Then Emmy said, with a rush, "Could I borrow your car, Jane?"

"Of course you can. What a good idea." I realized then that she had been plucking up courage to ask me, and that this accounted for the fact that she had sounded a little stilted and unnatural. I was pleased to have found the explanation. For a moment, obscurely, Emmy had worried me.

As soon as I had finished my coffee, I excused myself and hurried back to the studio. I carefully studied all the sketches I had made, and then settled down to make, from them, a composite drawing of Giselle's head as I intended to model it. This was not a dashed-off sketch, but a reasoned design. When I had finished the full-face version, I started on the profile. Dimly, with less than half of my mind, I registered the fact that my little car had gone climbing up the driveway to the main road; Emmy must be on her way. It seemed no time at all later that the Monteverdi was back, and Giselle with it.

This time I posed her carefully, showing her the drawings so that she would see just the angle I had envisaged. She nodded gravely, and composed herself with great intelligence to produce exactly the effect I wanted. I had forgotten that she was not only an actress but also a film star, and consequently intensely aware of lighting effects. It was a joy to see her, with no prompting from me, settling herself so that the sunlight fell in precisely such a way as to enhance the angles and shadows of those extraordinary facial bones. This time, there was no chatter. She was a professional, and so was I.

"So?" she said.

"Yes," I said.

After that, neither of us spoke. She sat, like an exquisite statue, immobile and uncomplaining. I began to work the pliant clay, drawing out the bones and muscles under the surface, feeling the planes and contours coming to life beneath my fingers. I was utterly absorbed, utterly concentrated, utterly happy.

EMMY

7

I don't mind telling you, Jane had me worried. I mean, Henry and I had known her for years, and she had always been what I call a nice person. When her husband, Simon, was alive, things had been easy for her, I suppose—but I've met plenty of people who have everything in life, and still make a complaining hash of it. Jane was comfortably off, happily married, and talented—and she made absolutely the best of it. She was a marvelous hostess, a witty conversationalist, a personality; she was also generous, unconventional, completely unsnobbish, and she never gossiped. Henry and I both loved her.

When Simon died so suddenly, she behaved just as well and bravely as I would have expected. He left her very inadequately provided for, because he had been something of a gambler in business and had never anticipated being struck down by a coronary in his early fifties. I happen to know that Jane had several unpleasant shocks to cope with after his death. She didn't tell me, of course, but I heard from other people.

For a start, the Chelsea house had not belonged to Simon, but was heavily mortgaged. Unable to keep up the payments, Jane found herself literally without a roof over her head. The Bentley turned out to be the property of the firm—another scrap of information which Simon had not thought fit to pass on to his wife. She also learned that he had opted for a pay-less-now pension scheme which would have provided quite handsomely for both of them had he survived until the age of seventy. As it was, he had gambled on longevity, and lost. Jane was left to manage on a shoestring.

As I said, I heard none of this from Jane herself at the time, and she made Meriel Blunt's offer of a Swiss chalet sound like a glamorous dream come true. In fact, it just about saved her bacon. Meriel told me afterward that they had been on the point of accepting a huge offer for the land, but had decided that Jane needed the house more than they needed the money. She had had to run the place down, she said, before Jane would accept it, in case it smacked of charity. Having seen Les Sapins, and knowing how land values are rising in Switzerland, I must say I don't think Meriel and Charlie were being quite so altruistic as they made out; but the point is that Jane, in disaster, was courageous, resourceful, and quite without self-pity. I admired her more than ever; and when I saw her bronze of Anne-Marie in the Bassingtons' London garden, I realized that she had progressed greatly as an artist since Simon's death.

Henry and I thoroughly enjoyed our first visit to Montarraz. Jane appeared to have settled down happily, to have adjusted from a life of luxury in Chelsea to the rigors of Les Sapins, and to have integrated with the local community. We had all laughed afterward about our bizarre evening at the Chalet Perce-neige, and Jane had shown a healthy lack of respect for the local celebrities. And now, suddenly, it was all different.

Naturally, I didn't blame Jane for accepting Sylvie Claudet's offer of her apartment—it was heavenly, and only a fool would have turned it down. Still, from the moment of our arrival there, I could sense a change in Jane. She wasn't relaxed any longer; she was as tense as a drawn bow, and had the same tendency to twang nastily if even slightly plucked. When she told us the story of Anne-Marie, I thought that explained everything. Now, I was unsure again.

For a start, that evening with Giselle Arnay and her ridiculous barbecue. Honestly, if you could have seen it. . . . Henry had told me exactly what he had seen through the binoculars after our *raclette* picnic, and it seemed to me that Giselle and Michel probably knew they had been overlooked, and were determined to scotch adverse criticism in the village. Which just shows what silly conclusions one can jump to—if Henry ever reads this, he'll make me rewrite that sentence. He has a passion for correct grammar, which I don't share.

Anyhow, the point is that Jane fell for the whole thing, hook, line, and sinker. I suppose it was flattering for her as an artist, having Giselle Arnay fawning all over her and begging to be sculpted; but I thought she'd have been level-headed enough to see through a ploy like that. But the more she talked, the more it seemed to me that Jane was going soft, was slipping into the role of yes-woman to the Verons and the Claudets. I didn't like it.

More than anything, I was haunted by the thought of that poor girl, Anne-Marie. I remembered her vividly—so gay, so young, so vulnerable, and on the brink of happiness.

Of course, I couldn't blame Jane for her part in the wretched affair—she had to tell the police the truth as she saw it. But was it really the truth? Was there no other explanation? There did not seem to be. Jane knew Anne-Marie well enough, and she had seen her going back to her chalet before five o'clock. All right, the girl must have been lying. That didn't necessarily make her a killer.

No, I didn't blame Jane, but I did blame Giselle Arnay—and it made me feel sick to see Jane fussing around her, more like a teenage fan than a grown woman. Meanwhile, down in the valley, Anne-Marie waited for her baby, entirely alone. When she went to the hospital, she would not have a single visitor, for the Sisters never left the convent.

It was true, of course, that Jane and Sylvie had both tried to visit Anne-Marie, and had been snubbed. Well, that was understandable enough. They had both, however unwittingly, contributed toward the verdict of guilty. But surely if an outsider, somebody quite unconnected with Robert's death, somebody she knew . . . That was when I decided to drive down to Charonne and see the girl myself.

I had intended to tell Jane about my plan at lunchtime, but she was so offhand, so wrapped up in herself and Giselle, that I thought better of it. So I just asked if I might borrow the car, and left it at that. I expect she noticed that I was a bit brusque—or perhaps it did not register. She was entirely concerned with getting back to that studio of hers.

I did tell Henry my idea, and he agreed that I should go alone. He thought I would have a better chance that way of getting to see Anne-Marie.

The drive to the valley was beautiful, revealing a series of glorious panoramas as the road snaked downhill. Soon I could see the steep red roofs of Charonne clustered below me, dominated by the square church tower. A little way outside the town, I could pick out the forbidding, barrackslike shape of the convent.

At close quarters it looked even more daunting. The garden was well kept but severe, and the whole place seemed deserted. The windows, set in regimented rows, were actually barred, like a prison. The whole building seemed to have turned its back on the world. With some trepidation, I grasped the iron bell pull and jerked it downward. I was answered by a mournful chime, which died away into the stillness of the interior. The dark oaken door, with its barred grille, remained firmly closed.

Then there was the sound of heavy footsteps on stone, the grating of a bolt, and the little door behind the grille shot open. I found myself looking into a pair of steady gray eyes, which studied me from beneath the white wimple and black veil of the order. The face, which was middle-aged, was calm but severe, not unkind, but with no softness, either.

"Yes?" said the nun. She did not smile.

I summoned what I hoped was an ingratiating smile, and my best French. "Good afternoon, Sister. I am sorry to bother you, but I have called for news of Anne-Marie Drivaz."

"You are a relative?"

I shook my head. "She has no relatives that I know of. I'm a friend."

"She has no friends," said the nun simply, stating a fact.

"That's not true." I was nettled, and my smile was wearing thin.

"When did you know her?" the Sister demanded, adding, "You are a foreigner"—as if it were an accusation.

"That's right. I'm English. I met Anne-Marie when she was *con-*

cierge at Panoralpes, in Montarraz. I was staying there." I had decided not to mention Jane, remembering the hostility with which she had been greeted. The nun considered this. "I see. Your name, madame?"

"Tibbett. Emmy Tibbett. Anne-Marie will certainly remember me." I paused. "How is she?"

"She is well."

"The baby . . . ?"

"Expected next week."

"Look, Sister," I said, "I would very much like to see Anne-Marie. I have made a special journey here. May I come in?"

Again the calm gray eyes appraised me. Then, without a word, the nun bent down, and I heard the noise of heavy bolts being drawn, and the groaning of an old-fashioned key in the lock. Then the door swung open, to reveal a long, bare, stone-flagged corridor. Silently the Sister stood aside to let me pass. I stepped into the chilly twilit bleakness.

The Sister led the way down the corridor, her heavy black shoes thudding on the stone flags like the footsteps of some medieval jailer. Near the end of the corridor she opened a door and said, "Please wait in here, madame." Then she had gone.

The room was small and cheerless. It contained a plain wooden table on which lay a black Bible, and four upright chairs. On the walls were a crucifix and a couple of bad reproductions of sentimental religious paintings. The small, high, barred window let in a little light, but no sunshine. I sat down and waited.

After about five minutes the door opened again, and the Sister returned, followed by a woman whom I could scarcely recognize as Anne-Marie. She was wearing a curious sort of floor-length apron, which made her look like an old-fashioned housemaid with a leaning toward holy orders, and under it her pregnant stomach was swollen and ugly. Her lovely hair was invisible beneath a hideous white cotton coif, like those worn by hospital nurses at the turn of the century. In the heat of the summer, she was wearing thick black woolen stockings and stout black laced-up shoes. Her face was as pale as her white headdress, but her hands were red and roughened by hard work and harsh kitchen abrasives. A huge black cross, made of some heavy material, clanked on her chest like fetters, and the weight of it seemed to drag on the back of her neck, so that her head was permanently bent forward, her eyes always on the ground.

"Well, Anne-Marie?" The Sister's voice was stern but not unkind. "Do you know this lady?"

Anne-Marie raised her eyes timidly and looked at me. I smiled warmly. There was a tiny answering flicker—no more than a momentary gleam. Then she looked down again and said, "Yes, *ma Soeur.*"

"Do you wish to speak with her?"

"Yes, *ma Soeur.*"

"Do you wish me to remain in the room with you?"

Anne-Marie hesitated. "If you wish to, *ma Soeur.* . . ."

"Do *you* wish it, Anne-Marie?"

In a whisper Anne-Marie said, "No, *ma Soeur.* If it is permitted . . ."

The nun showed no emotion. "Very well. I will return for you in ten minutes." She nodded briefly in my direction, and went out. Anne-Marie sat down on one of the hard chairs on the other side of the table, and we looked at each other for an endless, silent moment.

Then I said, "I'm staying in Montarraz, and I did so want to see you, Anne-Marie. How are you?"

"Very well, thank you, madame."

"Are you happy here?"

"The Sisters are very kind."

"Do you need help—of any sort?"

"No, thank you, madame."

We seemed to be getting nowhere. I said, almost roughly, "Anne-Marie, tell me the truth. You're not happy, are you?"

She burst out suddenly, "How can I be happy?" And then, lowering her eyes again, she whispered, "I do not deserve to be happy."

"Who says so?"

"Everybody. I have been wicked."

"Have you? Anne-Marie, look at me. Have you been wicked?"

There was a long silence. Then she said softly, "In my heart."

"What do you mean?"

"I wished that Robert was dead." Her voice was not passionate, not even emphatic. It was apathetic—a repetition which had grown stale. "I wanted him to die. So the court was right to call me guilty. In God's eyes, the thought is as evil as the deed."

"Who's been saying that to you?"

"Everybody. The good Sisters. They are right. They say I must be resigned. They say I deserve to be punished."

I was so angry that I didn't trust myself to speak for a moment. Then I said, controlling myself as best I could, "You have been punished enough, Anne-Marie. Now it is time for you to be happy again. After your baby is born . . ."

She began to cry very quietly.

I went on, "I know it will be hard to part with it, but it is for the best. Then, you must leave this place."

"But, Mme. Tibbett, I cannot." At last her voice, although choked with sobs, began to sound natural.

"Of course you can." I was growing reckless. "You have friends, you know. You mustn't think you are alone. Mme. Weston is your true friend, if only you will believe it, and so am I. I might even be able to arrange for you to come to England."

"No, no, madame. I cannot leave here unless I go to prison."

I could have bitten out my tongue for my tactlessness. I had completely forgotten that the girl was under the sentence of the court. A three-year term in prison, suspended only on condition that she stayed in the convent. In fact, the only way to get her away would be to prove her innocence and upset the verdict.

I said, "Of course. I had forgotten. We shall have to think what we can do. Meanwhile, I'd like to visit you again. Would you like that?"

"Oh, yes, madame." Anne-Marie extracted a handkerchief from beneath her hideous apron and blew her nose. She had stopped crying, and there was a distinct suggestion of her old self as she said, "You are so kind. It is wonderful to have a friend."

"But I tell you, Anne-Marie, you have many friends. Mme. Weston wants to come and visit you. . . ."

An iron curtain came down on her face. "I do not want to see Mme. Weston."

"And Mme. Claudet . . ."

"Nor Mme. Claudet."

"Anne-Marie, you mustn't blame them. The police asked them questions, and they had to tell the truth."

"They were lying, both of them," she said fiercely.

"Why on earth should they lie?" I said.

"How should I know? I'm just an ignorant girl, not a fine lady. I only know they were lying, and I think it is perhaps because they know who really killed Robert. Somebody they wish to protect. Some rich person." She spat the words out. Then she said, quiet again, "Forgive me, madame. The Sisters say I must learn humility, and it is true that I wished him dead."

"Now, I don't want to hear any more of that nonsense, Anne-Marie," I said. "If you didn't kill Robert, you didn't kill him, and you are innocent. Goodness me, I've often told Henry to go and jump in the lake. And meant it. That doesn't make me a criminal."

She even managed a tiny smile at that, and she was still smiling when the Sister came back.

"Have you finished your talk?" she asked me politely but coldly.

"Yes, thank you, Sister."

"Then run along back to the kitchen," she said to Anne-Marie. The girl jumped up, gave a curious little bob-curtsy, and went out of the room.

I said, "She is looking very ill, Sister."

The nun sniffed. "That is hardly surprising. She is near her time."

"I think she is overworking."

"Did she say so?" A note of sharp suspicion.

"No, no," I said hastily. Above all things, I didn't want to get Anne-Marie into trouble. "She didn't complain at all."

"I should hope not. She is a very lucky girl. If our good Mother Superior had not taken pity on her, she would be in prison." She did not actually add "as she deserves to be," but the implication lingered in the air.

On impulse I said, "Sister, do you believe that Anne-Marie killed her husband?"

She froze me with a look. "It is not for me to say, madame. The court found her guilty. The matter is closed." She held the door open pointedly, waiting for me to go out.

In the chilly corridor I said, "I should like to come and see her again. I hope that will be permitted?"

She tramped ahead of me in silence, her brogues pounding the worn stone flags. I thought she was going to ignore my remark altogether, but at the last moment, when I was already outside in the sunshine, she said, "I will ask the good Mother Superior." Then the massive door closed, and I heard the bolts being shot and the key turning in the ancient lock.

It was wonderful to be out in the sunshine again, away from the religious gloom and the smell of mingled disinfectant and incense. I drove down the road into Charonne, where I bought a number of small presents—a nestful of small, sweetly scented soap bars carved to look like roses; a bottle of eau de cologne; a pretty handkerchief in fine white lawn with a lace edge; and a little jointed wooden cow with a bell around her neck and an endearingly comic expression. Then I went to the largest fruit shop I could find, and got them to make up a basket of fruit, arranging the other little gifts among the apples, grapes, and bananas, and covering the whole thing with beribboned cellophane in the traditional Swiss style of gift wrapping. I could only hope that the rules of the convent and the humanity of the Sisters would allow Anne-Marie to keep my present, for I was sure that the trinkets would amuse her, and she certainly looked as though she could do with the vitamin C. Within an hour I was back on the doorstep again, ringing the iron bell pull.

I was relieved to see, when the grille in the door shot open, that the same Sister was still on duty. Her eyes widened when she saw the basket, but whether with disapproval or mere surprise, I could not be sure.

"I have brought this for Anne-Marie," I said. "Would you give it to her for me?"

"The order does not permit members to receive personal gifts," the nun said. But she did open the door.

"Anne-Marie isn't a member of the order, Sister," I said. "She's not even a novice. Just a domestic help."

There was a silence. The nun stood staring at the basket. Suddenly she smiled. "The cow," she said. She pushed it with her finger through the cellophane wrapping. "She has a funny face. One has to smile."

"I hope she will make Anne-Marie smile, too," I said.

The nun looked at me gravely. I had the impression that she had deliberately erased the smile from her face, but its softening effect lingered, transforming her. "I think it may be against the rules," she said, "but I will give the girl your gift."

"You are very kind, Sister."

"No," she corrected me, accurately, but without emphasis. "Not kind, madame. Our rules are poverty, chastity, and obedience." As she turned to go, holding the basket as if it were some precious relic, she added, "I have spoken to the Mother Superior. You may visit Drivaz again if you wish." Before I could say another word, she had gone, and the dark door had closed in my face.

When I got back to Panoralpes, the apartment was deserted. I presumed that Henry was still out walking, and that Jane was working in the studio. There was no sign of Giselle Arnay's car, so I imagined that she had had enough of posing for one day. I was in the kitchen, making myself a cup of tea, when the doorbell rang. I went to answer it, and was surprised to be faced by Chantal—Sylvie's young goddaughter.

"Oh," she said. "Hello." She walked past me into the drawing room and lay down full-length on the sofa.

"I'm afraid Jane isn't here," I said from the doorway.

"I know." Chantal sounded bored to the point of exhaustion.

"I think she's in the studio. Shall I go and . . . ?"

"Oh, don't fuss. I've brought Giselle's car. She'll be over from the studio in a minute."

"Oh," I said. "I see. Would you like a cup of tea?"

I got no answer. Chantal had rolled over on the sofa so that her back was toward me, and fallen into what appeared to be a graceful attitude of sleep. I shrugged and went back to the kitchen.

It was at the very moment that the kettle came to the boil with a high-pitched scream that the telephone began to ring. I quickly switched off the gas and came out into the hall, but by then the ringing had stopped. I was turning back to the kitchen, mentally castigating people who haven't the patience to wait for two minutes for an answer before hanging up, when I heard Chantal's voice, and realized that she must have answered the telephone in the drawing room. I could not follow the rapid flow of her French, but it was obvious that she was having an animated conversation. Oh, well, I thought, we're both only visitors here. She has as much right to answer the phone as I have. I went back to the kitchen and finally succeeded in making my pot of tea.

A minute or so later Chantal came into the kitchen. She looked excited—her eyes bright and a flush on her pale cheeks. She said, "That was Sylvie."

"Mme. Claudet? I thought she was on a yacht somewhere."

Chantal ignored my remark. "She's coming here. She arrives tomorrow. Isn't that wonderful?"

It did not strike me as wonderful. My first thought was that Jane, Henry, and I would have to move out of the apartment and back to Les Sapins, and I said as much.

"Oh, no." Chantal perched on the edge of the kitchen table. "Can I have some tea?" She was completely transformed from the listless, half-asleep creature of a few minutes ago. "No, Sylvie said you mustn't dream of moving out. She'll come and stay at Perceneige with us."

"Now, that's just silly," I protested. "This is her apartment."

"You don't know Sylvie," said Chantal. "She's . . . well, she's just the most fabulous person in the world. She'd do anything for anybody."

"Well," I said, "all the same, I think we ought to tell Mme. Weston straight away. You should have called her, Chantal, and let her talk to Mme. Claudet herself. It's a very awkward position."

"Oh, you are silly." Chantal took a gulp of tea, and at once put her cup down. "Ugh. Horrid. Sylvie would rather come and stay with Giselle and me." I noticed the rather curious omission of any mention of Michel Veron. "Sylvie just wants everybody to be happy."

"You're very fond of her, aren't you?" I said. Having started off by disliking Chantal, I found myself warming to the girl. Her enthusiasm was unexpectedly simple and disarming.

"Oh, yes. Everybody loves Sylvie, because she is so good. She is good even to that little slut Anne-Marie. Do you know that she paid all the lawyers' fees for her defense?"

"No," I said. "I didn't know that."

"Well, she did, but nobody knows, because Sylvie didn't want any thanks for it. And she's planning all sorts of presents for the baby. Just imagine. After what Anne-Marie did."

"What did she do?"

Chantal opened her eyes very wide. "Oh, you are silly. She killed Robert."

"Are you sure?"

"Of course I'm sure. The judge said so."

"Did Sylvie think she was guilty, when she arranged to pay for her defense?" I asked.

Chantal hesitated. Then she said, "It wouldn't make any difference with Sylvie. That's what I mean about her. She's always doing things for people. Like lending this apartment to poor Mme. Weston, and letting me drive her car and everything."

I was not sure that Jane would have appreciated the "poor Mme. Weston," but youth is brutally candid. To change the subject, I said, "You enjoy driving, do you?"

"Oh, yes. Very fast. In bare feet. Sylvie's Alfa—you know Sylvie's Alfa?"

"I don't think so."

"Everybody in Montarraz knows it. It's white with bright red leather inside, and it'll do a hundred and eighty."

"Good heavens. Miles per hour?"

"No, silly. Kilometers."

I did a quick mental calculation, which worked out at over a hundred and ten. I said, smiling, "Well, if you drive at that speed, I hope you keep your shoes on."

"I nearly had a big accident outside Versailles," she said with offhand satisfaction.

"I'm not surprised."

"A great big *camion* came out of a side turning, and my foot was wet and slipped on the brake. I did a big *dérapage,* and the car turned right around."

"That must have been frightening," I said.

She smiled faintly. "Oh, no. It was fun." She paused. "I have had many such happenings. I just remember that one, because of the day it happened."

"The day it happened?"

"Yes. Sylvie had to spend all day at some conference in Paris— ladies in hats, you know. So she said I could borrow the car all day. When I took it back in the evening, we were having a drink in the apartment when the police turned up, wanting to know if Sylvie had telephoned Anne-Marie about cleaning this apartment. Of course, Sylvie said she hadn't. They were very mysterious about the whole thing, but Sylvie made them tell us. Pierre is very important, you see. So in the end they told us that Anne-Marie had stabbed Robert that very afternoon. Poor Sylvie. She was so upset." Chantal smiled a little. "One of the gendarmes had the nicest brown eyes."

Before I could think of a suitable rejoinder to this, the front door opened, and there was a clatter of footsteps and voices. Jane and Giselle were back from the studio, and Henry was with them.

8 ✦♛

Jane, not unnaturally, was taken aback at the news of Mme. Claudet's imminent arrival, and at once began to protest that we would move back to Les Sapins at once.

"Don't be an idiot," said Chantal. She addressed all of us exactly as if we were her contemporaries, but with no apparent intention of being rude. "Sylvie would be bored to death here on her own." The implication was clear that Jane, Henry, and I at Les Sapins did not constitute company. "She wants to be with me . . . and Giselle," she added, as an afterthought.

There was a little silence; then Giselle Arnay said, in her quaint, abrupt way, "Sylvie will stay at Perce-neige." A simple, authoritative statement which nobody thought of challenging. "Come, Chantal, we go home." She turned to Jane and said, "I shall sit for you from eleven to twelve tomorrow morning. You will all come to Perce-neige for a drink tomorrow evening, before dinner."

Jane, a little flustered, said, "Well, now, Giselle, I'm not sure if . . ."

Giselle looked up solemnly at Henry, the little *gamine* again. "You will come, won't you, Henri?"

Jane looked hard at Henry, who shrugged his shoulders slightly. "Yes, Giselle," she said, and I heard once more that unpleasantly fawning note in her voice. "How very sweet of you. We'll come."

When Giselle and Chantal had gone, with a joyful roar of the Monteverdi, the three of us sat down to a quiet drink. I began to talk about my visit to Anne-Marie, but Jane seemed curiously uninterested. She was dreamy and withdrawn, as she had been at lunchtime, and I could only suppose that she was utterly absorbed in her new work. I always feel out of my depth with artists.

I dropped the subject of Anne-Marie, and said, "How's the statue going, Jane? Chipping away like mad?"

She gave me the sort of hopeless look that creative people reserve for Philistines, and said, "Oh, I've done nothing today but preliminary sketches in charcoal and a very tentative study in soft clay. I won't even be choosing the marble until the figurine is finished."

"I'd love to see the sketches," I said. "May I?" Surely there could be no harm in that.

Jane stood up. "No," she said. "No, Emmy dear, I'd rather you didn't. In fact, if you don't mind, I'd sooner nobody came into the studio. Even when I'm not working. You do understand, don't you?"

I said I did; but frankly, I didn't. I couldn't make out the change that had come over Jane—but then, I told myself, I wasn't used to living in the same house with an artist actually in the process of creation. As Jane withdrew to change out of her working overall, I made a mental vow to be sensible and to make allowances for her.

When we were alone, Henry said, "Now—tell me about Anne-Marie."

I did so, in all the detail I could. Henry listened in silence, and then said, "What do you think, Emmy? Did that girl kill her husband?"

I sighed. "I don't know. Really, I don't. She's had her head stuffed so full of woolly ideas about guilt—you know, the wish is as bad as the deed, and all that—that I don't know whether you can rely on what she says any more. It's even possible that by now she believes herself to be guilty—but I don't." I was surprised myself at the vehemence of my last words. Quite suddenly I was certain that Anne-Marie was innocent.

Henry smiled. "And they talk about my 'nose,'" he said, referring to his flair for intuitive detection that had acquired this nick-name at Scotland Yard. "You mean, you've no evidence except the impression the girl made on you."

"If she had killed him, she'd have admitted it before now—if only to ease her conscience. What has she got to lose? She's been battered and brainwashed, but she still knows the difference between the thought and the deed. She can't have killed him, Henry."

"In that case," Henry said quite lightly, "something had better be done about it. And we had better do it."

"What do you mean?"

"She's already been convicted, so the only way we can clear her is to demonstrate who *did* kill Robert Drivaz," said Henry.

"Look," I said, "be sensible. We're here for only another week, and the trail is cold. In another couple of years, Anne-Marie will be free from the convent—we might even get her out sooner, with Sylvie's help, by pulling strings. Then she can come over to England . . ."

Henry said, "Aren't you forgetting the baby?" I said nothing. He went on, "Anne-Marie will never be free, and neither will the wretched child. Can't you imagine the tales old Mother Drivaz will tell him—about his wicked mother, who murdered his father? She says she wants to adopt the baby, and it all sounds very suitable to the court officials—but I wonder just what widow Drivaz wants that baby *for?*"

I shivered. "It's a horrible thought."

"I agree," said Henry. He sounded cheerful. I recognized the signs. He was buckling down to a job. "So we'd better get going."

"Down to Charonne tomorrow to see Anne-Marie again?" I suggested.

"To Charonne," said Henry, "but not, I think, to see Anne-Marie. Much as I'd like to, I don't think she can help us at the moment. What I'm interested in is the local paper."

The next morning Jane was only too pleased to let us have the car—she was entirely engrossed with her sitting. By ten o'clock we were away, winding down the precipitous road to the valley. We soon found the offices of the *Gazette de Charonne,* and a smiling secretary told us we could have the run of the morgue, where back numbers of the paper were stored. Of course, she said, the Drivaz trial had been very fully reported. It had been of great local interest.

The reporters had certainly given front-page treatment to the affair. There were pages of newsprint and several photographs each day during the hearings. A wedding picture of Robert and Anne-Marie—the latter smiling up adoringly at her handsome bridegroom; Jane, eyes downcast, hurrying out of the courtroom; Sylvie Claudet, shielding her face with a newspaper against the cameras as she was ushered into a chauffeur-driven limousine; incongruously cheerful publicity photographs of Giselle Arnay and Michel Veron, who—although not called to give evidence—were in a way the stars of the show; an almost unrecognizable Mario, scowling at the camera; an only too cooperative Mme. Drivaz weeping at it (*Bereaved mother's unbearable ordeal, see Page 8*); defense and prosecution lawyers snapped on their busy errands, white jabots fluttering, heads together in conference as they walked; the Drivaz's chalet, taken from the outside, with a large white arrow indicating the "Kitchen of Death"; and so forth.

Sitting on hard chairs in the newspaper's archive room, with the yellowing pages spread out on an ink-stained table, Henry and I waded through the complete reportage of Anne-Marie's trial. I won't attempt to put you through the same grueling task, but here are a few verbatim extracts which proved later to have some significance.

> *Maître Dubois* (for the prosecution): At what time, Madame Weston, did you see the accused returning to her own house from Panoralpes?
>
> *Mme. Weston:* Shortly before five o'clock.
>
> *Accused:* That's not true!
>
> *The Judge:* Silence in the court! Proceed, Maître Dubois.
>
> *Maître Dubois:* Thank you, my Lord. Mme. Weston, how can you be sure of the time?
>
> *Mme. Weston:* Because I was just packing up my work in the studio. I always work until five o'clock, you see.
>
> *Maître Dubois:* But you said, madame, that you saw the accused *before* five o'clock.

Mme. Weston: Yes. I packed up a little early that evening, because it had become too dark to see properly. It had started to rain.

Accused: That's not true!

The Judge: If the accused does not hold her tongue, I shall have her removed from the court. Proceed, Maître Dubois.

Sylvie Claudet, as the wife of an influential French politician, had been treated with kid gloves. Her evidence had been brief in the extreme and was reported in full.

Maître Dubois: Just a few brief questions, Mme. Claudet—we shall not have to trouble you for long.

Mme. Claudet: Thank you.

Maître Dubois: Thank *you,* madame. Now, on April 14 last, did you make a telephone call from Paris to Montarraz?

Mme. Claudet: I did not.

Maître Dubois: Did you instruct any other person to make such a call on your behalf?

Mme. Claudet: No, I did not.

Maître Dubois: Did you intend to visit your apartment at Montarraz in the near future?

Mme. Claudet: Yes. The following weekend.

Maître Dubois: Did you, in fact, visit it?

Mme. Claudet: No. When I heard what had happened . . .

Maître Dubois: Quite, madame. Very understandable. Now, did you give any instructions that the apartment should be cleaned before your arrival?

Mme. Claudet: No.

Maître Dubois: Thank you, Mme. Claudet. That is all.

Maître Ronsard (for the defense): Mme. Claudet, I fear I must detain you for a few questions.

Mme. Claudet: Of course, Maître.

Maître Ronsard: You are acquainted with the accused, are you not?

Mme. Claudet: Of course. She is the *concierge* at Panoralpes.

Maître Ronsard: Are you in the habit of employing her to clean your apartment?

Mme. Claudet: When I am there, yes.

Maître Ronsard: Have you, in the past, telephoned from Paris to ask Mme. Drivaz to prepare the apartment for your arrival?

Mme. Claudet: Yes.

Maître Ronsard: But you did not do so on this occasion?

Mme. Claudet: I did not.

Maître Ronsard: And you did not instruct your maid to telephone?

Mme. Claudet: I have already said I did not.

Maître Ronsard: Nevertheless, someone might have telephoned the accused, impersonating your maid?

Mme. Claudet: I—

Maître Dubois: I object! That is not a proper question!

The Judge: Objection upheld. Mme. Claudet cannot be expected to conjecture on such a matter.

Maître Ronsard: My Lord, I am merely trying to establish—

The Judge: You have made your point, I think, Maître. Pray proceed.

Maître Ronsard: Mme. Claudet, will you tell the court where, in fact, you were on the afternoon of April 14?

Maître Dubois: Objection! The question is irrelevant.

The Judge: Objection upheld. Any further questions, Maître Ronsard?

Maître Ronsard: No, my Lord.

The Judge: Then the witness may step down. There is no need to detain her any longer.

The next extract comes from the cross-examination of Mario Agnelli.

Maître Dubois: You are employed by Mlle. Giselle Arnay as chauffeur and houseman?

Agnelli: And by M. Veron.

Maître Dubois: Where were you at five-thirty-five P.M. on April 14?

Agnelli: I was coming out of the building called Panoralpes.

Maître Dubois: And what were you doing there, if one may ask?

Agnelli: I'd just delivered a note from Mlle. Arnay to Mme. Claudet.

Maître Dubois: But Mme. Claudet was not there?

Agnelli: No. She wasn't expected till Saturday.

Maître Dubois: The apartment was empty, then?

Agnelli: As far as I know.

Maître Dubois: You did not ring the bell?

Agnelli: There's no sense in ringing the bell if the apartment is empty.

(Laughter)

The Judge: Silence in the court!

Mario Agnelli then went on to describe his encounter with Anne-Marie as she came running out of her chalet, "hysterical and with blood everywhere, on her clothes, on her hands." Maître Ronsard did not dispute this evidence, and made only a feeble attempt to jolt the witness—more, it seemed, from a sense of duty than anything else.

Maître Ronsard: M. Agnelli, are you aware that April 14 was a Wednesday?

Agnelli: Yes.

Maître Ronsard: And Mme. Claudet was not expected until Saturday?

Agnelli: That's right.

Maître Ronsard: Why, then, did you not simply post Mlle. Arnay's letter? Why did you go to Panoralpes in person?

Maître Dubois: Objection! The question is irrelevant.

The Judge: Objection overruled. Please answer the question.

Agnelli: First, it was a nice day, and I felt like going out. Second, if you know anything about the postal service in Montarraz—

(Laughter)

The Judge: Silence in the court! Does that answer your question, Maître?

Maître Ronsard: Yes, my Lord. Thank you, my Lord. No further questions.

The examination of the widow Drivaz, Robert's mother, was almost grotesque to read. The old lady's hatred of Anne-Marie, combined with her utter lack of comprehension of any rules of evidence, produced a situation of near-uproar, continually punctuated by angry interjections from the judge. At one point the witness and the accused had flown at each other's throats, figuratively speaking, and would undoubtedly have done so physically if they had not been separated by the stout woodwork of the dock and the witness box.

The Judge: The witness will kindly comport herself in a proper manner, or I shall adjourn the court! Is that clear?

Widow Drivaz: She murdered my son!

The Judge: Mme. Drivaz, you have no right to make such accusations. It is for the court to decide how your son died.

Widow Drivaz: Everybody knows she killed him! This trial is a farce!

The Judge: I will not have the court insulted! One more unauthorized remark from the witness, and she will be arrested for contempt. Do you understand *that,* madame?

Widow Drivaz: (An indistinguishable mutter)

The Judge: What did you say?

Widow Drivaz: Nothing.

The Judge: I am delighted to hear it. Proceed, Maître Ronsard.

Maître Ronsard: Thank you, my Lord. Mme. Drivaz, when did you last see your son alive?

Widow Drivaz: That day. The day he was murdered by that—

Maître Ronsard: What time of day?

Widow Drivaz: Midday. Around two o'clock.

Maître Ronsard: I see. He had been lunching with you?

Widow Drivaz: No.

Maître Ronsard: Then where did you see him?

Widow Drivaz: (After a pause) At the Café de la Source.

Maître Ronsard: I see. Are you in the habit of visiting the Café de la Source at midday, madame?

Widow Drivaz: That's none of your business!

The Judge: Answer the question, madame.

Widow Drivaz: Sometimes.

Maître Ronsard: I put it to you, madame, that it was most unusual for you to visit the café. I put it to you that you went there in order to persuade your son to leave, because you had been told that he was drunk and becoming violent—

Maître Dubois: My Lord! I object!

Widow Drivaz: It's lies! All lies!

Maître Ronsard: Mme. Bertrand has testified—

Maître Dubois: Objection! Objection!

Widow Drivaz: And if he did get drunk, it's no wonder, with a slut like that for a wife! Murdering harlot!

The Judge: Silence! I will have no more of these disgraceful scenes. Usher, clear the court! We will reassemble in half an hour.

Anne-Marie's cross-examination consisted of hectoring questions from the prosecution, and stubborn monosyllables of denial from the girl. She made no attempt to hide the fact that she and Robert had been quarreling, that he had come home drunk from the café and that she had upbraided him about it. It was while they were arguing, she said, that the telephone had rung, and the lady from Paris had asked her to go over to Panoralpes as soon as possible, as Mme. Claudet was arriving that evening.

Maître Dubois: How do you know the call came from Paris?

Accused: The operator said so. "I have a call from Paris for you," she said, and then the lady came on the line.

Maître Dubois: Did you recognize the voice?

Accused: No.

Maître Dubois: You told the police the call was from Mme. Claudet. Do you now withdraw that statement?

Accused: Yes. No. She said she was speaking for Mme. Claudet.

Maître Dubois: I put it to you, Drivaz, that this is a tissue of lies. There was no telephone call—

Accused: There was!

Maître Dubois: I put it to you that you first claimed to have spoken to Mme. Claudet, and then changed your story when you realized she could prove she had not telephoned. You went over to her apartment in order to try to establish an alibi for yourself—

Accused: No!

Maître Dubois: You knew that Mme. Weston would see you going over, didn't you?

(No reply)

Didn't you?

Accused: I—yes, I suppose so. I didn't think about it. She was always in the studio in the afternoons.

Maître Dubois: But you did not know that she would see you going back. You thought you had left it late enough, so that she would have left the studio and gone indoors.

Accused: That's not true!

Maître Dubois: Drivaz, why did you go back to your own chalet before five o'clock?

Accused: I didn't! It was nearly half-past!

Maître Dubois: Aha! Now we are getting to the point! You made a grave mistake, Drivaz. *You misread the time.* You deliberately planned to return when Mme. Weston would not see you—but your plan failed. Didn't it, Drivaz?

Accused: No! I mean, there was no plan! I went back and found Robert dead!

It was painful to read. Dubois ran circles around Anne-Marie, and nothing that Maître Ronsard was able to do could erase the impression that she was unsure of herself, that she had changed her story, and that it was in any case a highly unlikely one. With witnesses like Jane and Sylvie against her, she never had a chance. Her account, by the time Maître Dubois had finished with it, sounded like a ragged fabrication thrown up by a child to cover a misdemeanor. The jury took only half an hour to reach their verdict, and—having read the transcripts—I could only wonder why they had taken so long.

Henry read the trial reports first, and then handed each paper to me as he finished it. While I was busy on the account of the last day, Henry—for some reason of his own—looked at the copies of the *Gazette* for the day of the murder, and the days preceding and following it. Out of the corner of my eye I saw that he was making notes, but I was too absorbed in my reading to make out what they were.

Then he returned the papers to the filing cabinet, came back to the table, and said, "Finished?"

I nodded, putting aside the last depressing page. "I'm sorry," I said.

"Sorry? What for?"

"Because I've been a fool. I'm fond of Anne-Marie, and I'm sure she had every sort of provocation, but . . . well, you can't get around it, can you? She killed Robert, and she tried to cover it up in just the clumsy sort of would-be-cunning way that one would expect from—"

"From whom?" Henry's voice was sharp and almost unfriendly, and I knew I had put my foot in it.

"Well," I said, "poor Anne-Marie never had a chance in the world, did she? No proper education, no family background, no—"

"She was brought up by nuns," said Henry, still in that cold voice. "Do you think she doesn't know truth from lies?"

"I never said—"

"Oh, Emmy," said Henry. Suddenly he sounded not angry, but tired. "Even you."

"I've told you—I'm fond of Anne-Marie, and I'll do all I—"

As if I had not spoken, Henry went on, "Even you, with all your warmth and kindness—you're hopelessly prejudiced."

I felt cold. "What do you mean?"

"Anne-Marie is an ignorant peasant girl. Peasant. That was what you really meant, wasn't it? Peasants lose control of themselves and stab their husbands with carving knives. Peasants then try to do a clumsy cover-up which could never deceive an educated person. Peasants aren't like us—they're different. We don't understand what makes them tick. That's what you had in the back of your mind, isn't it?"

Every word burned me, because I knew that however much I might protest, Henry was right. Some prejudices lie so deep and so still that one isn't aware of them oneself—until somebody else prods them unmercifully out into the light of day. I couldn't say anything.

Henry said, very gently, "Just try reading some of those reports again. The bits I've marked, in particular. Tell yourself that it's Sylvie Claudet who is on trial, not Anne-Marie Drivaz. That it's Pierre

Claudet, the minister for whatever-it-is, who has been stabbed. Imagine that Anne-Marie is chief witness for the prosecution. Go on. Read them. Then tell me what you think."

I read the reports again, slowly. When I had finished, I looked up and met Henry's steady gaze across the stained wooden library table.

"Well?" he said.

"The witnesses," I said. "They were never properly examined at all."

"Which witnesses?"

"Sylvie, in particular. Jane. Even Mario."

"And what about the others?"

"There weren't any others. Except the expert witnesses—the police and doctors."

"Exactly," said Henry.

"What do you mean—exactly?"

"I mean the witnesses who weren't even called—Giselle Arnay and Michel Veron. Sylvie's maid. Chantal Villeneuve—"

"But—"

"I think," said Henry, "that we should reopen the case, don't you? From a different point of view. Do, by all means, visit Anne-Marie again, because she needs all the friends she can muster—but there's no need to talk to her about the case. For the purposes of my inquiry, I am going to assume that every word she spoke in court was the simple truth." He smiled, in a way I recognized. "It may be quite interesting."

9 ✿

*J*ane, Henry, and I arrived at the Chalet Perce-neige at half-past six that evening for our predinner drink. Mario opened the door to us, grinned, and said, "In the garden." He was wearing very tight jeans made of some snakeskin-printed material, and an orange silk shirt with full sleeves gathered at the wrist, like a Balkan gypsy. He certainly did not give the impression of being a domestic servant.

"Go on out," he said casually. "I'll bring more drinks." He strolled off in the direction of the kitchen, leaving us to make our way through the living room and out to the swimming pool.

We were greeted by a very decorous party. Sylvie Claudet, brown as a nut after her Mediterranean cruise, was stretched out on a blue canvas swing seat, wearing a minuscule bikini and enormous sunglasses and reading *France-Soir*. Giselle and Michel were both in the pool, splashing each other and giggling like children. Giselle wore a curious sort of striped garment, like a Victorian bathing suit out of which moths had nibbled large round holes in strategic spots. Michel, tall and thin, looked like a pale spider in his black swimming trunks. On the grass beside the pool, Chantal—dressed in some sort of flowing chiffon creation—sat cross-legged; she wore spectacles, and, almost incredibly, she was knitting what looked like silver string on a pair of huge needles. Hidden loudspeakers thrummed a background of guitars.

Sylvie jumped up as we approached, setting the canvas settee swinging, and ran to embrace Jane.

"Dar-leeng! See, I am here! Am I not clever? That poor Pierre, he is in Paris making the most boring speeches, and so hot, and *no-body* in town!"

"I thought you were on a yacht somewhere, Sylvie," said Jane—a little coldly, I thought.

"I was—and Pierre, too. But when he had to go back to Paris—phut! I go with him, and then come here as fast as the Alfa can drive. Oh, my Jane, that yacht! Boring, boring, boring. Sometimes I think I am always boring except in Montarraz."

"Always 'bored,' you mean," said Jane.

Sylvie laughed. "I hope I mean so," she said. "What is it you say in English? Many true words get spoke in a *blague*—no? But here I am with my friends, and I may be boring if I want to." She wheeled around toward Henry and me, still holding Jane's hand. "And what luck I have! Henry and Emmy are here! Such nice people to bore!"

I must admit, Sylvie had great charm. When I write down her words, they sound unremarkable; but close to her—say, within a radius of ten feet or so—one was in a charmed circle. I suppose the perfume helped, and the perfection of detail. I tried to imagine Sylvie with a broken nail or a spot on her face, but imagination promptly boggled. You have to admire it.

Mario soon appeared with a tray of bottles and glasses, and served drinks—after which, rather surprisingly, he stripped off his silk shirt and snakeskin pants to reveal a few square inches of swimming trunks underneath, and dived expertly into the pool. Michel Veron immediately broke off his fooling with Giselle, and soon he and Mario were engaged in swimming races—both of them doing a smooth and professional crawl. Giselle, quite expressionless, climbed out of the water and shook herself, like a puppy. Then she walked into the house, leaving a trail of wet footprints across the cream-colored carpet. Technically, we were her guests, but she did not address a single word to any of us. After a moment Jane put down her glass and followed Giselle indoors.

Chantal, totally absorbed, went on with her knitting. I sat down on the warm grass near Sylvie's swing chair, and after a few moments lay back and closed my eyes. I had seen Henry making for Sylvie, and I wanted to listen to their conversation without appearing to do so.

"May I join you, Mme. Claudet?" He sounded very English and correct.

"Mme. Claudet! Mme. Claudet!" mimicked Sylvie. "Oh, you English! You are Henry and I am Sylvie, and you shall sit beside me and tell me all you have been doing in Montarraz."

Henry told her about the *raclette* picnic—not, of course, mentioning his bird's-eye view of Perce-neige—and Sylvie made him promise to organize another and take her along. Then Henry said, "We've been down to Charonne, too."

"Have you? I think it is not a very interesting little town." Sylvie sounded bored.

"I agree with you. But we went for a special reason."

"A special reason. I cannot think what you could find in Charonne that you could not find in Montarraz, my Henry." Sylvie was teasing.

Henry said gravely, "Anne-Marie."

There was a short silence, broken only by the splashing of water from the pool as Michel and Mario started on another length. Then Sylvie said, in quite a different voice, "Oh, what a heartless woman I am. I had forgotten. Her baby must be due very soon. Did you see her?"

"Emmy saw her."

"How is she? Is she well?"

"She is—" Henry hesitated. "Emmy was worried about her. The nuns are kind but very strict, and the girl seems to be getting a guilt complex."

"Well—" said Sylvie, and then stopped.

"Well?" Henry prompted.

Reluctantly Sylvie said, "In the circumstances . . . of course, it was very human, very understandable, but . . ."

"I believe," said Henry, "that you paid for her defense."

"Who told you that?" Sylvie's voice was suddenly sharp.

"I did," said Chantal, without raising her eyes from her work. "I told his wife."

Sylvie laughed, not quite easily. "That was naughty of you, Chantal."

"Why? Are you ashamed of doing a good deed?" They had both lapsed into French.

"Of course not," said Sylvie. "It's just that—" She broke off, and then said, in English, "Forgive me, Henry. Of course, I do not mind that you should know, but I am not eager to—how do you say?—to make an advertisement of it."

"You paid for her defense, even though you considered she was guilty?" said Henry.

"I was so sorry for her. I did not know whether she was guilty or not."

"But now you are sure."

"Well—I can't challenge the court, can I? I did my best for the girl. That's all." Sylvie's voice changed again, became warm and eager. "Tell me, when will be born the baby? Can I go and see it—and Anne-Marie?"

"The baby is due next week," said Henry, "and anybody can see Anne-Marie—if she will see them."

"She would not see me before." Sylvie's voice was sorrowful. "I could not tell lies in the court, could I? No more than Jane could. Oh, I understand how Anne-Marie felt, but it hurt me, just the same. At least," she added, brightening, "I can send presents for her and the baby."

"I think you can do more than that, Sylvie," said Henry.

"More? How can I do more?"

"I've been reading the verbatim reports of the trial," Henry said.

"What has that to do with it?"

"I am not at all sure," said Henry, "that Anne-Marie did kill Robert."

"But . . ." Sylvie was sad and puzzled. "Oh, how I would like to believe that, Henry, but it just isn't possible. I'm sorry. I have to say it. The evidence was quite clear. And then—" Suddenly she changed vocal gears, and said loudly, "And you promise you will take me for a *raclette* picnic? Promise! Come on, promise!"

I opened my eyes and propped myself up on one elbow. Giselle Arnay had come out of the house again. Jane was with her, and they were talking animatedly. As they went over to the drinks table, Sylvie whispered urgently to Henry, "Please. No more. Not in front of Giselle."

"Why not?"

"It . . . she gets upset. You know that she was . . . well . . . involved, in a way."

"I'd like to talk to you some more about the case, Sylvie. If Anne-Marie—"

"Ssh. Please." There was no mistaking the seriousness in Sylvie's voice. Panic, almost. "I will come tomorrow to Panoralpes. We will talk then. Eleven o'clock."

Henry said, "If you will promise, I will promise."

"I will, I will," said Sylvie.

Giselle turned, glass in hand. "What is all this promises?" she asked.

Henry said, "I have promised to take Sylvie on a *raclette* picnic, if she will come and have a drink with me in her own apartment tomorrow."

"Oh." Giselle had lost interest. She turned back to Jane. "When will the figurine be ready? Tomorrow?"

Jane laughed. "I work fast, but not so fast as that. Give me a few more days."

"I too have to work fast," said Giselle. She took a long pull at her drink, and then said again, "Fast. Always fast."

Michel Veron and Mario came scrambling out of the pool, laughing and arguing over who had won the swimming contest. "You are a great liar, caro Mario," said Veron, and put his arm around the Italian's bare, wet shoulder. Giselle turned her head away and began talking to Jane about colors and textures of marble. Michel and Mario began toweling themselves down, laughing and indulging in mild horseplay.

There was nothing to it, of course; but Giselle Arnay was like a finely tuned, sensitive radio receiver, quivering to pick up the smallest tension, the hint of an emotion. And maybe amplify it? I could not be sure. Perhaps I was imagining the whole thing.

Once again I was beginning to experience that sense of unease, of not belonging, of being out of my depth, which always seemed to come over me at the Chalet Perce-neige. I could not for the life of me decide whether there was anything sinister about this group of people, or whether they were merely unfamiliar, with their fame and wealth and easy mastery of life. Was I like the psychiatric patient who was brutally told that his inferiority complex could easily be explained—he *was* inferior? I thought of the young ski instructors—Robert Drivaz and Jean Bertrand and Henri Whatever-his-name-was—and how easily and unselfconsciously they apparently had fitted into the Arnay-Veron circle. They had the virtues of simplicity. I was horribly middle-class, neither one thing nor the other. I couldn't adapt.

Anyhow, I was delighted when Giselle announced, in her usual abrupt way, that it was too cold to stay outside, and that she was going to change. At once I said that we should be going. We had only been invited for a drink, after all. Jane did not look too pleased, I thought, but nobody pressed us to stay.

As we were leaving, I heard Henry say to Sylvie, "Remember your promise?"

And she said quietly, "Yes, Henry."

Sylvie was as good as her word. Promptly at eleven o'clock the next morning she rang the doorbell of her own apartment—a beautifully mannered touch, for of course she had her own key. Henry and I were alone in the flat—Jane, as usual, being closeted in the studio with Giselle.

The first thing I noticed about Sylvie Claudet was that she looked worried. Not obviously, of course. Her precisely groomed surface was much too smooth to show the sort of ruffled nervousness which would betray an ordinary person. She greeted us charmingly, sat down on the sofa, and answered Henry's query by saying that she would love a glass of champagne. When Henry looked taken aback, she laughed and assured him that he would find a case of excellent Brut in the *cave,* and that she was offering us a bottle, as it was the only thing she liked to drink before lunch.

Henry went off to get the wine, and Sylvie shrugged off her silky broadtail jacket and lit a cigarette. That was when I noticed that her hand was just slightly unsteady, so that she had to flick the gold lighter twice before the cigarette was burning steadily, and her movements were just perceptibly quicker and jerkier than usual.

She took a pull on her cigarette, smiled at me slowly, deliberately stroking out any wrinkles in her behavior, and said, "Henry tells me you saw Anne-Marie. Poor girl. You must tell me all about her." She gave me no chance to do so, however, but went on at once. "Henry seems—I don't know—I had a feeling last night that he somehow disapproved of me. What have I done wrong, Emmy?"

"Nothing, as far as I know," I said. "It's just that Henry wants to do something for Anne-Marie if he can, and we thought you might be able to help."

"Me? How can I help?"

I smiled. "I'm not the detective. You'll have to wait till Henry comes back."

When the champagne had been poured, Henry sat down in an armchair opposite Sylvie, and said, "Thank you for coming, Mme. Claudet."

" 'Sylvie,' please."

"Sylvie. Emmy has told you . . . ?"

"What do you want to ask me?" The faint aroma of nervousness was back. "I don't see how I can help you."

Henry said easily, "First of all, we can run through just exactly what you did on the day Robert Drivaz was killed."

"Me? I was in Paris."

"I know you were. It's just to get a complete picture—"

"It's very simple," said Sylvie. "It was the day of the conference of the Federation of Women's Guilds—once a year, delegates come from all over France to this great meeting in Paris. It is of a boredom—you would not believe! But as Pierre's wife, I have to appear. I even made a speech—just a little one. I was there all day."

"You lent your car to Chantal, I believe?"

"How did you know that?"

"She told me. She says she had a near-miss accident near Versailles."

"She drives like a little demon when she . . . sometimes. I don't lend her the car any more." Sylvie wrinkled her forehead. "I worry about Chantal. She is more like a daughter to me than a goddaughter, especially since her mother died."

"But you let her have the car that day?"

"I knew I would not need it—I was the whole day at the conference, how you say, cooped up? I took a taxi home afterward—that must have been about six, I suppose. I had a cold meal by myself in the apartment—Pierre was away, you see, at some meeting in Vienna. Soon after ten, Chantal turned up, to return the car. She told me about her—her escapade. When the police arrived, I thought it must be about Chantal's accident—but no. They told us Robert Drivaz had been murdered."

"And the telephone call—could it have been made from your apartment in Paris?" Henry asked.

"Certainly not." Sylvie almost snapped out the words.

"How can you be sure? Your maid—"

"It was her day off. The manservant was with Pierre in Vienna. The apartment was empty."

"Does Chantal have a key to your apartment?"

Sylvie looked up suspiciously. "What has that to do with it?"

"I just wondered. Does she?"

There was a perceptible hesitation. Then Sylvie said, "Yes, she does."

Henry said, "Yours is a very fast car, I understand."

"It is a good car, yes."

"How long does it take you to drive from Paris to Montarraz, Sylvie?"

Sylvie laughed. "My car goes fast, Henry, but I do not—or very seldom. I always allow six hours, so that I need not hurry."

"But the car could do it in less time, couldn't it?" said Henry. "In—what? Five hours? Four?"

Sylvie considered seriously. "There are the Jura Mountains to cross," she said. "So much depends on the state of the roads. In winter, I suppose a lunatic driver could do it in five hours. In summer—rather less."

"It occurred to me," said Henry, "that Chantal could have driven down here and back that day, and still arrived at your apartment sometime after ten in the evening."

"But she was near Versailles, Henry—making a nonsense with a *camion*. She told you."

"So she did."

Sylvie put her glass down on the table, and sat up very straight. "I do not like," she said, "what you say. Chantal may be a little crazy, like all young people, but you hint that she—"

"I'm sorry, Sylvie." Henry rubbed the back of his neck with his hand—always a sign that he was concentrating. "You say Chantal is an orphan?"

"Yes. That is—Chantal may have a father somewhere, but she never knew him, and he has never shown any interest in her. Her mother was a great friend of mine. She was killed in an accident six years ago. . . . Henry, what has all this to do with Anne-Marie?"

Henry laughed, a little ruefully. "Nothing, Sylvie. Nothing at all. Chantal knew Robert Drivaz, didn't she?"

Sylvie shrugged. "In a place like this," she said, "everybody knows the ski instructors. But Chantal never . . . that is to say, it was Giselle . . ." She stopped.

"Ah, yes," said Henry. "Giselle. Who is now so sensitive about the whole subject. Why?"

"I should have thought it was obvious. She was . . . well, she behaved rather foolishly. Then Robert turned up in Paris and made a stupid scene. It was all very embarrassing for Giselle."

"You were there?" Henry was obviously intrigued.

Sylvie hesitated. Then she said, "No, I was not there. Giselle telephoned me and told me. She was very upset. She said he had been . . . most offensive."

"What exactly did Robert say to her?" Henry asked.

Sylvie blew out a long, lazy cloud of smoke from her cigarette. Then she said, "I really think you should ask Giselle that question, Henry. There is an English *mot* about a *poilu*—no? I have heard Pierre say it. What *le poilu* says cannot be in the court—is that it?"

Henry grinned. "What the soldier said isn't evidence," he said. "You're quite right. I'll ask her. You don't think she'll object?"

"How should I know?"

"I only ask because yesterday evening you were so very emphatic about not mentioning the Drivaz case in front of Giselle."

Sylvie smiled. "You did not quite understand, Henry. I think if you were to talk to Giselle *alone,* it might be different."

"You mean—Giselle's husband doesn't know about . . . ?"

"Oh, my Henry." Sylvie smiled slowly. "You are naïve, no? Just talk to Giselle. And now, is the interrogation finished? May the witness have another glass of champagne, Maître Tibbett?"

"Of course." Henry opened the eighteenth-century inlaid *secretaire,* which now housed an icebox, and brought out the bottle. He refilled our glasses, and then raised his. "To you, Sylvie. Thank you. You've been a great help."

"I have?" Sylvie laughed. "Oh, if it was always so easy to be a great help to somebody, how pleasant life would be."

"Why do you say that?"

"No reason." Sylvie sipped her champagne. "Well, Henry, I have kept my promise. Will you keep yours? The *raclette* picnic? Tomorrow?"

It was all very well for Sylvie to tell Henry that he should question Giselle Arnay directly, and alone; there seemed little prospect that the opportunity would ever arise. After all, Henry was not making an official investigation—he was merely, to put it bluntly, nosing about in other people's business. I said as much to Henry after Sylvie had gone, and he agreed rather gloomily. So we were both very surprised when, half an hour later, the doorbell rang, and there stood Giselle, looking like a guttersnipe in her faded jeans and old T-shirt. She strolled into the drawing room, sat down in a big armchair which seemed to engulf her, tucked up her bare feet under her buttocks, and said, "Jane will be in the studio for some time. She needs me not for the moment. Sylvie said you wanted to talk about Robert Drivaz and that girl. Why?"

A little taken aback, Henry said, "I am trying to help Anne-Marie."

"You are reopening the case, you mean?"

"I've no right to do that," said Henry. "This is purely unofficial. But if I come across any fresh evidence—"

"There is no way I can help you." Everything that Giselle said was a flat, direct statement, difficult to contradict.

"I think you can," Henry said. "That is, if you don't mind talking about your relationship with Robert Drivaz."

"There was none."

"I understood—" Henry began.

"You understand nothing. This is a small village. I am Giselle Arnay. If I engage a private ski instructor, of course there will be gossip."

Henry said, "But later, Robert came to see you in Paris."

"Yes—I believe he did."

"What do you mean—you believe he did?"

Giselle smiled slightly. "I was out," she said. "When I came home, Mario told me that Robert had come to the house. He was drunk and abusive. Mario sent him packing."

"That," said Henry, "is not my information."

Giselle sat perfectly still, but her eyebrows rose a fraction of an inch. "*Your* information? What is that, please?"

"That he did see you, that there was a stormy interview, and that you were very upset."

Quite expressionless, Giselle said, "I see. Sylvie has been talking to you."

"You know she has."

After a moment's hesitation Giselle said, "Sylvie is a silly woman. I suppose she told you lies because she is frightened."

"Frightened? Why should she be frightened?"

Giselle stretched elegantly and yawned. "Oh, you know. Pierre is a minister of the Republic. Caesar's wife must be above suspicion. Above all, from Caesar."

"What does that mean, exactly?"

"You are the policeman, Henry, not I. I am not a—what is it?—a sneaker. What Robert may have said to Sylvie in Paris—"

"Robert? He didn't see her in Paris."

"Didn't he?" Giselle yawned again. "Well, I expect you have *your* information. Poor Robert. He did not see me, he did not see Sylvie, and Mario was very rude to him. Perhaps he see Chantal?" Then, almost to herself, she added, "Perhaps so. Perhaps that is why Sylvie is afraid." Then, to Henry, "And then he came home, and his wife killed him with a carving knife. What a silly, silly boy. Is there more you wish to ask me?"

"Yes," said Henry. "I'd like to know just where you were and what you did on the day Robert was killed."

"So inquisitive, the little policeman. I don't remember what day it was."

"April 14."

"April . . . April . . . Oh, yes." She broke into a dazzling smile. "Of course, I was here. That is to say, at Perce-neige. With Mario. Just the two of us. Michel was in Paris, singing at Le Fromage Sauvage. Does that make me a—a suspicious?"

Henry said, "I know you were in Montarraz. I meant—what did you do on that particular day?"

"Oh, how can I remember? It was so long ago."

Henry said, "You must remember that day. When Mario came home and told you—"

"He did not."

"He didn't?"

"He was at the police station nearly all night. I went to sleep. I heard nothing of Robert until next day."

"All the same," Henry said, "in retrospect, that day must stand out. Don't you remember . . . ?"

Giselle stood up. "I don't remember. I shall go home now." She walked out of the apartment.

Henry looked at me and smiled. "Interesting, isn't it?"

"You're certainly stirring them up," I said, "but I can't quite see where it's getting us."

A few minutes later Jane came in from the studio. For a change, she seemed cheerful and sociable, accepted a drink, and started to talk with animation. When I asked her how her work was going, she smiled brilliantly and said it was fine.

"I've solved the problems—at least I think I have. For the moment, I can relax." She paused. "I owe you an apology."

"Whatever for?"

"I must have been impossible to live with the last couple of days. It's always like that when one is—how can I put it?—fighting. Knowing that something good is there, hidden in the clay, and struggling to get it out intact. Do you see what I mean?"

I didn't, of course, but I said that I did. I was delighted that Jane was back with us again. I had been really worried.

At lunch Henry steered the conversation around to Anne-Marie, and told Jane that he had been talking to Sylvie and Giselle, although he did not repeat what had been said.

Jane said, "So that's what Sylvie meant."

"What Sylvie meant?"

"Yes—she came barging into the studio about an hour ago, which didn't please me, but I couldn't very well object. Fortunately, I had nearly finished with Giselle for the day. Sylvie simply walked in and said to Giselle, 'When you're through here, go over to Pano-ralpes, will you, and have a word with Henry? He wants to talk to you.' Giselle said, 'What about?' and Sylvie just said, 'Your big blue eyes, darling.' Of course, Giselle's eyes aren't blue, but I suppose it was a figure of speech. Giselle laughed and said, 'What's he been talking to you about? Frivolities?' Sylvie looked quite put out, for some reason. She just said, 'Oh, don't be silly'—and pushed off." Jane helped herself to more salad. "Do forgive me, I've been so wrapped up in work, I haven't been functioning properly as a person. You've seen Anne-Marie, haven't you?"

"Emmy has," said Henry.

Jane immediately wanted to know how she was, when the baby

was due, what we could do to help. The change in her was quite astonishing. I told her all I could about my meeting with Anne-Marie, and then Henry took over.

"I'm trying to help her in the most practical way I can," he said. "I'm no good at knitting baby clothes, and in any case, I don't think that's the point. What I want to do is to prove that she's innocent."

A cloud crossed Jane's face. "Oh, Henry," she said, "you'll never be able to do that."

"Why do you say so?"

"Well . . ." Jane shrugged hopelessly. "Me, for one thing."

"What do you mean—you?"

"My evidence. You can't get away from it."

Henry said, "I'd like to talk to you about it, if you don't mind."

"Of course I don't mind. But what good can it possibly do? We might just as well talk about the weather."

Henry smiled. "It's funny you should say that!"

"Why?"

"Because that's exactly what I do want to talk about, Jane. The weather."

"The *weather?*" Jane looked at Henry as though he had taken leave of his senses. "What on earth . . . ?"

"The weather on the day that Robert was killed," Henry said.

Jane frowned. "I can't see what that has to do with—"

Henry said, "Just think back, Jane, and tell me about the weather that day."

Jane laughed, a little embarrassed. "Oh, really. How silly can you get? All right. It was a cold morning, but sunny. I remember, because Herbert went out during the night, and I woke up frozen. It got much warmer at midday, of course, but after lunch the clouds began to come up, and it got colder again. I lit the stove in the studio after lunch. It grew steadily more cloudy, and then it started to rain. That's when I packed up working, because there wasn't enough light."

"And it was also when you saw Anne-Marie going back from Panoralpes to her own chalet?"

"That's right."

Henry leaned forward. "Jane," he said, "are you absolutely certain it was raining?"

"Yes, of course I am. I told you—"

"How can you be so sure?"

"Well—because it was. That's all."

Henry said, "Mario remarked in court that it was a nice day."

"It wasn't a bad day," Jane conceded. "Earlier on, that is. But just before five it suddenly got dark and started to rain. Why would I have stopped working otherwise?"

"Look, Jane," said Henry, "I don't want to be rude, but Emmy and I have seen, these last few days, how you get completely and utterly wrapped up in your work when you're going flat out. Were you—like that—then?"

Jane had gone slightly pink. "I was working hard, yes."

"And so—forgive me—your evidence might be unreliable."

Jane put down her knife and fork with a clatter. "That's not fair, Henry. You know perfectly well that I'd have done *anything* to help Anne-Marie. If I'd had any idea how damning my evidence was going to be, I might even have cheated and kept my mouth shut. You can't imagine that I'd have made up false evidence—"

"No, no. Of course not, Jane. This is the way I'm thinking. You were absorbed in work, to the exclusion of everything else. It grew too dark to go on, so you stopped. And you jumped to the conclusion that it had started to rain. Why?"

"Because it *was* raining." Jane sounded near to exasperation.

"No," said Henry.

"What?"

"I said 'No.' It couldn't have been raining."

"What on earth are you talking about?" Jane demanded.

I must say, I was with her. How could Henry know it had not been raining?

Henry said, "The police made a great point of the fact that the murderer must have approached the chalet along the swept path, because there was unbroken snow lying on the fields around about."

"I know that," said Jane.

"When we were in Charonne, in the newspaper office," said

Henry, "I took a look at the copies of the *Gazette de Charonne* for the day of the murder and the day after."

"Oh," said Jane with disdain. "Journalistic nonsense. Sensational—"

"I looked," said Henry, "at the weather reports. The forecast, and the actual conditions. I noted down the figures." He pulled out his notebook and opened it. "On April 14, the limit of zero degrees was at eight hundred meters, and didn't rise above that level all day."

"Well?"

"Montarraz village," said Henry, "is at an altitude of fifteen hundred meters. If anything had fallen here, it would not have been rain. It would have been snow."

There was a long silence. Jane was nodding her head slowly as she worked out the implications. "Yes," she said at last. "Yes, you're right. And there was no snow—otherwise the police would have admitted that footprints might have been covered up. Anyway —well, I know it didn't snow." She sounded deeply puzzled.

"So," said Henry, "I ask you to think again. What gave you this conviction that it was raining?"

Another long pause. Jane said, "I don't know . . . I can't think . . ." And then suddenly, "Of course! The umbrella!"

"What umbrella?"

"When Anne-Marie came past the studio door, back from Panoralpes to her chalet, she was running and sheltering under an umbrella. So naturally I assumed it was raining."

Henry looked at her. There was a long silence. Then Jane said, "Oh, my God. All right, Henry, don't bother to say it. You're right. I didn't actually see her face. But it was Anne-Marie."

"How do you know?"

"Well—she was wearing her blue overall—the one she was wearing when she went over, earlier. . . ."

"The one she always wore for housework," Henry pointed out. "Which is obtainable at any branch of the local chain store."

Again Jane said, "Oh, my God."

"Dear Jane," said Henry, "don't be so distressed. You may have been right. It may have been Anne-Marie you saw. On the other hand, it may not. It could have been anybody—anybody of about Anne-Marie's height and build, dressed in a blue overall, hiding her face under an umbrella." He leaned across the table and took Jane's hand. "Jane, Jane. Don't cry. Don't you see—this is the breakthrough? *It could have been anybody.*"

SYLVIE

Extracts from the private diary
of Mme. Sylvie Claudet
(translated from the original French)

10 ♛

Tuesday, 8 September

I'm so terribly worried about Chantal. Sometimes it seems that for years I've been trying to shield her from the consequences of her own foolishness—and I suppose that this in itself is an admission of failure. If I had succeeded, I would have been able to stop her from being foolish in the first place, instead of eternally trying to patch things up afterward.

There's this drug thing. Oh, I know that people like Giselle and Michel and Mario and—yes, let's face it—like me haven't made things easy for her. But I'm reasonably sure she's been on the hard stuff for some time. I've never mentioned it, of course. Neither has she. We love each other too much to risk hurting each other. She manages very well, I must say. I mean, it's not obvious. Not yet. Still, I can't help worrying.

It wouldn't matter if it wasn't for this business of poor Anne-Marie. Heaven knows, I did all I could—paid thousands for the girl's defense, and so on—but now this extraordinary little Englishman is stirring it all up again. Why? If he were a Frenchman, I'd think it was political—trying to get at Pierre through me. Can it be that he's employed by one of Pierre's political enemies? We must be very, very careful. I must be careful. I must protect Pierre, and myself, and Chantal. Whatever she may have done. God knows what she may have done.

That day—the day Robert Drivaz was killed. Chantal had my car. Did she really have a near-miss with a lorry at Versailles? Where was she? The Englishman said she could have driven to Montarraz and back. So she could—it hadn't occurred to me. I tried to make it sound impossible when I talked to him, but I know it's not. Chantal could have driven here and back.

Tomorrow, we all go up the mountain for something called a *raclette* picnic. It will be horrible, that I know. But I must go, because I must know what this Englishman is doing, what he is thinking, and how it affects Chantal. Thank God Pierre is safely in Paris. Did I say "safely"? I hope so.

Then there's Giselle. What did she mean, talking about frivolities? I'm fond of Giselle, there's no harm in her, and she did as I asked and posed for Jane and made a fuss of the English couple. But Michel is a different matter. Michel and Mario. There's danger. I should never have let Chantal go and stay at Perce-neige without me—but how could I stop her, when I was on a ghastly yacht in Menton? What has she been saying? How much does Mario know? What did he mean when he telephoned me in Paris?

"Giselle is very concerned about Chantal. She thinks you should come to Montarraz at once." Of course I came. Now Giselle says she isn't in the least worried about Chantal, and she had no idea Mario had rung me; and all he will do is smile, and walk away. I wish Pierre were here.

Wednesday, 9 September

Well, the *raclette* picnic is over, and it was just as grisly as I feared it would be. Chantal, very sensibly, refused to come; so did Michel. But for some reason Giselle developed an extraordinary enthusiasm for the beastly outing—so of course she persuaded Jane to take a break from work and come along too. So there were five of us, the Tibbetts, Jane, Giselle, and myself.

The weather was lovely—and when you've said that, you've said everything. Thank God, I insisted on driving up—at least, as near as one could get to the place. Apparently, they usually walk. It was quite a pretty clearing in the trees, and Henry started piling up stones to make a hearth, while the rest of us were told to collect firewood. This was utter disaster to my hands—I had a manicure only yesterday—so I left Giselle and the Tibbett woman to do it, and went with Jane to fill the saucepan at a nearby stream.

I don't know what's the matter with Jane. She's usually a nice enough creature—not very . . . what can I say? . . . not very *mondaine,* but a good-hearted, *useful* sort of woman. Today she was almost unfriendly. She looked at me in the strangest way. Or am I imagining things?

Anyhow, we filled the damned saucepan—in the process I splashed my new Pucci shirt. I had to make a joke of it, but of course it's ruined. Then we were all expected to sit on the grass around this filthy, smoking fire—I suppose I shouldn't have worn my white silk trousers, but it never occurred to me we wouldn't even have a rug to sit on. Giselle, of course, was in her element—she wore her old blue jeans, and soon had her face smeared with charcoal; she also removed her shoes and walked around barefoot. She is a curious girl. Anyhow, she did toast my cheese for me—the grisly idea is that everyone does their own, so that you all end up like chimney sweeps.

When the grim rites were finally over, Jane and Emmy lay down under the trees and went to sleep. Giselle wandered off on her own, the way she does—which left me with the Englishman. I can't make him out. *Petit bourgeois* and insignificant, I thought at first—now, I'm not so sure. One thing—he's persistent. Why couldn't he leave it alone, instead of stirring up . . . what? Oh, Chantal. . . .

I played it as cool as I could—after all, there's no sense in wrecking a Pucci shirt and a pair of silk pants for nothing. I said, "Did Giselle talk to you yesterday?"

"Yes," he said. Just like that. Nothing more.

I tried again. "Did she tell you what Robert said to her in Paris?"

"No." He was filling his pipe with that awful deliberation that Englishmen use when they want to be awkward.

"Oh, well," I said, "I expect she will one day. Giselle is a funny girl. You have to catch her at the right moment."

That did produce a response of a sort. He said, "It would be surprising if she told me, considering that she denies ever having seen him in Paris."

I suppose it was wicked of me, but my heart gave a little jump of joy. If Giselle was going to tell such transparent lies, she was bound to attract suspicion to herself. Away from Chantal. How could I convince this Tibbett that Giselle had been lying, without seeming eager to denounce her? I said, "I told you, she's a strange person. For her, the truth is what she wants it to be, at any particular moment. It's all part of the artistic thing."

"Is it really?" His voice was dry and edged, and I realized—I simply hadn't noticed before—that we were speaking in French. I must remember to be careful what I say in front of him; one assumes a foreigner will not understand.

"And then—" I said, and deliberately hesitated.

"And then what?"

"Well." I smiled. "Giselle and Michel put up an impeccable front, of course. They have to, because of the publicity. But actually, some of their parties are . . . well, a bit wild. It's just possible that she might have seen Robert, and not even remembered afterward."

He looked at me sharply and said, "You told me she had telephoned you with an account of the meeting."

It was true—so I had. A slip there. I said, "That's quite right, but it was late at night. She said he had just left. It's possible she doesn't remember anything about the telephone call, either."

Tibbett said, "Giselle denies that Robert Drivaz was ever anything more than her ski instructor. She agrees that he turned up at her house in Paris, demanding to see her. But she says that she was out, and that Mario sent him packing. She says that Drivaz was drunk and abusive."

"How does she know that, if she wasn't there?" I tried to make it sound casual.

"I presume that Mario told her."

"Oh, Mario." I sighed, and was silent. What could I say about Mario that wouldn't . . . well . . . lead this Tibbett man deeper into things that were no concern of his. I went on, more brightly, "In any case, this is all academic, isn't it? I mean, we're all fearfully sorry for Anne-Marie, and we'll do all we can for her and for the baby—but there's no doubt that she killed Robert." I paused again. "After all, three years in the convent isn't forever. My husband is not a poor man, and he has a lot of influence. You can rest assured that we will do . . ." I hesitated, choosing my words; ". . . that we're in a position to do more for Anne-Marie than . . . anyone else. If it seems desirable, we'll get her baby back from its grandmother—in due course. There's no sense in rushing things. Surely for the moment it's best to leave things as they are, and not stir up trouble."

There was a long silence. Tibbett puffed at his pipe and looked steadily out over the valley, at the mountains beyond. Then he said, "Perhaps you're right, Sylvie. But all the same . . ."

"Oh, please," I said, "don't let's spoil this heavenly afternoon with dreary talk like this." Heavenly! May I be forgiven! I gave him one of the slow, dazzling smiles. "It's been such fun having you and Emmy here." This was a bit tricky. I had to get my timing right. As if it had just occurred to me, I added, "Pierre and I are so busy, our apartment at Panoralpes stands empty most of the time. Such a waste. Anytime you feel like taking a break—well, I do hope you'll use it. Just drop a line to say you are coming."

He took his pipe out of his mouth slowly, and looked at me. Long and hard. His eyes are dark blue, and somehow they seemed to see right through me. I felt as if—I don't know—as if I'd been caught trying to bribe a policeman, which, I suppose, was just what I had been doing. Oh, my little Chantal . . . why do you force me into situations like this? If I only knew just what you had done. . . .

Then Henry Tibbett smiled at me—a warm smile, almost conspiratorial, as if he understood and sympathized. God knows, perhaps he did. He said, "You really are very kind, Sylvie. We might take you up on that."

Then Giselle came wandering back, with a huge bunch of alpine flowers and a filthy face, and Jane and Emmy woke up and started to be practical—dousing the fire and packing things up—and we all walked down to the cars and drove home. As I've said, it was *not* my idea of a gay afternoon—but in a curious way I felt that perhaps the Pucci shirt had not been sacrificed in vain.

It was a relief to get back to Perce-neige, back inside the comforting fences, back into the world I knew. All the same, I was uneasy, because I knew I must speak to Chantal, and I didn't know what I was going to say. People like us don't talk to each other. We don't need to. We share a way of life, a complicated web of conventions which covers almost every situation, making speech unnecessary except as a decoration to life. This was different. There were no flip clichés to convey what I had to say to Chantal.

I found her in her bedroom, asleep as usual. If Chantal is not involved in some frenetic activity, she just goes to sleep. Not a bad idea. She woke up when I came in, and I was relieved to see that she appeared quite sober and rational.

"Hello, Sylvie," she said, rolling onto her back and holding out her hand to me. "Was it ghastly?"

"Yes," I said. I took her hand, and it lay in mine, like a little bird. Then I gave it back to her, with a definite gesture, and said, "Chantal, I want to talk to you."

"Talk away," she said, closing her eyes.

It was even more difficult than I had foreseen. I said slowly, "Chantal . . . you're grown up now . . . you have your own life to lead. . . ."

She closed her eyes and gave a little impatient sigh. I tried again. "I've never asked you to tell me . . . things . . . because I knew that we understood each other. There was no need."

Her eyes still shut, she said, "No need, Sylvie. No need at all."

This was getting me nowhere. Making a big effort, I said, as briskly as I could, "Well, I'm going to ask you something now, Chantal. Straight out."

She opened her eyes. "Well? Go on—ask!"

"It's about the day Robert Drivaz was killed."

"You do surprise me," she said in a totally unsurprised voice. And then, "You're frightened, aren't you, Sylvie?"

"Of course I am! Everything was all right . . . it was all over . . . and now this Tibbett man has to come along. At the time, the police were very—very kind to me. And you weren't questioned at all—were you?"

Chantal yawned. "No. Not at all. Of course, I was there in your apartment when the gendarmes came. Do you remember the one with brown eyes?"

"Chantal," I said, "this is serious. Please believe me. I'm not going to ask you what you did that day—"

"But you know what I did, Sylvie." She sounded amused.

I went on, as though she had not spoken. "—but I am going to ask you what you've been telling Tibbett. Don't you real- ize . . . ?"

Chantal propped herself up on one elbow and looked at me. "I told him that you lent me your car, and that I drove to Versailles and nearly had an accident with a lorry. I told him I was with you when the gendarmes came in the evening. I told him you were the whole day at a boring conference. Nothing else." A little pause. "He didn't ask me anything else."

I said, "He suggested to me that you could have driven down here in the Alfa, killed Robert, and driven back to Paris. I told him it wouldn't have been possible, but—"

"But of course it would," said Chantal calmly.

"He also knows," I said, "that you have a key to my apartment in Paris."

"You told him, I suppose?"

"He asked me point-blank—I couldn't deny it, could I? Oh, my little Chantal—all I'm asking is that you should be careful. Careful. He's not half as naïve as he looks, you know. Whatever you did, whatever you've said, you know that I love you and I'll do anything to keep you out of danger. But *you must be careful.*"

"Oh, Sylvie!" Suddenly she was like the little twelve-year-old I used to know, *ma petite Chantal.* She threw her arms around my neck and kissed me. "I will. I promise. I will be careful. You trust me, don't you? Say you trust me!"

"I trust you and I love you," I assured her, stroking her silky blond hair. "And if you don't want to tell me—"

She lifted her head from my shoulder and gazed earnestly into my eyes. "But I've told you, Sylvie. I've told you."

"Then that's all right," I said as cheerfully as I could. "We'll say no more about it."

I wish I could be sure it is all right. But it's clear she won't tell me any more.

Thursday, 10 September

This evening Giselle made an unpleasant scene. She had been down at Les Sapins all day, sitting for Jane, and she came back to dinner in an extraordinary mood. Of course, Giselle makes her own rules as she goes along, and we're all used to the way that she just withdraws from human society, sometimes for days on end. Usually, though, she just wanders off on her own, or stays in her room smoking, or drives off somewhere in the Monteverdi and reappears several days later—and nobody dreams of asking her where she's been. That's just her way.

Today, however, was different. She came back from her sitting with Jane, not withdrawn, but on the attack. That's very rare. Her little face was hard, and her eyes were not dreamy but glinting like diamonds. She spoke to nobody, but kept looking at us, each in turn, like a small tiger waiting to pounce. It was very unnerving.

Mario served dinner and then sat down with us, and he and Michel began talking and fooling, pretending that nothing was wrong. But of course, something was, and we all knew it—Giselle made sure of that. What made it all the more awkward was that Chantal had brought back that young man, Jean Bertrand. He had been giving her a tennis lesson—or so she said. I wish she wouldn't . . . but what can you expect?

Anyhow, Giselle just sat there, eating nothing, with her chin practically resting on her plate, glaring at us all. Then, quite suddenly, she picked up a knife and began pointing it at each of us in turn, chanting to herself, "Eeny, meeny, miny, mo"—the way children do.

"What's the game, Giselle?" I said, trying to make it sound as if I was lightly amused.

She didn't answer me, of course. Just went on pointing and chanting. Suddenly Michel couldn't stand it any longer. He had been smoking, and he was in a nervous, violent temper. He jumped up, shouted, "Shut up, you little bitch!"—and threw his wine glass at the window. Fortunately, the plate glass is toughened and did not break; but the wine glass shattered, and the red wine spattered the pale wooden paneling.

Giselle took absolutely no notice. She went on, monotonously, "Eeny, meeny, miny, mo. . . ."

Chantal remained completely unmoved—she didn't even look up from her plate; but Jean Bertrand was sitting there gaping, with eyes like saucers. The story will be all around the village by tomorrow. Mario, as if glad of an excuse to break out of the magic circle of Giselle's malevolence, jumped up and began clearing up the broken glass. I had expected Michel to stalk out of the room after his outburst, but to my surprise he sat down again and muttered something about being sorry.

I said, "For heaven's sake, Giselle, let us into the joke. What's the idea? What are you up to?"

At that, she stopped chanting and looked full at me. "I'm not up to anything," she said. "I wonder, though, who *was* up to something, one day last April." And she started again. "Eeny, meeny, miny, mo . . . catch a killer by his toe . . . if he's rich enough, let him go . . . eeny, meeny, miny, mo. . . ."

I have heard people talk about their blood running cold, but I had never experienced the sensation until then. I literally felt that I was freezing, and I began to tremble—not from fear, but from cold. I tried not to look at Chantal. Giselle went on, "I say 'him'—but it could be 'her.' Probably was. It would have been easier for a woman to impersonate Anne-Marie, wouldn't it, Sylvie?" she added, directly to me.

"What on earth are you raving about, Giselle?" I had control of myself now, and I hope I hit the right note—somewhere between impatience, incredulity, and tolerant amusement.

"Jane did not work well this afternoon," said Giselle, suddenly conversational, switching the subject with her usual abruptness. "She was upset, I could tell at once. I'm like that myself on the set sometimes. After an hour, I saw it was no use going on. So I told her to stop working and tell me all about it."

She paused. There was dead silence at the table. Giselle looked at each one of us in turn, and smiled, slowly and maliciously. "You're interested, aren't you? All of you."

"Well, for heaven's sake, get on with it," I said. "What did Jane have to say?"

"Oh, she didn't want to tell me anything—she thought it wouldn't be ethical, or something." Giselle was now rolling small pieces of bread into little balls and balancing them on her knife, with the concentration of a small child with a toy. "I couldn't get the whole story out of her. But it seems that Henry Tibbett has torn a great, big, gaping hole in Jane's evidence against Anne-Marie. He's proved—or Jane thinks he has—that although she *believed* she was telling the truth at the trial, she might perfectly well have been wrong. It wasn't necessarily Anne-Marie she saw going back to the chalet before five o'clock. It could have been anybody of about Anne-Marie's size, wearing a blue overall." Suddenly, very fast, she added, "Eeny, meeny, miny, mo—and out *you* go!" And swung so that her knife pointed at Michel.

He gave a little ironic bow. "I am honored but not surprised," he said. "That is, if you are implying that it could not have been me. Why not?"

"Too tall," said Giselle laconically. Her eyes rested briefly on Mario, who had come back to the table. "It could have been Mario, though. He's so slim and pretty. Or Sylvie, or Chantal—"

"Or you!" Mario spat out the words.

"I was just going to say—or me. It's interesting, isn't it? I won-der who it was?"

I didn't dare look at Chantal, although I knew from experience that she was capable of playing any scene with complete cool. Then I heard her voice, calm and apparently amused, saying, "Or it could have been the so-correct Mme. Weston, couldn't it?"

"Don't be idiotic, Chantal." It was Michel who spoke, sharply. "How could Mme. Weston have seen herself go past?"

"Oh, you are silly. Supposing she didn't see anybody? Supposing she made the phone call, and got Anne-Marie out of the way, and then went to the chalet and killed Robert? Afterward, of course, she said she had seen Anne-Marie going back. The court only had her word for it, after all—but who would doubt the word of the so-cor-rect English lady? If Tibbett has now shown that her story might not be true—well, she has every reason to be upset. That's all."

Chantal, having delivered herself of this unusually long speech, returned to her dinner. There was a moment of silence, while every-one considered the implications of what she had said. I confess, I had never thought of Jane as a murderess, of Jane as a deliberate liar. Now I suddenly found myself wondering. Had Chantal, with her absolutely unintellectual instinct, stumbled on the right answer?

Giselle was concentrating her intense gaze on to Chantal's face, thinking hard. At last she said, "Very ingenious. Go on. Why should Jane wish to kill Robert?"

Chantal shrugged. She was perfectly self-possessed. "How should I know? Perhaps she was in love with him herself."

"That's ridiculous," I said quickly. I mean, it obviously was. "But Jane was very fond of Anne-Marie, and I know she . . . she rather blamed herself for the break-up of the marriage." I carefully did not look at Giselle. "I mean, she was instrumental in getting Anne-Marie the job at Panoralpes, talking the widow Drivaz into con-senting, and . . . and all that. . . ." I ended lamely.

"And so it didn't work out, and so Mme. Weston goes and stabs Robert Drivaz with a carving knife, and carefully frames her proté-gee, Anne-Marie, and gives damning evidence against her. Really,

Sylvie, you'll have to think again." It was Michel who spoke, and there was a nasty, malicious note in his voice.

Giselle was looking at Michel, long and hard. "Oh, so interesting," she said. "Eeny, meeny, miny, mo . . . out goes Michel, so he can afford to be oh, so objective. But Michel had good reason to hate Robert Drivaz . . . didn't you, chéri? The great Michel Veron wouldn't stain his hands with blood, of course—but he could arrange for his friend Mario to do the dirty work."

Michel was on his feet. "How dare you . . . ?"

"I'm not saying that's what happened, chéri." Giselle was leaning back now, smiling. "I'm just pointing things out. All quite untrue —but supposing the press got hold of them. Let's go around the table, shall we? I've just pointed out why Michel might have wanted to kill Robert, and how easily Mario could have done it for him." She pointed the knife at Chantal next, and the candlelight glinted wickedly on its blade. "Now we come to Mlle. Chantal. Our innocent little girl, who amuses herself in such strange ways when she comes to the mountains. As M. Bertrand can tell us." She was speaking very softly, and poor Jean Bertrand jumped as if he had been bitten when the knife suddenly swung to point at his heart. "Nobody knows what may have gone on between our little Chantal and Robert Drivaz."

"I was in Paris, Giselle. Ask Sylvie." Chantal sounded gently amused.

"We will see. So many things are possible." The knife moved again, and I realized that it was pointing at me. "And Sylvie. Kind Sylvie, who paid for Anne-Marie's defense. I wonder why she did that? Sweet Sylvie, who is Caesar's wife. The police were so very delicate with her. No awkward questions. Supposing this Tibbett starts asking them? What will Sylvie do then?"

"Oh, for heaven's sake, Giselle." I was really angry. "Apart from the fact that everybody knows I was at that benighted conference in Paris—"

"Michel could have operated through Mario," said Giselle thoughtfully. "Sylvie could have operated through Chantal." She looked around the table and smiled brightly. "Hands up," she said

136

like a cheerful schoolmistress, "anybody here who was not heartily delighted when Robert Drivaz died."

This really was too much. I said, "If you are determined to be offensive, Giselle, I think it should be pointed out that you had more motive and better opportunity than anybody else for killing Robert. You know perfectly well that you were bored with him, and that he had turned up in Paris and made a nuisance of himself. You told me yourself—"

"I was making it up," said Giselle, perfectly calmly. "I was a bit high. I never saw Robert in Paris. I was out when he came around, and Mario sent him packing. Isn't that so, Mario?"

Mario was looking at her with cynical amusement. "If madame says so, it is the truth," he said, deliberately exaggerating his Italian accent.

"So if you ask me," Giselle went on thoughtfully, "I would say that it would be better for all of us if we decided that Mme. Weston herself killed Robert—unless Anne-Marie did, of course." She looked slowly around the table, at each of us in turn. "Well?"

Horribly conscious of Jean Bertrand's goggling presence, I said as lightly as I could, "I think this silly game has gone on long enough. Everybody knows that poor Anne-Marie had a terrible time, and nobody really blames her for what she did—but there's no doubt that she did it. The main thing now is to see that she and the baby are well cared for. I've arranged for baby clothes and flowers to be sent to the hospital, and Pierre is going to see that she is looked after financially. I hope the rest of you are going to do something constructive for the poor girl, instead of amusing yourselves by pretending that she didn't kill Robert, which is about the cruelest thing you could do to her at this moment in time."

"Oh, bravo," said Giselle. "Oh, well done, Sylvie." But she was not smiling. "We will drown Anne-Marie in red roses and hand-knitted matinée jackets. We will stop her mouth with hundred-franc notes and lull her to sleep with champagne. We will sing her a sweet lullaby of charitable care, and she will quite forget that she has been convicted of murder and must give away her child. That's the most constructive thing we can do, isn't it?"

And with that she got up and stalked out of the room, leaving her dinner untasted. From what I know of her, I don't imagine we'll see her again for several days.

Oh, Chantal. . . .

Friday, 11 September

All last night I lay awake trying to decide what to do for the best. I didn't come to any definite conclusion, except that I must talk to Henry Tibbett again. So this morning I went to Panoralpes. My excuse was to tell Jane that Giselle was ill and couldn't sit for her. Actually, of course, she's locked in her room, smoking.

But when I got to Panoralpes, I found nobody there except the little Italian girl, Lucia. She told me that Jane was working in the studio, and that Henry and Emmy Tibbett had left. Yes, it was unexpected, she said. No, she didn't know whether or not they were coming back. Mme. Weston had not said. They went off on the evening train yesterday, she thought.

So I went over to the studio, where Jane was working on the clay prototype of Giselle's head. I told her Giselle was ill, and she simply said in an offhand way that it didn't matter, as she didn't need her for the moment. When I asked about the Tibbetts, she just said shortly that they had gone back to England.

I wonder if that's true. If only I knew what I should do. . . .

EMMY

11 ♕

Henry was very thoughtful when we got back from the raclette *picnic.* I'm afraid it wasn't much of a success. Sylvie put up a brave show of enjoying herself, but I don't think she really did—anyway, who ever heard of wearing white silk pants to make a campfire? I suppose she throws them away as soon as they get dirty, like she buys a new Alfa when the ashtrays are full. Oh dear, now I'm being bitchy. Let's face it, I'm jealous. I try not to be, but it's hard. They say that money doesn't bring happiness, but I just wish I had the chance to find out. Actually, come to think of it, Sylvie hasn't been very chirpy these last couple of days. I suppose even she has her worries.

As for Giselle, I simply can't make her out. She changes from moment to moment, like the pattern in a kaleidoscope. It's fascinating to watch, but it makes one a bit dizzy. The really astonishing thing is that somebody like me should be calling a film star by her Christian name—but I can't think of her as a star any more. Next time I see her on the screen, I'll be saying to myself, "But it's only Giselle."

Then there's Jane. Jane has changed, and I don't like it. At first I thought it was just this frantic concentration on her work, and then she seemed to snap out of it and become her old self again; but since Henry showed her that she could have been mistaken about Anne-Marie, she's been behaving very oddly. I suppose it's natural for her to be upset if she thinks her evidence might have been wrong . . . but you'd think she'd be only too eager to help Henry, and to find out who it was she actually saw. But she isn't. That's what's so odd. She shies away from the subject, and she's as nervous as a kitten. I wonder. I wonder whether—now that Henry has put the idea in her head—she fancies that she knows who it was. Oh dear, what a mess it all is.

I had just written that when Henry came in to the sitting room, looking very grim.

"You'd better go and pack," he said. "We're leaving."

"Leaving? What on earth do you mean?"

"We're taking the evening train to Paris."

"Does Jane know?" I asked.

"She does," said Henry in a hard voice.

"Oh, Henry—you haven't quarreled with Jane, have you?"

"No. No, it's not that." He gave me a worried smile. "It's just that Jane has been . . . indiscreet."

"What has she done?"

He sighed. "I've just been up to the studio," he said. "I found Jane there, alone and in tears."

"Good heavens. What on earth had happened?"

"Apparently Giselle noticed that she was nervous and over-wrought, and suggested abandoning the sitting and having a chat instead. She doesn't miss much, our Giselle. She then proceeded to wheedle out of Jane just what was upsetting her. Jane had the rudimentary good sense to realize she ought not to talk about it—but Giselle can twist her around her little finger. Before she knew it, Jane was telling her all about the snow limit and the umbrella, and how she wasn't certain any longer who it was she had seen. Apparently, it had an extraordinary effect on Giselle."

"It upset her?" I asked.

"No—that's what Jane is so bothered about. Giselle seemed—not exactly delighted, but terribly excited at the news. She was fairly sparkling, Jane says—but in a malicious sort of way. She jumped up, kissed Jane, said *that* would put the cat among the pigeons—and rushed off in that great car of hers, back to the Chalet Perce-neige at a hundred miles an hour. Now, of course, Jane bitterly regrets having told her, and is afraid she's put her foot in things properly. That's why she was crying."

"Oh dear. But I don't see why we have to rush off to Paris."

"Because, my dear Emmy," Henry explained, "if we want to follow up any leads there before they're tampered with, we've got to do it at once. We may be too late already."

So I packed our bags, we said good-bye to a subdued and still red-eyed Jane, and by suppertime we were in the dining car, eating our way across the broad plains of central France. We arrived in Paris at eleven o'clock, and checked into our favorite small hotel. I was tired after the journey, and I was appalled when Henry calmly announced that we were going out to a nightclub.

"Oh, Henry—not now. I'm whacked."

"We must, love—there's no time to waste."

"You mean, this is a business call?"

"It is," said Henry. "We're going to Le Fromage Sauvage— where Michel Veron was appearing in April."

Le Fromage Sauvage was very small, very dark, very crowded, and very expensive. The cabaret was about to begin, and as we groped our way through the gloom to a table, the already inadequate lights dimmed still further, as a brilliant spotlight made a fiery circle of the center of the small dance floor. There was a crash on the timpani, and a small man in evening dress stepped into the spotlight. He flashed a toothy smile around the audience, and announced dramatically, "Mesdames et messieurs . . . I have the great honor to present to you . . . Gaby Labelle!"

The small man then disappeared into the darkness like an eel into the mud, and from behind a black velvet curtain a woman in a glittering dress made entirely of blue sequins stepped into the limelight. There was a big wave of applause, and the woman, her beautiful face haggard beneath her glinting hair, blew kisses right and left. Then she grasped the microphone as if it had been a lover—or a lifebelt—and began belting out a sad song of the Paris streets in a powerful, husky, low-register voice, while the pianist and guitarist thrummed unobtrusively in the shadows.

"She still looks marvelous, doesn't she?" I whispered to Henry. "She must be over fifty. I never thought I'd see her in the flesh."

Henry was not listening, either to me or to Gaby Labelle. He was looking to the left, straining his eyes to see in the darkness; and as I looked too, I was able to make out the figure of the small, toothy man. He was making his way slowly between the tables, exchanging a smile here, a whispered word there. He gave us a brief glance, dismissed us as nonentities, and would have passed our table if Henry had not stopped him.

"May I have a word with you?" Henry said quietly. Gaby Labelle had sobbed out the last phrase of her song, and was now acknowledging the warm applause.

The small man looked displeased and said, "After the cabaret, if you please, monsieur." He prepared to move on.

Rather unfairly, Henry whipped out his police identity card. "I'm from the English police. Scotland Yard. I must speak to you."

The small man looked distinctly alarmed. He glanced around nervously and then said, "I will come to your table when the cabaret ends." He turned his back on us, flashed a smile at a bejeweled woman sitting at a nearby table, and moved off.

Gaby Labelle sang two more songs, and followed them up by one of her old hit numbers, the first note of which was greeted by a storm of clapping. She then disappeared behind the curtain, allowed herself to be recalled, did two encores, and finally vanished definitely. The subdued pink lights came up to the point where it was just possible to see the bottles in the champagne buckets, the piano-guitar combination resumed its insistent beat, and conversation swelled up. I wondered if the small man would keep his promise. I had a distinct feeling that if he had not seen Henry's identity card, we would not have seen him again; but, as it was, he came.

"Well, now, Chief Superintendent . . . Tibbett, is it? . . . what can we do for you?" He favored us with his lighthouse-beam smile. Without waiting for an answer, he poured himself a glass of champagne from our bottle, hailed a passing waiter, and ordered another.

"You are Jules Renoir, the owner of this *boîte?*"

The man gave a little affirmative bow. "At your service. You are making official inquiries in Paris, Superintendent?"

Henry sidestepped this. "I am investigating a crime which occurred last April. On Wednesday the fourteenth, to be exact."

Renoir frowned. "That is a long time ago," he said reproachfully. "It is not easy to remember."

"Nevertheless, I am sure you can help me," Henry said. "It was the week when Michel Veron was appearing here."

"Ah, yes. What a talented young man! Of course, we engage only the top names."

"I realize that," said Henry. "I imagine some stars are temperamental, aren't they?"

"Very few. Very few. Temperament is the resort of the second-rate. The top artistes are true professionals."

"Michel Veron?"

"A case in point," said Renoir. "He rehearsed every tiny detail of his act with our stage manager and electrician. A perfectionist. But I am sure you did not come here to discuss Michel Veron."

"As a matter of fact," said Henry, "I did."

"You did?" Renoir was amazed. "But—"

"What time are the cabaret appearances here? Are they the same each week?"

"Yes, yes. Always at the same times. First at eleven, and then a second appearance at one o'clock. The one you have just seen."

"Michel Veron did not miss a performance?"

"Dear me, no. The reverse, if anything." Jules Renoir laughed.

"What do you mean?"

"Well, I told you how thoroughly he rehearsed. All Monday afternoon he was here, running through lighting effects, checking the mike and so on. All well and good. We expect that before a first performance on Monday night. But, if you'll believe it, on the Wednesday—that's the day you are interested in, isn't it?—yes, I remember now that on the Wednesday he turned up again after lunch. He had decided to introduce a new song into his act, and he insisted on rehearsing it, with lighting effects. I had quite a business getting hold of the stage manager and electrician."

"So Veron was here all the afternoon?"

"That's right. From three until—well, after six, anyway."

"And these other men could confirm that?"

Renoir laughed. "I should say so. They were far from pleased at being called out in the afternoon, but Veron insisted."

Well, that certainly seemed to be that. Apart from the fact that Veron was far too tall to impersonate Anne-Marie, he could hardly have been simultaneously at Le Fromage Sauvage and in Montarraz. All the same, it did seem almost too good to be true that he had decided on extra rehearsal on that particular day, just at the crucial time. Establishing an alibi? If so, he had certainly succeeded.

Henry was thanking Renoir, and assuring him that there was no more help he could give. Renoir, looking bewildered, was on the point of departure. And then two things happened. The fresh bottle of champagne arrived, and, close on its heels, Gaby Labelle.

She had changed out of her sequined dress into an elegant silk trouser suit, and she had a magnificent mutation mink stole slung carelessly around her shoulders. She looked older but no less striking at close quarters. She sank gracefully into a chair and said, "Give me some champagne, Jules. I'm parched. And introduce me." Her voice sounded like a purring cat with a sore throat.

There was nothing Renoir could do but accept the situation, for many eyes had now turned to our table. He said, "This is Mr. Tibbett from London, my dear. And Mme. . . . ?" he added on a note of inquiry.

Henry quickly confirmed that I was, indeed, his wife. Gaby Labelle smiled ravishingly at us, and hoped we had enjoyed her performance. We made appropriate noises of appreciation.

"From London?" Gaby Labelle regarded us gravely over the rim of her champagne glass. "You are in Paris on business?"

"Not entirely," said Henry carefully. "As a matter of fact, we are on our way home from a holiday in Montarraz."

"Montarraz? Oh, that is where Sylvie Claudet has an apartment. Do you know Sylvie? She is an old friend of mine."

"We certainly do," I said. "We were actually staying in her apartment."

"Well, well." Gaby Labelle relaxed, apparently delighted to find herself among friends. "So you are friends of Sylvie's. You must know Giselle and Michel, too."

"Yes, indeed," said Henry. "We spent several evenings at the Chalet Perce-neige."

Renoir was a study in bewilderment and apprehension. He laid a hand on Gaby Labelle's arm. "Gaby, chérie, I am sure you must be—"

She shook it off impatiently. "No, no, Jules. I want to hear news of my friends. How is Sylvie?"

Henry hesitated. Then he said, "Very well, I think. Perhaps a little worried."

Gaby Labelle nodded seriously. "Yes. I felt the same thing." There was a little pause, and then she said, "Why did she have to go to Montarraz? Do you know?"

Henry said, "I don't think she *had* to go there. She and her husband had been cruising in the Mediterranean—you know M. Claudet, of course?"

"Do you know, it is strange, but I have never met him. He is always away on important government business, and then Sylvie and I get together and talk of old times."

"Well," said Henry, "I gathered that Pierre Claudet had to cut short their holiday because of, as you say, important government business, and so Sylvie decided to come down to Montarraz instead."

Gaby Labelle looked puzzled, and shook her head. "No, no," she said. "She had arranged to come and dine with me, but she telephoned the evening before, saying that she had had a message from Montarraz—something about the apartment—and must go down there next day. I thought she sounded upset."

Henry said easily, "Oh, well, perhaps I misunderstood. Anyhow, I don't know what took her down there. You're an old friend of hers, I gather?"

"Oh, yes." Gaby Labelle encompassed us both with the sad, sweet smile which has enchanted audiences all over the world. "I have known Sylvie for many years." She laughed throatily. "Oh, now we are both *femmes du monde*—jewels and furs and champagne —but it was not always so, you know. It is not so long ago that I was singing for my supper in cheap little cabarets, and Sylvie was selling hats at Frivolités."

"Frivolités?" Henry repeated the word casually, but I could not stop myself reacting, and I was pretty certain that the man Renoir noticed. Anyhow, he stood up, and said, almost roughly, "Come along, Gaby. You know you must sleep if you are to do good work."

"But Jules—"

"Superintendent Tibbett is a busy policeman from England," said Renoir, with a lack of subtlety which must have been born of desperation. "He is in the middle of an investigation, and must be tired."

Gaby Labelle's thin, painted eyebrows went up. "A policeman? How fascinating. Sit down, Jules. I am intrigued to talk to a policeman who is a friend of Sylvie and Giselle."

"My dear Gaby, I must insist." Renoir was almost dancing with nervousness.

"Frivolités is the name of a hat shop, is it?" said Henry.

"Gaby . . ." I really felt sorry for Renoir. However, luck was on his side. Suddenly, with immense relief and in a different tone, he said, "Look, my dear, there is the Marquis d'Avenet, with Cyrus G. Kloppenheimer, the American impresario. They are inviting us to join their table." He waved and smiled toward a dark corner of the nightclub.

Slowly, Gaby Labelle turned her head to look. Sure enough, two smoothly opulent middle-aged men were raising their glasses to her across the room. She sighed, and stood up gracefully. "It seems I must go. I am still a working girl, you see. I hope we meet again, M. le Gendarme." She held her hand out to Henry, and as he took it, she added softly, "Rue des Lapins, twenty-one. It's disappeared now, of course." And she turned and followed Renoir across the room to the other table.

We were in the Rue des Lapins by nine o'clock the next morning. It was a small street in the Eighth Arrondissement, between the Rue de Rivoli and the Madeleine, narrow and very chic. It reminded me of Beauchamp Place in London. There were a couple of small, trendy restaurants and a spattering of obviously expensive boutiques, as well as a few discreet and desirable private houses. The whole district exuded an aroma of wealth and luxury, which pervaded the street like perfume.

Number 21 was not a hat shop, but a boutique selling handmade jewelry, silk shirts, and *avant-garde* beach wear. The window display consisted of a single, shapeless garment, a few glittering jeweled belts, and a rose, tastefully arranged around an abstract plastic sculpture, which appeared to represent, if anything, a series of naked female breasts. The name of the establishment was Denise.

Henry looked at me and grinned. "Go on," he said. "Be brave."

"It's not my sort of place at all," I protested.

"Still less mine," said Henry. "In you go. I'll wait for you in that café on the corner."

"But—what am I to say?"

"Play it by ear—there's nothing else you can do."

"You won't come in with me?"

"Of course not. I'd spoil everything."

Henry gave me an encouraging grin, and walked off down the street. Timidly, I pushed open the door and went into the shop.

I was greeted at once by a formidable lady of uncertain age, skeletally thin and heavily made up. Her hair was dyed lilac-pink, and she clanked as she moved from the weight of assorted junk jewelry she wore. Her sharp black eyes assessed me—not, I thought, in very flattering terms. She said, as tersely as a schoolmistress, "Madame?"

I said hesitantly, "I . . . I think perhaps I've made a mistake. I was given this address . . ."

"Yes, madame?" Her voice was even sharper.

"You see, I was hoping to . . . to buy a hat. I understood this was a hat shop."

"You can see that it is not, madame."

"A hat shop called Frivolités . . ."

It seemed to me that there was a subtle change in the woman's attitude. Not exactly a softening, but a heightened awareness, almost a feeling of conspiracy. I couldn't exactly put my finger on it. She said, "There was a shop of that name here, madame, but it closed down some years ago. However, I think we may be able to show you some interesting merchandise. Will you step into the salon? This way . . ."

She led the way to the back of the shop, and through a doorway draped with curtains. I found myself in a small room, furnished with several imitation Louis XV sofas, a few gilt chairs, and many long mirrors. There was also a gramophone turntable and a cocktail cabinet. Mme. Denise went first to the turntable and flooded the room with a discreet but blanketing swell of soft music. Then she opened the cocktail cabinet and offered me a drink.

At that hour in the morning, I wanted a drink about as much as I wanted a hole in the head, but something prompted me to say yes. Mme. Denise poured out two large brandies, gave one to me, and then put a beringed hand on my arm and guided me to one of the chaise-longues. She sat down beside me.

"There, my dear," she said. "Now we can talk. You are interested in Frivolités?"

"Yes. You see, I once had a friend who—"

"I quite understand. Unfortunately, you are several years too late. You had not heard?"

I shook my head.

"You do not live in Paris, perhaps?" There was a note of suspicion.

"No, no. I'm English. I come from London."

"Ah. That would explain it." Mme. Denise raised her glass. "Your health, my dear. Well, I won't go into details, but Frivolités ran into—certain difficulties. It was all managed discreetly, but the shop was forced to close. Now, we do not provide the same . . . facilities. Obviously, on these premises, it would be unwise. However, occasionally I get a visit from an old client of Frivolités like yourself, who wishes for the same sort of . . . service . . . and I have an address which I can give you. It is a hairdressing establishment, and I am sure that it will give you every satisfaction."

"You're very kind," I said, "but I don't—"

"You will not find it cheap, but then, extra special service always has to be paid for, hasn't it?" She smiled at me, like a snake. "The address will cost you a thousand francs," she added, on a business-like note.

"As a matter of fact," I said, "I'm not really inquiring for myself."

At once she became suspicious. "In that case, madame, I fear I have been wasting your time. This is a very personal service—"

"I'm trying," I said, "to trace a friend. A girl who used to work at Frivolités. Her name was Sylvie."

"Why do you wish to trace her?" demanded Mme. Denise sharply.

"Oh—just that I haven't seen her for years, and I'm visiting Paris from England . . ."

"What was her surname?"

This was a poser. I had no idea of Sylvie's maiden name. Lamely, I said, "It sounds silly, but I never knew her second name. I just knew her as Sylvie."

For some reason this answer seemed to please Mme. Denise. She nodded slowly, and then said, "How old is she?"

Surprised, I said, "Well . . . let's see . . . she must be in her late forties by now."

Almost to herself, Mme. Denise said, "I see. Not one of the little ones. Sylvie . . . no, madame, I fear I cannot place her." She paused, and then said, "She worked in the shop, you say?"

"That's right. Selling hats."

Mme. Denise drained her drink and stood up. She looked furious, as though I had mocked or insulted her. "I am sorry, madame. I cannot help you. You will not be requiring the address I mentioned?"

"Thank you, no. I was looking for a hat shop, you see. Not a hairdresser."

She shot me a look full of suspicion and distrust, but all she said was, "I hope you are successful in locating your friend, madame, but since you do not know her name . . ."

I felt I should have replied *"Touché"*—but I did not. Instead, I escaped thankfully from the claustrophobic atmosphere of the boutique and hurried to the café, where Henry was drinking coffee and reading *Le Monde* from a roller stick.

"Well?" he demanded.

I reported my strange conversation with Mme. Denise. "It was really creepy, Henry. Heaven knows what went on—the shop must have been a front for something pretty nasty. At first I thought it was probably a place where married women could meet their lovers —you know the sort of thing. You say to your husband, 'I'm just going to buy a new hat, darling'—and there's the boyfriend waiting in a back room. But then she made that sinister remark about the little ones. Should I have bought that address for a thousand francs —not that I have that much French money."

Henry shook his head. "No, no. Let the French police clear up their own cess pits. It's nothing to do with us, and we don't want to make people suspicious. Of course, it could all be perfectly innocent. . . ."

"Innocent?" I echoed. "Very special personal service, and a thousand francs for the address? Don't be silly, Henry."

"What I meant was," he explained, "that Sylvie's connection with the shop may have been innocent. According to Gaby Labelle, she was just a salesgirl. She may not have known what was going on—and for all we know, the racket may not have started up until after her time there. On the other hand, why did Giselle bring it up?"

"Pure mischief-making, I should think," I said. "Remember Sylvie's position as Pierre's wife. Even if her connection with the place was innocent, there's obviously a nasty smell attached to Frivolités, and she wouldn't want it known that she worked there."

"Well," said Henry, "the next thing is to find out more about the story. Mme. Denise said it was discreetly hushed up, but somebody must know."

"Jules Renoir?" I suggested. "Gaby Labelle?"

Henry considered. "Very likely," he said. "Renoir was on tenterhooks last night. But he'd never talk. No—I have it. The very person. Pierre Claudet."

"*What!* Henry, you can't—"

Henry laughed. "The International League of Women in action again? Darling, give me credit for a little tact. Of course, I wouldn't dream of mentioning to M. Claudet that his wife had been involved in any way."

"But—"

"Look, Emmy—the very fact that Sylvie is so sensitive about Frivolités shows in itself that her husband doesn't know her previous connection with the place. She's afraid he may find out. Right— I certainly don't intend to tell him. But if there was a scandal which involved people in high places—and it almost certainly did, if it was hushed up—then Pierre Claudet is just the man to know about it. Finish your coffee, and we'll set about contacting him."

12 ♛

*Of course, it was no easy matter arranging an interview with a govern-*ment minister, especially as we had never met him before. A telephone call to the ministry produced, predictably, no result at all, except a cold official voice advising us to submit our request in writing, when it would be considered. Fortunately, however, Jane had given us the private, ex-directory telephone number of Sylvie's Paris apartment, and this was more fruitful. The phone was answered by a maid, who told Henry that Monsieur was expected home for lunch. He was entertaining a small party of political colleagues. Madame was still away in Switzerland.

Henry said, "I shall call around in a few minutes and leave a note for M. Claudet. Will you make sure that he reads it when he comes home to lunch?"

"Yes, monsieur."

We found a stationer's shop, and bought writing paper and envelopes. Then we went into a café, ordered more coffee, and Henry laid a sheet of paper on the table and brought out his fountain pen.

"What are you going to say?" I asked.

Henry didn't answer. He wrote quickly on the paper, and then passed it to me to read.

Dear M. Claudet,

I have just come from Montarraz, where I have been staying in your apartment, thanks to the hospitality of Jane Weston and your wife, Sylvie. I would very much appreciate an opportunity of talking to you privately. You can reach me at the Hotel Ste. Jeanne anytime this afternoon. I shall be leaving Paris tomorrow.

Yours sincerely,
Henry Tibbett, Chief Superintendent,
C.I.D., London.

"You think that will get him?" I asked.

"I think it will intrigue him," said Henry.

"So what do we do now?"

"We deliver the note," said Henry, "and we wait. Not, I hope, for too long."

Henry was right. It was not yet one o'clock, and we had just arrived back in our hotel room with the rolls, cold ham, and wine which we had bought as a snack lunch, when our telephone rang, and the hall porter informed Henry that a gentleman wished to speak to him. The gentleman had not given his name.

Henry took the telephone, and said, "Hello . . . yes, Tibbett speaking . . . good afternoon, M. Claudet . . . it's very kind of you . . . yes, yes, I quite understand how busy you are . . . three o'clock? Yes, that will suit us very well . . . oh, my wife . . . didn't I mention . . . ? Yes, she is with me . . . No, I wouldn't exactly describe it as official . . . you know how such matters are arranged, I am sure . . . until three, then . . . good-bye. . . ."

"Well?" I said as he rang off.

Henry grinned at me. "Smooth as silk," he said, "but he's dead scared. He wants us to go to his apartment this afternoon at three. He says he can spare us half an hour after his lunch guests have gone."

"Oh, well," I said, "that gives us two hours to burn."

"That's where you're wrong," said Henry. "It gives me less than two hours to get hold of a whole lot of information."

Henry was lucky. Considering that it was lunchtime, he could hardly have expected success in tracking down a French journalist friend in a matter of minutes—but fortunately the man's secretary knew at which café he was lunching. Henry rang the restaurant, and lured his friend away from his meal to the telephone. After ten minutes of conversation, to which Henry's contributions were little more than the occasional "Yes? . . . Really? . . . And then what? . . . Ah, I see," he rang off and turned to me with a sigh of satisfaction.

"Good old Georges," he said. He sat down on the bed and took a bite of buttered roll.

"All the lowdown on Claudet?" I asked.

"Not all of it, of course—but Georges is as well informed as anybody.".

"Well?"

"No scandal," said Henry. "Not a breath. Never has been. Brilliant academic record, qualified as a lawyer, went briefly into practice, and then took to politics. Not rich himself, but married a girl of immense wealth and powerful family—"

"But Sylvie—" I began.

"No, no." Henry took another mouthful, and spoke indistinctly through it. "First wife. Married her thirty years ago, when he was a young man. Her money and family connections launched him on his political career. They had two children, a boy and a girl—now both grown up and married, of course. Six years ago Mme. Claudet was killed in a motor smash. Two months later Pierre Claudet married Sylvie."

"Still no scandal?"

"No . . . but quite a lot of criticism, especially from his first wife's family and friends. He'd inherited all her money, of course. Nobody knew anything about Sylvie. Pierre Claudet just produced her from nowhere. Of course, snobbery is officially out these days, especially in politics—however powerful a force it may actually be. Claudet made a public virtue of the fact that his new wife had been a simple, hard-working woman, and nobody could challenge the moral rectitude of that. In fact, it did him some good at the polls, I gather. And then, Sylvie turned out not to be vulgar and gauche, but elegant and charming, which pleased everybody. Also, she at once became tremendously active in good causes and women's organizations and so on—a model minister's wife. She was soon accepted by everybody."

"Everybody?"

"Well." Henry grinned. "I daresay there are some people who wouldn't be heartbroken if she slipped up publicly—but it's generally agreed that she's doing a good job. At least, she's not doing anything to hinder Claudet's ambitions."

"His ambitions being . . . ?"

"Oh, President of the Republic, without a doubt, according to Georges. Meanwhile, he has already achieved junior ministerial rank, and his immediate objective is to be transferred from his present rather insignificant ministry to something really powerful, like Foreign Affairs. There's rumored to be a cabinet reshuffle in the offing, and Claudet's name is being mentioned for a big job."

"He must have enemies," I said.

"Of course he has. Georges says there's an influential group who are fighting tooth and nail to keep him out. A juicy scandal, whether it affected him personally or just Sylvie, would be exactly what they want to discredit him."

"I see," I said. "No wonder Sylvie is frightened. Did the Drivaz murder case affect Claudet's reputation, by the way?"

"Not really. Georges says his enemies tried to make something of it—but Sylvie's part in it was so patently innocent, and she made such a good impression in the witness box, that it left them with no ammunition. Anyhow, the whole thing took place in another country. By now, it's dead and buried as far as the French press is concerned."

"And Frivolités?" I asked.

Henry hesitated. "It didn't seem to register at all with him at first," he said. "I had to repeat the name several times, and give him a few hints. Then he remembered. He's a journalist, with a filing-cabinet mind. Oh, he said, a very minor affair. A hat shop used as a front for a brothel, as far as he remembered. The sort of thing that was bound to crop up after the closing of the official *maisons de tolérance.* He couldn't imagine why I should be interested in it."

"Sounds like a skillful piece of hushing up," I said.

"Perhaps," said Henry. "Or perhaps it really was unimportant. Oh, well. I hope we shall find out more from Pierre Claudet."

The Claudets' apartment was a penthouse suite, on the top floor of an old-fashioned apartment building not far from the Champs Elysées. As we stepped out of the slow-moving, ornate lift, we could see through the corridor window an impressive panorama over the gray rooftops of Paris. Typically, the hallways and corridors of the building were bleak and almost shabby, but when the very correct manservant opened the apartment door in answer to our ring, we stepped into a world of extraordinary luxury and opulence, which— even if it was somewhat conventional—proclaimed wealth and good taste at the top of its voice.

The furniture was Louis XV, and it never occurred to me to doubt that it was genuine. The curtains were pure silk, the carpets handmade in *grand point.* An ormulu clock ticked majestically on its marble plinth, and a few pieces of exquisite Sèvres porcelain were carefully displayed to their best advantage. The flower arrangements were obviously professional, and all the visible books were leather-bound and gold-tooled. Standing in the Claudets' Paris apartment, I suddenly realized that, to them, the Montarraz flat was, indeed, just a simple country retreat. It's all relative.

The butler said, "Monsieur requested that you should wait in the study, M. le Superintendent. He will be with you in a few minutes."

He ushered us into a book-lined room, furnished with a huge leather-topped desk and a beautiful antique revolving globe of the world. After a minute or so, we heard a door opening onto the corridor outside, and a rich spate of masculine voices spilled out, accompanied by the aroma of Havana cigars. The luncheon guests were on their way. There was more talk and laughter as coats were donned and farewells said; then the front door closed definitively, and there was a momentary silence. Then came rapid, heavy footsteps in the corridor, the study door opened, and Pierre Claudet came in, his hand extended and his face smiling welcome.

"Superintendent Tibbett? And madame? *Enchanté,* madame. Forgive me for having kept you waiting—an official luncheon, I'm afraid. The sort of thing which I have to endure, and which Sylvie finds so boring—so she wisely escapes to Montarraz. I only wish I could do the same. May I offer you a cognac? A cigar?"

When we had accepted brandy and Henry had refused a cigar, Pierre Claudet settled us comfortably into two leather armchairs, sat down behind the desk himself, and said, "And now you must tell me how I can help you, monsieur. I understand you have been staying with Sylvie in Montarraz. Is it . . . is it about Sylvie that you wish to speak?" His voice was as smooth as oiled silk, and he was still smiling, but I thought I caught an undertone of uneasiness.

"No, no," said Henry quickly. "I'm afraid I rather unscrupulously used your wife's name as an introduction to you, sir. We are old friends of Jane Weston's, you see, and we have been staying with her in your apartment. . . ."

"In my apartment?" Claudet was clearly puzzled. "I am sorry, I do not quite follow. Mme. Weston lives in the little chalet, surely?"

I said lightly, "Oh, didn't Sylvie tell you? She very kindly lent the apartment to Jane while you were both away for the summer."

Pierre Claudet's mouth set in a hard line of displeasure. He said, "No, she did not tell me. But Sylvie is in Montarraz now—she went down there nearly a week ago. There can hardly have been room for all of you in the Panoralpes apartment."

The last words were spoken on a definite note of interrogation, and I suppose my hesitation in replying was absolutely explicit, because Claudet went on at once, "I see. Sylvie is staying at the Chalet Perce-neige, I suppose."

"Well," I said fumblingly, "now that we've left, I'm sure she'll—"

"I understand the situation perfectly, madame." It was obvious that he also disapproved of it. Then, with an abrupt change of tone, he turned to Henry and said, "Now, let us get to business, M. le Superintendent. I fear my time is short. What do you want with me?"

It was all pretty daunting, but Henry did not intend to be bullied. I recognized the way in which he deliberately settled back in his chair and sipped his drink, before he said, "It's only a small matter,

M. Claudet, and it won't take long. I expect you would first like to see my credentials." He pulled out his wallet, extracted his official identity card, and laid it on the desk.

Pierre Claudet did not even glance at it. "Any friend of Mme. Weston's . . ."

"Ah, but I want to ask you for information which you might not wish to divulge to an ordinary member of the public, M. Claudet. I am conducting an inquiry into the affair of the hat shop in the Rue des Lapins known as Frivolités. The police closed it down six years ago."

There was a moment of dead silence. Pierre Claudet leaned forward very deliberately and picked up Henry's identity card from the desk. He studied it for a moment, then flicked it almost contemptuously with his right forefinger, and laid it down again. In the stillness, the small noise of his fingernail against the cardboard sounded unnaturally loud. He said, "An official inquiry, on behalf of Scotland Yard?"

"No," said Henry. "That is why I have come to you in this unorthodox way, instead of going to your police. I believe that you can tell me more than appears in the official reports."

"Indeed? What makes you think that?"

Henry smiled. "The fact that so little is officially recorded about the affair. And yet, some people near the top of the pile clearly know more than they are prepared to say. So I have come to the very summit for information."

There was another pause. Then Claudet said, "What is your interest in Frivolités? It is ancient history."

"I can assure you," said Henry blandly, "that I have no intention of raking up old scandals. On the contrary, I am concerned above all with discretion, and with making sure that unsavory facts are not published—perhaps in another country."

That obviously made Claudet think. Without saying anything definite, Henry had sown in his mind the possibility that scandalous revelations might be made outside France, and that the very fact that our visit was unofficial was something to be thankful for.

Henry can be quite wicked when he wants to be, and it's a mistake to underestimate him—as people have often found to their cost.

Claudet said, "As a matter of fact, I was slightly concerned with the case—I was at the Ministry of Justice at the time. But—"

"Good," said Henry. "That means we can talk. I will tell you all I know, and you can correct me, or elaborate, as you like." Before Claudet could protest, he went on. "Frivolités was, on the face of it, a small, chic hat shop in the Rue des Lapins. Actually, it was a front for a number of illicit goings-on. The most innocent of these was to provide an opportunity for society ladies to meet their lovers, under the pretext of a shopping expedition. They paid highly for the service, and I do not believe that they were blackmailed. Is that correct?"

"Of course." Claudet was expressionless. "You must know that it was on these grounds—allowing the premises to be used for immoral purposes—that the shop was closed."

"Exactly," said Henry. "But, as I said, this was merely the most innocent of the vices. A double front, if you like. Behind this relatively charming and romantic illegality, there was a darker picture. It concerned the little ones."

"What do you know about it, M. Tibbett?"

"Not very much," Henry admitted cheerfully. "That's why I came to see you. The little ones were young girls—perhaps boys, too, I don't know. Ah, I see you can enlighten me. Boys, too?"

Claudet nodded briefly. Henry went on. "These children were kept there to gratify the unusual desires of—well, important people. People who could not afford a scandal. People who were prepared to pay enormously for that elusive commodity—trust."

"I do not understand you, monsieur."

"I think you do. Somebody—perhaps several people—knew the identity of Frivolités's clients. This person—or people—had a perfect blackmail weapon to hand, but did not use it. The clients believed, rightly, that if they paid enough, they would not be threatened. Unfortunately for them, somebody broke this trust. An honest person, who did not even consider personal gain by blackmail, but who went straight to the police." Henry paused. Claudet had gone very pale. "Was that person you, M. Claudet?"

"I do not intend to have my name dragged into—"

"Of course not, M. Claudet," said Henry patiently. "I thought I had explained that my interest in the matter is to be as discreet as possible. But if I do not have the facts myself . . ."

"Very well." Claudet reached a quick decision. "What I am about to tell you is in the strictest confidence. That is understood?"

"Of course."

"Well, you are right. It was I who exposed Frivolités to the police. The whole matter came to my notice through—a friend. That need not concern you. I reported it to a—a very senior police official. As his inquiries progressed, he grew more and more concerned at what he found. At last, he came to me privately and asked for my advice. It seemed that a number of very prominent men in public life were involved. The country was in a precarious state politically, and a scandal of that sort could have had grave consequences for France and her people. The men concerned had undoubtedly learned their lesson, and would never be so foolish again. I felt that the welfare of the nation was paramount. I agreed with the police official that Frivolités should be closed down quietly, on a charge of 'use of premises for immoral purposes.' The whole thing was managed with great discretion, and that was the end of it. And I don't mind telling you," Claudet added, with an almost noble defiance, "that I would do the same thing again in similar circumstances."

"And what happened," Henry asked, "to the owner of the . . . enterprise?"

Claudet frowned. "That was the only unsatisfactory aspect of the affair," he said. "The woman who nominally owned and managed the shop was fined and given a heavy suspended prison sentence. That ensured her discretion, for she had only to step once out of line to find herself behind bars. However, the police were convinced that she was only a—how shall I put it?—a nominee. I doubt if she even knew enough to be a great danger. We never laid hands on the man—or woman—behind the whole unpleasant racket. Any attempt to track this person down threatened to involve some eminent public figure. It was an impasse, and has remained so." There was a little pause. Then Claudet added, "I trust that your visit does not imply that this . . . this creature is becoming active again. On your side of the channel, perhaps."

"I hope not," said Henry. He stood up. "Well, thank you very much, M. Claudet. You have helped me a great deal. I won't keep you any longer—I know what a busy man you are."

"Just a moment, M. Tibbett." Claudet spoke quietly, a man accustomed to exercising authority. "Please sit down." Henry sat down. "I have been very frank with you. Now you will kindly be frank with me."

"I have told you—"

"You have told me nothing at all," Claudet pointed out, accurately. "You have used me to confirm what I believe was largely guesswork on your part. You have extracted information from me. Now—just what is your interest in the matter?"

I could not resist a sidelong glance at Henry, to see how he would react to this. It was, after all, an eminently reasonable request, and since Henry had admitted that his inquiry was not official, he could hardly shelter behind the stockade of professional secrecy. I was beginning to feel considerable respect for Pierre Claudet. Very neatly, and giving the impression of admirable frankness, he had not only cornered Henry, but put him squarely in the wrong. I waited with some anxiety to see how Henry would return this beautifully placed ball.

To continue the tennis analogy, Henry now played a well-judged lob. He said, "My interest is very simple, M. Claudet. I have reason to believe that . . . somebody . . . has had the idea of reviving this old scandal by means of blackmailing people who may have had some connection with Frivolités. I am anxious to put a stop to this, and I am sure you are, too."

Claudet considered for a moment. Then he said, "This—person. Is he the man we never caught, the actual owner of the enterprise?"

"I can't be sure of that," said Henry.

"But you know the identity of the blackmailer?"

"Yes," said Henry, "but at the moment I can't prove it, so naturally I can't make accusations. Meanwhile, M. Claudet, if anybody should approach you with demands for money—"

"Me?" Claudet's voice was as sharp as a whiplash. "Why should anybody approach *me*, M. Tibbett? My part in the affair was absolutely honorable. I have nothing to hide."

"I realize that, M. Claudet. Nevertheless—"

This time it was Pierre Claudet who stood up. "I wish you every success with your investigation, M. Tibbett," he said, "but I am unable to help you further. If you imagine that I will name the eminent men involved, you are mistaken; I did not do so six years ago, and I will not do so now. So I fear your visit has been fruitless." He glanced at his watch. "I have to go now. I have a meeting at four o'clock. Good day to you."

When we were out in the street again, I said to Henry, "I'm glad that's over. You did splendidly, darling."

"Thank you."

"I must say, I'd no idea you were such an accomplished liar."

"Liar?" he said. "What do you mean?"

"Well—all that stuff about blackmail, and knowing who was behind it all, and—"

"I wasn't lying," said Henry.

"You—weren't? You mean, somebody really *is* blackmailing eminent people about Frivolités? And you think it all has some extraordinary connection with Anne-Marie?"

Henry smiled at me. "Just for the moment," he said, "I'm not telling you or anybody else what I think. Just take it from me that I told Claudet no lies. Now—what was the name of the organization whose conference Sylvie was attending on the day of the murder?"

The Federation of Women's Guilds had its headquarters in a trim modern office on the Left Bank. The organizing secretary was a small, fussy woman with untidy gray hair who gave the impression of having been ten minutes late for an appointment several years ago, and never having caught up. However, she was keen to be helpful, and most interested when I explained that I wished to find out about the Women's Guilds of France so that I could give a talk on the subject to my own Townswomen's Guild at home. (This was no lie, either; I actually gave the lecture a few weeks ago.) Soon I was inundated with pamphlets, accounts of projects, welfare schemes, voluntary work, day nurseries, fund-raising, and so forth. It was quite some time before I managed to steer the conversation around to the annual conference.

"Ah, yes. That is the highlight of our year, madame. It is held every April, here in Paris. Delegates come from all over the country to exchange views and report progress. We have some very distinguished speakers, too. This year, the conference was opened by Mme. Claudet—the wife of the minister, you know. Such a delightful woman, and so very interested in our work. We felt really honored, knowing what a busy person she is." The secretary beamed complacently.

I said, "Yes, indeed. For someone in her position to devote a whole day to a conference must be—"

She interrupted me. "Well, of course, she couldn't stay the *whole* day. We quite realized that—we would not have expected her to. But she gave a most interesting opening address, and then stayed until midday listening to the other speakers. We had been hoping to entertain her for lunch, but unfortunately she had another appointment. Still, I think I may say that the conference was a great success. Now, I do want you to take a leaflet about our play groups for preschool-age children of working mothers. . . ."

Back at the hotel, Henry sat down on the bed and began to rub the back of his neck with his hand—a sure sign that he was deep in thought. He said, "She could have managed it."

"But she didn't have her car," I pointed out. "She had lent it to Chantal."

Henry shook his head. "She couldn't have done it by car," he said. "Not even the Alfa, if she didn't leave the conference until twelve. But if the plane times are right, it could have been done by flying to Geneva and hiring a car there." He picked up the bedside telephone. "Reception? Do you have airline timetables? . . . Good . . . Paris to Geneva and back . . . in the afternoon . . . can you find out and ring me back? Thank you."

"I can't believe it," I said. "I mean—Sylvie, of all people. She's so gay and so gentle. . . ."

Henry was not listening. He had taken out the small notebook which he always carried, and was making rapid notes. A moment later the telephone rang.

"Yes? . . . Yes, I've got that . . . what time does it arrive?" He scribbled rapidly. "And Geneva to Paris? . . . Yes. . . . Yes, thank you . . . no, I don't want to make a booking. . . ."

He rang off, drew a line under the figures he had written, and said, "It's perfectly possible. There's a flight from Orly at one o'clock, getting in at ten to two. Plenty of time to pick up a hired car and drive to Montarraz. The return flight leaves Geneva at seven, and gets back to Paris at ten to eight. By nine o'clock, she could easily have been back in her apartment, waiting for Chantal. Pierre Claudet was away, with the manservant, and Sylvie herself told us it was the maid's day off."

"And the phone call to Anne-Marie?"

"Made from a call box on the way to Montarraz. It's perfectly easy to disguise one's voice on the telephone."

"But Henry—in heaven's name, *why?* Frivolités . . . ?"

"Shut up," said Henry. "I'm thinking."

13 ♔

As Henry has often remarked, it's one thing to conduct an investigation from his desk at Scotland Yard, with all the facilities of a superbly organized police force at his fingertips—and quite another to get involved in these unofficial investigations into which his inquiring nose is always leading him. One thing we both knew from experience was that even officialdom could not extract from an airline a list of the names of passengers who had traveled on a particular short-haul flight six months previously—for the good reason that such records are not kept.

There was a faint hope, however, that the car-hire firms at Geneva airport might be able to trace back a hiring made earlier in the year; so it came as no great surprise when Henry announced that we would be leaving Paris for Switzerland by the midnight train. Meanwhile, he said, we had one more job to do in Paris—and he asked the hotel switchboard to connect us with the Claudets' private number. This time I picked up the telephone when it rang.

"M. Claudet's residence, good afternoon." The voice was brisk and feminine.

I said, "Is that Mme. Claudet's maid speaking?"

"Yes, madame. Can I help you?"

"I hope that you can. I am a journalist from England"—all right, one has to tell fibs sometimes in this business—"and I am making a private inquiry into the Drivaz murder, for my magazine."

There was a short silence, and then the voice said, "I do not see how I can assist you, madame."

"You were working for Mme. Claudet at the time?"

"No, madame. I started here in May."

"Oh." This was a poser. "You don't know how I could contact your predecessor? My editor wishes me to interview her, and would be prepared to pay for any information—"

"I am sorry, madame." She did sound genuinely regretful. "Perhaps I could . . ." I became aware of background noises—a door banging, a distant masculine voice. Speaking away from the telephone, the maid said, "Yes, monsieur . . . no, monsieur . . . an English lady . . ." And then there was a muffled silence, as if she had put her hand over the mouthpiece. A few seconds later her voice came back to me, crisp and clear. "Forgive the interruption, madame. I am afraid I cannot help you at all. Good-bye, madame." She rang off.

I turned to Henry. "Well," I said, "that was an abysmal failure. The girl is new—only been there since May. And even if she did have a line on her predecessor, Claudet—I suppose it was him—stepped in and shut her up. I'm so sorry, darling."

To my surprise, Henry was smiling. "Don't be sorry," he said. "It was what I expected, and I hope it will have the desired effect."

"And what is that?"

"To stir things up," said Henry.

We were lucky enough to get a couple of *couchettes* on the night train, sharing a four-berth compartment with a couple of dour French businessmen. As the express roared and rattled its way through the night, I lay sleepless on my upper bunk, thinking about Sylvie Claudet, about Chantal Villeneuve, about Giselle Arnay and Michel Veron, about Jane Weston and Anne-Marie Drivaz. In the faint glow of the blue night light I could see Henry on the opposite bunk, sleeping peacefully. I thought of all the other journeys which we had made, hurtling our way across Europe in pursuit of information, or criminals, or to try to save a life—always impelled by Henry's unquenchable passion for justice. Perhaps it's easier for a man to be so single-minded. Of course, when I thought about Anne-Marie, I longed to be able to bring her, with her baby, out of the gloomy cloisters and into the sunshine; but when I thought about Sylvie, and Jane, and Chantal . . . well, to put it mildly, I wondered if I was really cut out for the role of an Erinys.

By the time we arrived at Geneva in the early hours of the morning, I had fallen into a restless sleep, in which I dreamed that I was wide awake, still in the train and lying on my bunk; but on the opposite bunk, instead of Henry, was Chantal—lying there and staring at the ceiling. I kept on asking her, "What actually happened, Chantal? What actually happened?" But all she would reply was, "Oh, you are silly."

Then, suddenly, I was in the dark corridor of the convent at Charonne. At the far end of it, there was a woman walking away from me, and I knew it was Sylvie. Then I saw that she was being followed by a man—a dark, sinister figure, slipping from shadow to shadow after her. I knew she was in terrible danger, and I ran to catch the man, to stop him—and as I grabbed him and he turned to face me, I saw that it was Henry. I must have called out his name, because I woke myself up. Henry was lying on his bunk, smoking a cigarette and gazing at the ceiling. He held out his hand to me across the compartment and said, "It's all right, darling. Don't worry. I'm here. Were you having a nightmare?"

I couldn't bring myself to take his hand. Looking at him, I felt frozen and frightened. He said, "It *must* have been a bad dream. You're looking at me as though you've never seen me before."

I snapped out of it then, and made myself smile back at him— but the feeling of tingling fear and revulsion took a long time to fade. Less and less did I relish the errand which had brought us back to Switzerland.

We arrived in Geneva in time for an early breakfast at an old-fashioned café near the station. It was all just as I remembered it from previous visits—the tall gray houses; the café tables with checked gingham cloths covered for each new customer by a crisp white paper mat; the waitresses looking permanently pregnant, for they wore, under their frilly white aprons, bulky leather purses on straps around their waists. Above all, there was the smell which characterizes a city—in this case, milky coffee, fresh bread and cherry jam, with faint overtones of the *kirsch* and *prunelle* with which some Swiss workmen like to start their day. When we had finished breakfast, we took a taxi to the airport, to begin our inquiries at the self-drive car-hire counters.

Once again we were hampered by the lack of any official backing. Henry could not simply produce his identity card and demand to see the company's files. We had to resort to guile, and it was not very easy. For a start, we picked the smallest of the three companies advertising cars for hire, shunning the big international concerns and choosing the local firm. Then Henry went into his impersonation of a fussy, indecisive but demanding British tourist—just the sort of difficult but not impossible customer who provides a challenge to a conscientious receptionist.

First, he demanded to know the exact procedure for hiring a car. The girl explained politely that formalities were minimal—she needed only to see his valid driving license and, in the case of a foreigner, his passport. Henry at once handed over the documents. The girl scrutinized the license carefully to check that it was, indeed, valid—and then flipped open the passport to compare the two signatures. She handed the papers back with a smile.

"Thank you, monsieur. That is quite in order."

"But if the hirer is Swiss, you don't have to see his passport?" asked Henry fussily.

"No, monsieur. Of course, Swiss driving licenses carry a photograph of the holder, which makes them a surer form of identification. In fact, British licenses are just about the only ones without photographs—so we compare the signature. Now, which model of car do you wish to have? When you have decided, there is a form to be filled in, and you pay the daily hire rate and a deposit. The kilometer rate is, of course, paid when you return the car—according to the distance you have driven. And of course, you receive your deposit back. Here is a list of the cars we have available, with the different rates." She handed us a brochure.

Henry made a great performance of poring over it, and finally turned to me. "Can you remember which model Sylvie had? Was it the Mercedes or the Opel?"

"I really don't know, Henry," I said. "I just remember what a splendid car it was."

"Exactly. It's most provoking to have forgotten the make." He turned to the receptionist. "A friend of mine, a Mme. Claudet, hired a car from you in April, and my wife and I rode in it with her. We were greatly impressed by its performance in the mountains, and I am quite determined to have the same model. Mme. Claudet—a very attractive French lady with fair hair. Surely you must remember her?"

The receptionist did her best, assuring us that all their cars were chosen for their good hill-climbing qualities—but Henry was not to be fobbed off. If he could not get exactly the model that Mme. Claudet had hired on April 14, he would not hire a car at all, but would take a train to the mountains.

I was greatly struck not only by the girl's patience and good humor, but by the fact that she did not seem to find this exigence extraordinary. I suppose people who have to deal with the general public all day come across more eccentric and difficult characters than one ever imagines. At length, sooner than lose our business, she agreed to look up the records for April 14. We held our breath as she produced a big box file and began sorting through piles of printed forms.

"Let me see—April 14, you said? . . . April 12 . . . April 13 . . . ah, here we are." She detached a slim batch of papers from the folder—about ten in all. "What was the name again?"

"Claudet. Mme. Claudet, from Paris. A French lady—very attractive, with fair hair . . . about five-foot-four. . . ." Henry's impersonation of a bore was so accurate as to be maddening.

The girl consulted each of the papers carefully, and finally said, "You're sure it was April 14?"

"Of course I'm sure. It was my wife's birthday. I'm hardly likely to forget my own wife's birthday, am I?"

"That's right," I put in. "It was my birthday, and we flew over in the afternoon from London. Mme. Claudet met us in the car which she had just hired from you, and drove us to the mountains."

The girl was still patient and unruffled. "Then I am afraid, monsieur, that you must be mistaken about the firm from which your friend hired the car. It certainly was not from us."

"Excuse me, miss, it certainly was. She told us distinctly. The fact of the matter is that your organization does not keep proper records." Henry appeared to be losing his temper. "It is quite disgraceful that you cannot trace a simple transaction of that sort, dating from only a few months ago. I have a good mind to complain to your head office."

At last the girl's smooth manner began to crack with exasperation. "I tell you, monsieur, nobody of that name hired a car on April 14!"

"And I assure you that she did. You haven't heard the last of this!"

"All right!" The girl almost threw the sheaf of papers at Henry. "Look for yourself! Those are records of all the hirings on that day, and you can see for yourself that your friend's name is not there. Only one of the clients was a French lady, and her name was quite different!"

Henry was riffling through the forms, and I peered over his shoulder. Mr. Johnson from London. M. Bercy from Brussels. Mr. and Mrs. Rockbeeker from New York. At the next form, Henry suddenly stopped dead, and a curious silence descended on that small corner of the airport. The form was made out in the name of Mlle. Chantal Villeneuve from Paris. She had hired a small blue Volkswagen for one day only, and had returned it that same evening at ten minutes past six, with two hundred and thirty-two kilometers on the clock. Just the distance to Montarraz and back.

Henry's pause was only momentary, just long enough to take in the relevant details. Then he quickly went on to inspect the rest of the papers, which he then pushed back across the desk to the receptionist, saying pettishly, "There is certainly no record of the hiring here, but that does not mean it did not take place. Your system is evidently most inefficient. However, by good luck I have remem-

bered what car it was. It was a Volkswagen, was it not, my dear?"
He appealed to me.

"That's right! How clever of you, Henry! Yes, it was certainly a
Volkswagen—a little blue one."

The girl, understandably, could not repress a small sigh of exasperation mixed with wry amusement. To have gone through all this
pantomime to end up with the smallest, most popular, and least expensive car on the list! Clearly she was convinced that Henry had
never had any intention of hiring one of the more expensive cars,
and had created this ridiculous diversion out of a desire to appear
important. Oh, well—he wasn't the only one. She'd had to deal
with plenty like him, and worse.

"So you will take a Volkswagen, monsieur?"

"Yes," said Henry pompously. "A blue one, if possible."

The girl smiled with real amusement. "Certainly, monsieur, if we
have a blue one available. Now, if you will just give me the details . . ." She had a virgin form on the desk in front of her, which
she proceeded to fill up, as Henry spelled out his name, home address, type of insurance cover required, and so on. The girl then
consulted a list, and announced that a blue Volkswagen was available. Henry scrawled his name at the bottom of the form, and the
girl took a set of keys from a board behind her. I managed to
glimpse the registration number on the tag. I recognized it. We
were to have the identical car in which Chantal Villeneuve had
driven up to Montarraz to murder Robert Drivaz.

Before we actually took possession of the car, Henry announced
abruptly that he had a telephone call to make. He suggested pointedly that I might like to avail myself of the facilities of the ladies'
cloakroom. I know Henry well enough to take a hint, so I made
myself scarce. When I got back to the car-hire desk, some ten minutes later, Henry was waiting for me. He did not volunteer any information about his telephone call, so I was careful not to ask him.

Of course, there was nothing in the least sinister about the little
car. If it had ever contained clues in the form of bloodstains or carelessly dropped handkerchiefs, all had been thoroughly cleaned and
cleared away months ago. Numerous other drivers had occupied the

driving seat since that April afternoon. Even more than a hotel room, a hired car is utterly anonymous, until its temporary proprietor has had time to impose his own characteristic clutter of maps and baggage on it. All the same, it was an eerie feeling, as Henry took the wheel and headed the car for the Lausanne autoroute—the same road that Chantal must have taken five months ago.

I said, "In a funny way, I'm not surprised. I mean, I find it quite easy to imagine Chantal as a killer. What does baffle me is—why? What was Robert to her, or she to Robert?"

"I daresay we shall find out," said Henry.

"She must have left Sylvie's car at Orly Airport and taken a plane down here," I said. "I suppose she thought she might not have time to drive the whole way."

"If she had any sense," said Henry, "she would never have contemplated driving down."

"But if she'd driven," I pointed out, "we'd never have found out. I mean, there's no trace at the Customs posts when one comes and goes by car. She wouldn't have had to show her driving license and fill in that form."

"Agreed," said Henry, "but just think for a moment. Sylvie's car is very distinctive, and it's well known in Montarraz. More than likely, somebody would have spotted it, with its red upholstery and French number plates and all. As it was, she arrived in Montarraz in a completely inconspicuous vehicle. I daresay there are a hundred blue Volkswagens in and around the village. No—the Alfa would have been too big a risk."

"I suppose so," I said. And then, "But Henry—*why?* I suppose it really was Chantal?"

"My dear Emmy," Henry said, "she had to produce her passport and her driving license—and French driving licenses have photographs on them. As to why—nobody knows what Robert Drivaz got up to when he was in Paris. We know nothing about Chantal, come to that, except that she's an orphan, Sylvie's goddaughter, and a very tough little character indeed."

"So what do we do now?"

For several moments Henry concentrated on the white ribbon of road ahead, frowning. Then he said, "I really don't know. It all depends what we find in Montarraz."

The church clock was chiming eleven as we drove through the village. We went first to Panoralpes. Everything was quiet and serene in the sunshine. Jane's little chalet and studio were apparently deserted. There were no cars in the driveway outside the block of flats. In the marble foyer, Lucia, the *concierge,* was on her hands and knees, scrubbing energetically. She scrambled to her feet as we came in.

"Oh! *Signore* . . . Mme. Weston did not say . . . I did not know . . ." She was obviously dismayed to see us.

Henry said reassuringly, "Don't worry, Lucia. We weren't expected back."

"But . . . there is nobody here. Mme. Weston is out, and Mme. Claudet's apartment is all shut up."

"But you have a key, haven't you?" said Henry. "You go in to do the cleaning."

Lucia blushed scarlet. "*Si, signore* . . . but I have instructions from M. Claudet . . . *nobody* is to be allowed into the apartment without his express permission. . . ."

"These are new instructions, are they?" Henry asked.

"*Si, signore* . . . M. Claudet was here yesterday evening, and he told me himself . . . of course, he did not know that you would be coming back, but his instructions were most definite, and I don't like to—"

"Of course, Lucia. We quite understand. M. Claudet has left again, then?"

"Oh, he did not stay long, *signore.* He just came and knocked on my door—it must have been about eleven o'clock in the evening— and gave me these orders. Of course, I thought that he would want the apartment made ready and the beds prepared, but he said no, he was not staying. He and madame drove away again in the white motor car. I do not know where they went, *signore.*"

"And Mme. Weston?"

"Oh, she will be coming back quite soon. She has gone to the *carrière* outside Charonne, to select a piece of marble. For Mlle. Arnay's statue, so she told me."

"You also have a key to her chalet?"

"Si, signore."

"And no new instructions?"

Lucia smiled. "No, *signore*. Mme. Weston always tells me to admit any visitors who come if she is not there. Do you want to go into Les Sapins, *signore?*"

"No, no, I just want to leave a note for Mme. Weston. If I write it now, will you leave it on the kitchen table in Les Sapins, where she can't miss it?"

"Of course, *signore*."

Henry tore a page out of his notebook and scribbled rapidly on it, holding the paper against the pink marble wall. When he had finished, he handed it to me to read.

Dear Jane,

We are back, after an instructive visit to Paris. We are now going to the Chalet Perce-neige, where I think we will find all the characters in this drama. You must do whatever you think is best, but if you do not hear from Emmy or myself by three o'clock this afternoon, I most earnestly ask you to go to the police and tell them all you know. Believe me, this will be for everybody's good. Think of Anne-Marie, dear Jane, and I know that you will come to the only possible decision.

Henry

P.S. It is kind of you to be so hospitable to unexpected visitors. We do appreciate it.

I read the note, and then said to Henry, "You think Jane knows the truth?"

"I'm reasonably sure she does."

"Has she known all along?"

"Darling," said Henry, "I'm not a mind reader. I don't know, and it doesn't matter." He folded the paper, wrote Jane's name on the outside, and handed it to Lucia.

"I will put it in the kitchen at once, *signore*," said Lucia. "Will you be coming back this evening, *signore?*"

"I wish," said Henry, "that I knew, Lucia."

As we drove up the hill toward the Chalet Perce-neige, Henry said, "I wish I didn't have to involve you in this, darling."

"Don't be silly," I said. "I'm involved, and that's all there is to it. Nothing to do with you. These people are my friends."

"That's not what I mean." Henry sounded unusually serious. "This is going to be the showdown, and it may be dangerous. What I'd really like to do would be to park you safely in the Hotel Mirabelle for lunch, and come back to collect you when it's all over."

"Just you try," I said.

Henry did not seem to hear me. "The trouble is," he said, "that I need you there. I need you as a cover, I need you as a witness, and I may even need you as an escape route."

Suddenly I felt cold.

"They could quite easily dispose of me," Henry went on, as though talking to himself, "but two of us makes it more difficult. With two, we have a hope against them."

"What do you mean—them?" I said. "Surely it's only Chantal—"

Henry said, "The trouble is, we haven't a shred of real evidence."

"What do you mean? The umbrella—the hired car—"

"Look," said Henry, "the fact that I've shown it *might* not have been Anne-Marie whom Jane saw doesn't prove that it wasn't her. She was just as capable as anybody else of hiding her face under an umbrella. As for the hired car, Chantal can simply deny it. I daresay there's more than one Chantal Villeneuve in Paris, and it's a very long shot that the receptionist would recognize her again—she probably took care to wear her hair differently and put on dark glasses. And even if the girl thought she remembered her—just try proving it in a court of law."

"She had to sign the hire form," I said.

"Yes—with some sort of scrawl which she could disclaim afterward. Didn't you notice, when we hired the car—the girl compared the signature on my driving license most carefully with the one on my passport, to make sure that it was really me. But she didn't even glance at the one on the form. In fact, I deliberately made it quite different. In any case, even if we could prove beyond all doubt that Chantal hired that car, where would that get us? Chantal never lied to the police, for the good reason that they never asked her any questions. She might have had all sorts of reasons for slipping down to Geneva and keeping quiet about it. Don't you see—if we could have produced this evidence *before* Anne-Marie's trial, it might just have weakened the prosecution's case; but now, as far as the police are concerned, the matter is closed. Anne-Marie has been tried, found guilty, and sentenced. Quite apart from anything else, no policeman likes to have to admit in public that he was wrong. I know, believe me. I'm one myself. No—it takes really stunning proof to get a case reopened and retried."

"Then what on earth are we going to do?" I asked.

"We are going to try," said Henry, "a colossal bluff." Suddenly he sounded more cheerful. "Now, listen carefully. When we get there, this is what I want you to do. . . ."

A few minutes later we were nosing the little blue car up the lane which led to the iron gate in the forbidding fence enclosing the Chalet Perce-neige. Henry parked the car some way from the house, having turned it to face downhill toward the village. He switched off the engine and put the ignition key into the unlocked glove compartment. Then we both got out, leaving the car doors unlocked, and walked toward the gate. We could see through its stout iron railings that three cars were parked outside the chalet's front door. The Claudets' white Alfa, Giselle's stunning yellow Monteverdi, and an inconspicuous beige Mini.

Henry took my hand and gave it a quick squeeze. "It seems," he said, "as if we have a full house. So much the better. Come on."

I had half-expected the iron gate to be locked, but it was not. A solid-looking padlock hung from it, but the gate swung easily and noiselessly open as Henry pushed it. The next moment we were standing under the porch, and the chime of cowbells rang out as Henry pressed the bell push.

Everything was quiet. Had it not been for the cars, one would have imagined that the house was deserted, and I realized again how isolated it was, how bleak and forbidding when viewed from the road. For a moment nothing happened. Then the small door behind the eye-level iron grille was opened from the inside, and we found ourselves looking into the surprised face of Mario.

Before he could react, however, he was pushed aside, the front door flew open, and there stood Giselle, as tiny and lovely as ever. Surprisingly, she was formally dressed, in trousers and a long tunic made of some soft, silvery silk material. Her face broke into that enchanting, world-renowned smile.

"Henri! Emmie! We thought you had deserted us! Oh, this is good to see you! Come in!"

Come into my parlor. Well, there was no turning back by then. We stepped into the pine-scented hallway. As we did so, Mario slipped past us and out to the front gate. I just had time to hear the padlock clicking firmly shut before the front door closed behind us.

14 ♛

The spider's web was as attractive as ever, but the sinister image lingered in my mind as we followed Giselle out onto the sunny lawn, where the two arms of the house encircled the brilliant focal point which was the swimming pool. Around the pool the people whom Henry had described as the characters in the drama were grouped in apparently carefree ease; but Henry's simile had been apt. Not only did the whole scene look theatrical and contrived, but the very atmosphere was like that on a stage, in those first few moments of the play before the suspension of the audience's disbelief.

"See, everybody! Henri and Emmie have come back to us!" Giselle stepped aside, with an upstage gesture. We made our entrance.

Pierre and Sylvie Claudet were sitting side by side on the blue canvas swing seat. Each of them held a tall, flute-shaped glass full of pale golden liquid, and a champagne bottle stood in an ice bucket at Pierre's feet. Sylvie was wearing yet another of her beautiful Pucci trouser suits, but Pierre Claudet looked incongruous in very formal dark gray. Both of them were tense and nervous.

Michel Veron was sitting astride a rustic bench, which had been artfully contrived out of a vertical slice of tree, bark and all. His guitar was slung around his neck, and he was strumming it idly but expertly, providing just the background music that a good *metteur en scène* would have arranged. He looked angry rather than worried.

I turned my head quickly to look at Giselle, who had stepped back to usher us out onto the green lawn. She looked as insubstantial as a ghost, framed in the dark doorway; she also looked apprehensive. At that moment, Mario appeared behind her, and put a hand on her shoulder. His face was completely expressionless.

The only person who appeared utterly relaxed was Chantal. She was wearing a tiny white bikini, and her slender body was deeply tanned, so that her fair hair looked almost white against the bronze of her forehead. She was lying on her back on the grass beside the pool. Her eyes were closed, and her arms flung wide on each side of her. She looked as innocent and as vulnerable as a child asleep, and her only reaction when Giselle announced our arrival was to stir slightly, and put one brown arm across her eyes, as if to protect them from too bright a light.

Pierre Claudet, predictably, was the first person to overcome the instant of shock and displeasure which our arrival had obviously caused. He stood up, held out his hand, and said, "Superintendent Tibbett! What an unexpected pleasure. You have concluded your investigations in Paris, then?"

Shaking the outstretched hand, Henry smiled and said, "Not exactly. I'd say, rather, that my inquiries had led me back to Montarraz."

"What do you mean, your inquiries?" Sylvie sounded nervous.

Claudet said, "The superintendent came to see me in Paris yesterday, my dear. He is on the track of an international blackmailer, if I understood him aright. I am afraid I was not able to help him. At any rate," he added, smiling at Henry, "I presume that your visit here is purely social. May I offer you some of Giselle's excellent champagne?"

I glanced at Henry. He, too, was smiling. "Thank you. We'd love some." Mario came forward, expert and unobtrusive, and poured us a glass each. You would never have taken him for more than a well-trained servant.

Henry took his glass and sat down on the grass beside the pool. Taking my cue from him, I did the same. He raised his glass and said, "Your good health, Chantal."

"Oh, shut up," said Chantal, without opening her eyes. She rolled over onto her face.

Giselle said, "And now you chase this international blackmailer in Montarraz? That is exciting."

Henry ignored her. He said to Sylvie, "We met a friend of yours in Paris, Sylvie. Gaby Labelle. She was telling us about the old days, when you were still working, and before she was famous. It's funny how people's lives change, isn't it?"

Sylvie said shortly, "I haven't seen Gaby in years. As a matter of fact, I never knew her very well."

"I'd no idea you knew her at all." Pierre Claudet was looking at his wife in surprise. "I'm a great admirer of hers. You must invite her to dinner when we get back to Paris. I must say, you've kept very quiet about knowing her."

"Perhaps because I was afraid you might admire her even more at close quarters, chéri." Sylvie was smiling and teasing. She leaned over and kissed Pierre's cheek.

Michel Veron strummed a chord on his guitar, and said, "Is Labelle still around? I'd have thought she was past it by now."

"Thank you very much, Michel!" Sylvie was mock-indignant. "She's not so very much older than I am."

"She's very much still around," said Henry. "She's currently packing in the customers at Le Fromage Sauvage. Twice-nightly cabaret."

Michel Veron stopped playing, laying his fingers on the guitar strings to kill the reverberating sound. He looked hard at Henry. "You went to Le Fromage Sauvage?"

"We did."

"Any particular reason?"

"Yes."

"What reason?"

"I was interested," Henry said, "to hear about your appearance there. M. Renoir was most helpful."

Michel Veron exchanged a quick glance with Mario, who moved quietly to a position just behind Henry, where he lit a cigarette and lounged against the wall of the house.

Sylvie said, "You had a busy time in Paris, Henry. What else did you do?"

"Not very much." Henry seemed quite unaware of Mario's presence. "I had a long talk with an old friend of mine who's a journalist—that was most interesting. And of course, M. Claudet was kind enough to spare me some time, as he has told you."

"What did you really go to see Pierre about?" Sylvie asked, a little too elaborately casual. "I really don't believe in your international blackmailer."

Before Henry could reply, Claudet said hastily, "Oh, just an old scandal, my dear. Something about a fraudulent hat shop which was closed by the police. Nothing you would ever have heard about."

There was an electric silence. It was broken by Chantal, who, without opening her eyes, said, "Oh, you are silly."

"Who is silly?" Sylvie's voice was edged with anxiety.

"All of you. Henry wasn't doing any of the things he says he was. He was digging the dirt about the Drivaz case." And she settled herself more comfortably on the grass.

Claudet said grimly, "A strange thing happened after you had been to see me yesterday, Superintendent."

"Really?"

"Yes. A foreign woman telephoned my apartment, using my private number. She said she was a journalist from England, writing an article on the Drivaz case. She was trying to get hold of Sylvie's maid—the girl who was alleged to have made that nonexistent telephone call to the Drivaz girl."

"That's right," I said. "That was me."

They all looked at me then, and Claudet said, "If that is true, Mrs. Tibbett, I must say that it hardly reflects to your credit."

Giselle let out a ripple of laughter. "Oh, Pierre, don't be so pompous. You're not in the Chamber of Deputies now." To Henry she said, "So Chantal's right, is she? You're after a murderer, not a blackmailer."

"You might say—both," said Henry.

"And have you caught him?"

"No."

"But you know who it is?" Giselle's question hung in the air, emitting sparks.

Henry said easily, "Oh, yes. I know." He put down his glass, and glanced at his watch. "Well, it's been fun seeing you all, but I'm afraid we must go. Jane is expecting us for lunch, and I promised we wouldn't be late."

"No. You are not going." It was Veron who spoke. He stood up and laid down his guitar on the bench.

"I'm afraid we must."

"I mean—" Michel Veron looked embarrassed. "I mean, you can't just walk off and leave us on tenterhooks. You must tell us who the murderer is."

All eyes were on Henry now, and the tension was almost tangible. Mario took a step forward, so that he was standing immediately behind Henry, full of menace. Nobody even noticed when I murmured, "Excuse me," and slipped away into the house.

The telephone was in the hall. I picked it up and dialed Jane's number. As I listened to the ringing tone, I imagined the bell shrilling in the tiny sitting room at Les Sapins, and Jane coming out of the kitchen to answer it. Or perhaps she was in the studio—where she had had an extension bell fitted. It shouldn't take her more than a minute to get back to the chalet. But the telephone rang on unanswered, and suddenly I saw Mario coming in from the garden.

Ignoring the ringing tone, I said into the receiver, "Yes, at Perceneige . . . oh, about five minutes . . . no, don't bother, we have a car . . . unless we don't turn up, of course . . . yes, I'll tell Henry. See you soon. Good-bye, Jane." I rang off, and turned to face Mario.

He was smiling slightly, and gave me a curious little bow, as if of acknowledgment and admiration. I stuck my chin in the air and walked past him and out into the garden, looking—I hope—braver than I felt.

Henry was on his feet now, ringed by the others. He smiled at me and said, "Ah, there you are, darling. Did you ring Jane?"

"Yes," I lied. "I told her we were here, and to expect us in five minutes."

"Good," said Henry. He surveyed the circle of tense faces. "Jane is going to Charonne this afternoon, so Emmy and I will have Les Sapins to ourselves. Personally, I'm hoping to get some rest—I never can sleep on trains."

Mario had come out of the house again, and I saw him nod, barely perceptibly, to Michel Veron. I fervently hoped that this meant that the iron gate was now unlocked again.

Henry added, "Meanwhile, I'm sorry I can't satisfy your natural curiosity—but I'm sure you'll realize that it would be quite unethical. You'll all know soon, I promise you."

He took my arm, and we walked together into the house. I felt like a traveler in a jungle, who knows that he is being stalked by a man-eating tiger, and that to show fear would be fatal. The circle of eyes seemed to burn holes in my back. But nothing happened. The gate was open, and we made our way to the little blue car. However, it was not until we were in it, and halfway down the hill to Les Sapins, before either of us spoke. Then Henry let out a big sigh of relief and said, "Well done, darling. You were splendid. What did Jane say?"

"Nothing."

"What do you mean?"

"She wasn't there. There was no reply. Then Mario came out, and I had to pretend to talk to her."

"In that case," said Henry, "even better done. I confess, I had some nasty moments."

"But, Henry," I said, "you surely can't mean that all those people—our friends—are in some sort of conspiracy against us?"

"For a start," said Henry, "I wouldn't describe them as our friends. To go on with, they are all famous people—which makes them both powerful and vulnerable, and that's a dangerous combination. If a particularly sordid murder could be proved against one of them, the others would be implicated in some measure. And if I'm not mistaken, all of them have plenty to hide. It only takes one crack in the façade, the press gets its chisel in—and the whole lot crumbles. And behind it—who knows? Drugs, irregular sex of one sort and another, tax evasion, bribery—all sorts of nasty things that people in the public eye prefer to keep locked in the woodshed.

They made a great mistake, that little lot, when they let people like us get a foot into the door of their tight little world—and now they know it. They're closing their ranks against us."

I shivered. "It's terribly hard to believe."

"That's why there had to be two of us," Henry went on. "If I had been alone, and if they thought I was the only person with evidence to clear Anne-Marie—well, I think they might have preferred the risk of an unfortunate accident happening to me on their premises to a big scandal blowing up in their faces."

I found myself glancing nervously over my shoulder, half-expecting to see the Monteverdi, with Mario at the wheel, chasing us, crowding us, edging us off the narrow mountain road and over the precipice. I said, "What will they do now?"

"That remains to be seen," said Henry. "My hope is that they will try persuasion before they resort to violence. I think we can expect some visitors this afternoon."

Jane was in the studio when we arrived at Les Sapins, having just returned from Charonne with her block of marble. She had chosen a dark color—almost black, but with threads of red running through it, like trickles of blood. The clay figurine from which she would work was standing on a board in the studio—life size, pale gray, and still, a severed head of Giselle. I tried to imagine the smooth lines and contours of it translated into dark, shiny marble—and decided that the result would be beautiful, but sinister, too. I wondered what Giselle herself would think of it.

Jane greeted us with a big smile of relief. "Oh, I am glad to see you both. And I love unexpected visitors. . . ."

Henry said, "You're always so hospitable, Jane." For a moment I thought I caught a strange look passing between them, but I may have been mistaken.

Then Jane said, "Let's go over to the house and have a drink."

Sipping Fendant in the tiny living room, Henry said, "You understood my note, didn't you, Jane?"

"Well, it had me a bit worried—about the police and—"

"Jane," said Henry quietly, "please. You know very well what I meant. You would have told the police?"

"I . . . I don't know."

"Of course you would. And what's more, you must promise me that if anything should happen to me in the next few days, you'll go down to Charonne and tell them."

"But, Henry, what could happen to you?"

"I could have a motor smash," said Henry. "I could be on a plane that crashed. I could climb a mountain without proper equipment and fall over a precipice. You'd be surprised at the things that could happen to me."

He and Jane looked at each other for a long moment, and again I had the feeling that they shared a secret. Then Jane said, "All right. I promise."

"Good." Henry was cheerful again. "Well, what's for lunch?"

"Lunch?"

"Didn't I mention that we were inviting ourselves?"

"But—" Jane looked nonplussed. "I had a snack in the Source on the way up. There's nothing to eat in the house!"

In the end, a search of the kitchen produced some bread, butter, and cheese, and a tin of sardines, from which we made ourselves a frugal meal. I was glad that we had had a good breakfast in Geneva. We were just finishing the last crumbs, and Henry was saying, "Now, Jane . . . about this afternoon . . ." when the telephone rang.

Jane looked inquiringly at Henry, who motioned her to answer it. She went into the hall.

"Hello . . . yes, this is Mme. Weston speaking . . . who? Oh, yes, Sister . . . yes, of course . . . at once . . . about twenty minutes, I should think . . . give her my love . . . tell her not to worry . . . yes, as quickly as I can. . . ." She rang off and came back into the kitchen.

I said, "Anne-Marie?"

"Yes. It was the Sister from the convent. The baby is on its way, and the doctor says Anne-Marie should go into the hospital at once. I'm going down to collect her and take her in my car."

"But—"

"I arranged it a couple of days ago." Jane was struggling into her coat. "After you'd seen Anne-Marie. I couldn't bear the thought of her going into the hospital alone. The Sister agreed."

"And Anne-Marie? I thought . . ."

"Oh, I know she wouldn't see me before, but your visit evidently made a big impression on her, Emmy. She actually sent a message thanking me and saying she'd be pleased. Must go now. Good luck." And Jane had gone, like an excited whirlwind. All her nervousness seemed to have dropped away from her. Clearly, as far as Jane was concerned, the dead could bury their own dead. Her preoccupation was with the new life which was on its way. Henry and I washed up our plates and glasses, and sat down to wait.

Our first visitor arrived soon after three o'clock. Looking from the sitting-room window down into the forecourt of Panoralpes, I saw the small beige Mini being neatly parked between two painted white lines, even though the car park was empty. Then the door opened, and the lank figure of Michel Veron climbed out. He was wearing the huge dark glasses which had appeared in his wedding photographs, and between them and the long hair falling over his eyes, it was impossible to judge the expression on his face as he climbed up the path to the chalet.

I opened the door in response to his knock. He paid no more attention to me than if I had been a hired maid, but walked straight in through the open door of the living room, with that famous slouch which sets the fans yelling before he even opens his mouth or touches his guitar. I followed him into the room. Before Henry had time to speak, Veron said, "Good afternoon, Superintendent. I imagine you are expecting visitors."

"It did cross my mind," said Henry.

Michel Veron sat down at the table. "I've come to see you," he said, "because I'm the one person you can't possibly accuse of this murder."

"Really?"

"Really. For a start, if you visited Le Fromage Sauvage and spoke to Renoir, you'll know without any doubt that I was in Paris for the whole of that day."

"For extra rehearsal," said Henry. "Was that really necessary?"

"Of course. I put a new number into the act."

"Very well. You have an alibi. Go on."

"Secondly, as even my wife has remarked, I am far too tall to have impersonated Anne-Marie."

"Don't you agree," said Henry, "that if a man employs an agent to kill another man, he is just as guilty as the actual killer?"

"Of course. And I know what you are driving at. But you are wrong. You see, I had no motive for killing Robert Drivaz."

Henry's eyebrows went up. "No motive? My dear Mr. Veron, Drivaz and your wife—"

Michel Veron made an impatient movement. "I'm afraid you have not grasped the situation, Superintendent. My marriage to Giselle is, you might say, one of convenience to both of us. I don't think I need to say more. This is strictly off the record, of course."

"I could have a hidden tape recorder," Henry said. I saw he could not repress a slight smile.

Veron smiled back. "I think not. You would never be so . . . ungentlemanly. No, as a matter of fact, I liked Drivaz. He kept Giselle amused, and he was a pleasant character."

"Until your wife dropped him, and snubbed him in Paris. He could then have turned into a blackmailer," Henry pointed out.

"A ski instructor?" Veron seemed to find this very funny. "Oh, he might try to sell a story to the gutter press, but nobody would take it seriously, and there's no such thing as bad publicity."

"All right," said Henry. "You've made out your case for not killing Drivaz, or causing him to be killed. Why are you here?"

"Because," said Veron, "it would be more agreeable for me and for other people if the case against Anne-Marie was not upset. After all, she got off very lightly. When the three years are up, she will be well provided for. Giselle and I are prepared to set up a substantial fund for her and for the baby. She will be financially secure, and that is all that matters for people of that sort. Then, I realize that your investigations must have left you considerably out of pocket." I thought he might have had the grace to sound a little embarrassed, but he did not. Presumably, he classed Henry with Anne-Marie as the sort of person to whom financial considerations are paramount.

Henry said nothing. Veron put his hand into his pocket and brought out two small pieces of paper, which he laid on the table. "This," he said, "is a check for twenty thousand Swiss francs, made out in your favor. This is a receipt for the money, stating that you have accepted it as payment for expenses incurred in investigating the Drivaz case. It also mentions that you are now satisfied that the verdict of the court was correct. If you will just sign it, we can forget the whole thing, can't we? I am sure it will be a great relief to everybody."

"Except Anne-Marie," said Henry. He spoke quietly, but I have seldom heard him sound so angry.

"My dear Tibbett, I have already explained that she will be looked after." He stood up, smiling contemptuously. "I'll leave the check and the receipt. I quite understand that you will need to . . . persuade yourself. To grab at the money might damage your self-respect. Just let me know when you've made up your mind." He looked at both of us as if we were less than dirt and stalked out of the room, leaving the two slips of paper, the pink and the white, lying on the dark table.

As soon as the front door had slammed behind him, I burst out, "Of all the rotten . . . !"

Henry smiled gently and said, "Don't waste your breath, darling. It's all according to plan."

"What do you mean?"

"Give them plenty of time. Let Veron go back and report. Then we'll make the next move."

"You talk as if it was a game of chess," I said.

"In a way, it is," said Henry.

Nearly an hour had passed, with unbearable slowness, before Henry walked out into the hall to the telephone and dialed the number of the Chalet Perce-neige.

"Chalet Perce-neige? May I speak to Mme. Claudet, please? . . . Tibbett . . . yes, I said Mme. Claudet . . . that's right . . .

Mme. Sylvie Claudet." There was a pause. Henry grinned at me over the receiver. Then he said, "Sylvie? Henry here. Would you be kind enough to tell Michel Veron that I do not accept his check? . . . Oh, I think you do understand . . . yes. . . . No, I would rather you told him . . . yes, I know exactly what I'm doing. I'm going to the police. I think they will be interested in the check and the receipt, as well as other information I have for them . . . yes, I agree it was foolish of him, but . . . what? . . . Well, if you hurry . . . there's not much time . . . very well, ten minutes. . . ."

He rang off and turned to me. "You'd better make some coffee. The next contingent is about to arrive."

"What did she say?"

"Oh, she started off by pretending she didn't know about the check, and then changed her tune and said she had tried to stop him being so foolish. I imagine there's a certain amount of consternation at the Chalet Perce-neige just now. And some recriminations, if they have breath left for them."

"Henry," I said, "we're alone here. Jane is in Charonne. Suppose they decide that the answer is violence?"

"They are almost certainly discussing that possibility at the moment," said Henry calmly. "However, it would be messy, risky, and a last resort. Let us see what we shall see."

15 ♛

Pierre and Sylvie Claudet arrived together in the white Alfa. Claudet looked thunderous, and Sylvie haggard with worry. There was no beating about the bush. They sat down at the table, and Claudet said at once, "Tibbett, my wife is extremely distressed at this business of Anne-Marie, as you can see for yourself. Is it really necessary for you to continue with it?"

"I think so," said Henry.

"I have already made financial arrangements for the girl." Claudet became businesslike, the man of affairs. He opened a slim black briefcase and drew out a document. "You might like to look at this. After speaking to Sylvie on the telephone, I had my lawyer draw it up in Paris yesterday evening, before I flew down here. My lawyer holds a copy. It is a binding document, not an empty promise."

Henry took the paper and studied it gravely. Then he looked up and said, "This is a most generous settlement, M. Claudet. I am delighted to know that Anne-Marie will want for nothing. May I ask why you suddenly decided to take this step?"

There was a small hesitation. Then Claudet said, "I cannot take the credit. It was Sylvie's idea. I told you I had spoken to her on the telephone. She has been thinking a lot about the Drivaz girl."

"I know she has," said Henry.

"We are all sorry for her. I had been intending to make some such gesture, but I had not got around to it. Sylvie prompted my conscience—and now it is done. In two and a half years' time, when Anne-Marie leaves the convent—"

"I think she will be leaving sooner," said Henry.

"Alas, she cannot. The court ordered—"

"M. Claudet," said Henry, "I think I have made it clear that I intend to get that verdict set aside, by proving the identity of the actual killer. So your generous gift will be put to good use almost at once."

There was a heavy pause. Then Claudet said, "Now, Tibbett, naturally I am interested in seeing justice done, but this all seems rather unnecessary. The girl is well provided for. I happen to know that the Verons are also prepared to help her. When she is free again, she can start up a new life—maybe open a little business. . . ."

"Like a hat shop?" Henry's words cut the conversation like a knife. There was a moment of utter silence. Then Sylvie began to cry.

"You know, don't you?" she sobbed. "You know about Chantal. . . ."

Quickly Claudet said, "My wife, Tibbett, has a notion that her goddaughter is somehow mixed up in this affair, and that it is Chantal whom you propose to accuse. Sylvie would do anything in the world to protect her—and so, for Sylvie's sake, would I. Sylvie has admitted to me that it was for Chantal's sake that she persuaded Michel Veron to visit you with a . . . a proposition, which you refused. Now we are here ourselves. Can't you at least tell us whether or not it is Chantal whom you suspect?"

Henry said, "It sounds to me as though it is Sylvie who suspects Chantal. I must confess that the possibility crossed my mind—but with the total lack of motive . . ."

"You're bluffing," Sylvie sobbed, near-hysterically. "You're trying to trap us! You know very well about Chantal and Frivolités and that blackmailing brute Drivaz . . . you said yourself she could have driven to Montarraz that day in the Alfa. . . ."

Claudet said, "Frivolités? What are you talking about, Sylvie?"

"Oh, darling . . . I didn't ever tell you . . . I didn't want to upset you . . . Chantal was one of the . . . one of the girls. I . . . I got her out of that terrible place before it closed down, and I've tried to make it up to her . . . tried to help her to forget . . . and then Drivaz found out and began to persecute her. . . ." Sylvie's voice was rising dangerously.

Claudet, looking thoroughly shocked, put his arm around his wife's shoulders. Henry said evenly, "So you think that Chantal Villeneuve drove down here in your car on April 14 and killed Robert Drivaz, because he was blackmailing her? Is that correct, Mme. Claudet?"

Sylvie was crying quietly by then. "What else can I think? But Henry, I beg you . . ."

Henry said, "She did not drive your car down here, Mme. Claudet."

Sylvie's head came up, in surprise. "She didn't? Then how—"

"She left your car at Orly Airport," Henry said, "flew to Geneva, and hired a car there. Yours is so well known that it might have been recognized."

"You know this?" Sylvie's voice was a whisper.

"I know it," said Henry, "but I can't prove it." Then, surprisingly, he turned to Pierre Claudet. "M. Claudet, do you happen to have your driving license with you?"

"My driving license?" Claudet looked astonished.

Henry said, "Yes—I'd very much like to take a look at it. I don't think I've ever seen a French license, and it would be interesting, for reasons of comparison—"

"You are a policeman, my friend," said Claudet, with a heavy attempt at humor, "and the policeman's first instinct is to ask for name, address, and driving license, as we all know." He reached into his breast pocket, pulled out an alligator-skin wallet, and extracted the license, which he handed to Henry.

Henry studied it for a moment, and then said, "This photograph —forgive me, M. Claudet—but this photograph must have been taken some years ago."

"Of course it was—when I was in my twenties. In France, a driving license never has to be renewed, so long as it remains clean."

"But a passport does?" Henry queried.

"Naturally. Every ten years."

"So that a man may appear to be twenty-five on his driving license and fifty on his passport?"

"Quite possibly. What of it?" Claudet sounded irritated by this irrelevance. "The driving-license photograph is a mere formality. Any checking can be done by comparing the signatures. There must be many Frenchmen who no longer resemble the photographs on their licenses. Just what are you getting at, Tibbett?"

"Nothing, nothing. Thank you very much." Henry handed the license back to Claudet, who replaced it in his wallet with a flourish.

"Well, now," Henry said, "I think the time has come for plain speaking. I know this must be very distressing for you, Mme. Claudet, but believe me, it will be best for everybody if you tell me all you know. For a start, I will be frank with you. I have proof that Chantal did fly to Geneva on the day of Robert Drivaz's death, and that she hired a car from the airport. The car was returned the same evening, with the exact mileage to and from Montarraz on the clock. Now, I think you can fill in the details for me."

Sylvie had started to cry again, but she pulled herself together, blew her nose, and said, "I suppose I always knew it, really. I have been so terribly worried . . . it's a relief to be able to talk about it. . . ."

"I'm sure it is," said Henry sympathetically.

Suddenly, in a rush, Sylvie said, "Chantal isn't really my goddaughter at all. She was . . . oh, I don't know where to begin. I've always been interested in social work, you see—long before I met Pierre. I worked for an organization which helped young girls and children in Paris. We heard rumors about this shop—Frivolités— but we had no proof to take to the police. I even took a job there to try to find out more about it. All the children—they were only children, you see, boys and girls—they were all kept most carefully secluded, nobody could get near them. But in the end . . . oh, it's a long story, and I won't bore you with it, but in the end I got Chantal out. It was horrible . . . she had been literally forced into prostitution at the age of twelve. You may think she's a strange girl. I can assure you, Henry, the wonder is that she is not very much stranger. Can you imagine the effect of such experiences on a child of that age? I . . . I more or less adopted Chantal. I told everybody that she was my orphaned goddaughter."

"So you rescued Chantal," said Henry, "but there were still the others, weren't there?"

"Of course. I couldn't simply go to the police—I realized by then that the place was being protected by highly placed influence. The only hope was to play those monsters at their own game. So I managed to get Pierre Claudet interested in the matter."

"You—what?" Claudet's astonishment was ludicrous. "You didn't even know me then! You had nothing to do with Frivolités!"

Even in her distress, Sylvie managed a glimmer of coquetry. "Chéri, I work in my own ways."

"But—"

"You were told about Frivolités by your secretary, Jacques Lamaire, no?"

"That's right. And—"

"And a little later on, Jacques introduced you to me, didn't he?"

"You know very well that he did. But you never—"

"I did not want you to think I had anything to do with the horrible place," said Sylvie. "I made Jacques promise not to tell you where his information came from. All the same, I did so want to meet you—especially when you were so brave and so determined to clear all that filth away."

"Well, I'll be damned," said Pierre Claudet. And then to Henry, with unmistakable pride, "And I thought I knew my wife after six years of marriage! What a woman!"

Sylvie gave him a little smile, and went on, "Well, there you are. Pierre's first wife had recently been killed in an accident, and Pierre and I got married. Chantal was better, psychologically, and I settled her in a little flat of her own. Everything seemed to be all right, and Frivolités was mercifully fading into oblivion. And then—it happened. Here in Montarraz."

"What happened?"

Bitterly, Sylvie said, "That creature happened."

"Robert Drivaz?"

"No, of course not. Not Robert. Mario Agnelli."

"Mario?" Henry sounded surprised. "What on earth had Mario to do with it?"

"Just this." Sylvie's mouth was set into a hard line. "I didn't know it, of course, but Mario had been one of the boys at Frivolités. When the place was closed down, he was sent to an orphanage—nobody could trace any family for him, you see. But he had been ruined—he was vicious and perverted and bitterly malicious, too. He ran away from the orphanage. Heaven knows how he got himself picked up by Giselle and Michel, although I can guess. Of course, I had no idea who he was—I didn't know all the children by sight. But he and Chantal recognized each other at once. And, naturally, he took a delight in telling Michel and Giselle the whole story. He knew I had had a hand in the closing down of Frivolités, and he hated me for it."

"And so he blackmailed Chantal?" Henry asked.

Sylvie shook her head. "No, not Mario. He had no need. He's doing all right for himself with the Verons. There's nothing Chantal could give him that he hasn't got. He just amused himself. He knew I was frightened of him, and of what he might do or say. Oh —not for myself. But the two people I care about are Pierre and Chantal, and he was in a position to do terrible harm to both of them."

"But where," Henry asked, "did Robert Drivaz come in?"

"Giselle took up with Robert, as you know, and he started to hang around the Chalet Perce-neige. I don't know who told him about Chantal's past. It could have been Mario himself, it could have been Giselle, when she was—in one of her moods. Anyhow, somebody told him. You know what happened next. The Verons went back to Paris, and one day Robert turned up, drunk and offensive, demanding money. Naturally, they simply laughed at him and threw him out. Well—you can imagine the rest. There he was in Paris, humiliated, penniless, determined not to creep back to his wife with his tail between his legs. Where could he get more money in Paris? Why, from Chantal, of course. By blackmailing her. He didn't know that she had none to give him, poor child. To Drivaz, we were all millionaires."

"You know he did this?" Henry asked quietly.

Sylvie nodded. "She told me. She made a joke of it. She said she laughed at him and sent him away. But . . . I wondered and I worried. I couldn't help it. Then came this conference of the Women's Guilds. Chantal begged to be allowed to borrow the car that day. I knew she loved driving the Alfa, and I hoped it might cheer her up. I said she could have it. Later on, I regretted it. I had a dreadful sort of premonition . . . I don't know how I sat through that morning of dull speeches. At lunchtime, I made an excuse and slipped away. I looked everywhere for Chantal. I searched Paris for her. I rang friends . . . nobody had seen her. Nobody knew where she was. I was in desperation—I just knew that something terrible was happening. I nearly cried with relief when Chantal arrived at my apartment that evening, about half-past ten. She looked tired, but—I don't know—excited. She told me some story about nearly having hit a lorry near Versailles. And then—the police arrived."

Sylvie shuddered at the memory. "I thought I would die. I could hardly speak. They told me that Robert Drivaz had been stabbed—murdered. They asked me if I had made a phone call to Anne-Marie. Gradually, I realized that they weren't after Chantal. That they thought Anne-Marie had killed Robert. I just told them the truth—that is, I answered all their questions truthfully; but I knew . . all the time I knew. And Chantal herself . . . so cool and collected. Flirting with one of the gendarmes. It was—uncanny. Ever since then . . ." Sylvie seemed on the verge of breaking down completely, then pulled herself together again. "I told myself she couldn't have done the journey in the time—and then you pointed out that she could have—"

"You didn't think of checking on the mileage of the car?" Henry asked.

"Oh, Henry, I am just a silly woman. Of course I thought of it, but I had no idea what the figure had been when Chantal took the car. Then the case came up, and the evidence against Anne-Marie seemed so strong. When Jane gave her evidence, that made it sure. You'll never know how relieved I was. And then—"

"And then I came along and stirred up all your doubts again," said Henry.

"Yes. Oh, forgive me, Henry—but I hated you for it. And now—" She gave a hopeless sigh. "Now, all is over. I know it. Chantal killed Robert, and I can't cover up for her any longer. Oh, my little Chantal. . . ."

Sylvie had just buried her face in her hands again, when there was suddenly the sound of the front door being flung open and slammed. And in the open doorway of the sitting room stood Chantal, her eyes glittering, her face so distorted with fury that she looked demented. But her voice was steady and ice cold, as she said, "Very touching, Sylvie. Not a dry eye in the house. I could almost believe it myself, if I didn't know it was a pack of Goddamned lies!"

Chantal had changed out of her bikini and into a sort of flowing black robe, with scarlet embroidery and big bell sleeves. It was because of these sleeves that it took me a moment to realize that she was holding a small, businesslike revolver in her right hand.

16 ♛

"*Chantal!*" *The word came out of Sylvie's mouth as a sort of* scream, and she jumped to her feet.

Chantal made a small, decisive movement with the gun. She said, "Sit down, Sylvie. And keep quiet, or you'll get hurt."

Sylvie subsided into her chair, dabbing at her eyes. Pierre Claudet, in a fine mixture of the paternal and the ministerial, said, "Now, Chantal, my dear. I know you are overwrought. Why don't you lie down and . . . take a pill. One of the ones you like so much, eh? Have a nice quiet sleep and . . . now, my dear, mind what you're doing with that gun. It could be dangerous. Chantal!"

"And you, you fat slob," said Chantal. "Don't think that I'd hesitate to kill you, because I wouldn't. Sit where you are and put your hands on the table."

Claudet had gone as white as dough. Without another word he laid his well-manicured hands on the dark, polished table. The diamond in his gold signet ring glinted in the afternoon sunshine.

I sat still, rigid and terrified. If this was what Henry had intended to provoke, I could only hope that he had also considered how to get us out of it.

Henry himself appeared perfectly and maddeningly at ease. He smiled and said, "Hello, Chantal. Nice to see you."

Keeping her gun trained on the Claudets, Chantal said, more rationally, "I was listening. From the balcony outside."

"I know," said Henry.

"You couldn't have known."

"All right. I deduced that you would. I'm not always as silly as you think."

She almost smiled at that, then became fierce again. "Did you believe what she said?" Chantal indicated Sylvie by a slight gesture of the gun.

"I must believe it, mustn't I?" said Henry.

"What does that mean?"

"All the evidence goes to substantiate Mme. Claudet's account of what happened."

At this, Chantal's unfocused attention swung back to Sylvie with ferocious concentration. "You filthy bitch," she screamed. "You thought of everything, didn't you? Everything except this."

Henry was on her so fast that it was only afterward that I realized it had been a deliberate ploy of his to arouse Chantal's fury against Sylvie, and that he must have started moving the instant Chantal's gaze was off his face. As the gun came up, Henry's fingers were around Chantal's wrist, wrenching it upward, and the bullet thudded into the wooden ceiling. Sylvie jumped up, screaming, as Pierre Claudet sprang to help Henry. Chantal fought like a spitfire, scratching and biting, but she had no chance. Within a minute or two Henry had the gun and Claudet had immobilized Chantal efficiently, with both her arms pinioned behind her back.

Sylvie said, "Oh, it's all so horrible. I can't bear it. I'm going—"

"No!" said Henry, and it was as decisive as the shot had been. There was dead silence, and then he went on, "I'm sorry, Chantal, but the gun was dangerous." He picked it up, broke it, and extracted the five remaining bullets, which fell with deadly softness into his hand. "There. That's better. Now we can sit down and discuss this matter quietly. Please let Chantal go, M. Claudet."

"But—"

"I said, 'Let her go.' " Henry's voice carried such quiet authority that Claudet did as he was told. Then he went back to the table and sat down beside Sylvie, taking one of her hands protectively in both his. Chantal rubbed her wrists in a marked manner and glared at us all. Henry went on, "Please sit down, Chantal."

"I'd rather stand."

"As you please. What I want to hear now is your version of what really happened."

My dream on the train came flooding back to me. "What really happened, Chantal?" And, as in the dream, Chantal replied, "Oh, you are silly."

"You said just now," said Henry, "that Mme. Claudet's account was all lies. That's not true, is it?"

"Of course it is!"

"No." Henry spoke sharply. "Mme. Claudet's account was substantially correct. Otherwise you wouldn't have broken in here, threatening us with a loaded gun."

"She was lying!"

"You were one of the girls at Frivolités, weren't you?" said Henry. "You don't deny that?"

"That has nothing to do with—"

"Right. The point is established. We can go on. You were one of the girls, and Mario was one of the boys, and you recognized each other when you met at the Chalet Perce-neige. Correct so far?"

Again Chantal said nothing. Henry went on, "Robert Drivaz knew all this, having been told by someone in the Veron household. And so, when he came to Paris, he called on you with the idea of blackmailing you."

"No!" shouted Chantal.

"No? Then perhaps you will tell us your version, as I suggested."

"It was her!" Chantal pointed a white, accusing finger at Sylvie; in her flowing black robe, she looked like a witch designating her victim. "If Robert Drivaz blackmailed anybody, it was her!"

"How do you know?" Henry asked quietly. Sylvie had gone very pale, and was twisting her handkerchief between her fingers.

"Well, I know he went to her apartment, because I met him coming out one day as I was going in, and he looked very pleased with himself. And now, if she tells you he was blackmailing me—where would she have got the idea, unless it was from personal experience?"

Sylvie said, "Oh, Henry, please be . . . please understand. Chantal is hysterical. She doesn't know what she is saying. What on earth could Robert Drivaz have blackmailed me about?"

"Frivolités!" shouted Chantal.

"But, Chantal dear, it was I who took you away from there. It was I who had the place closed down."

"I wonder," said Chantal with an ugly sneer.

"You wonder," put in Claudet icily, "but you do not know. So far, M. Tibbett has the choice between your wild accusations and Sylvie's proven facts. Go on."

"On the day before the murder," said Chantal, "Sylvie told me she had to go all day to this conference, and asked me if I wouldn't like to borrow the car."

"Oh, Chantal," Sylvie protested, "you know that's not true. You begged to be allowed to—"

"She told me," Chantal went on unsteadily, "to bring the car back and come in for a drink that evening—but not before ten, as she wouldn't be home. And that's what I did—and then the gendarmes arrived—"

"Oh, Henry," said Sylvie softly, "don't you see? My poor Chantal—she is utterly confused and not responsible for what she does. Can't you understand how I tried to protect her, even when I felt sure of the truth? And now her poor demented brain spins around and accuses *me* . . ."

"Chantal," said Henry, "did you happen to notice the car that was parked outside the chalet? The one Emmy and I hired in Geneva."

"The blue Volkswagen?" Chantal was offhand, uninterested. "What about it?"

"You don't recognize it?"

"Why should I?"

"Of course she recognizes it!" Sylvie burst out. "She knows very well it's the one she hired that day—"

"Are you crazy?" Chantal demanded.

Henry said, "No, Chantal. Mme. Claudet is not crazy. You have put up a good fight, but facts are facts."

"What facts?" Chantal demanded.

"I have proof," Henry said, "that that particular car was hired by Mlle. Chantal Villeneuve from Geneva Airport on the afternoon of April 14, and returned on the same evening, with the distance to and from Montarraz on the clock. With the other evidence we have just heard, I don't think any court would hesitate to decide that it was you, and not Anne-Marie, whom Jane Weston saw going into the Drivaz chalet just before five o'clock. There seems to be—"

Chantal was moving slowly toward Sylvie. Suddenly she threw back her head and let out an unearthly scream of hysterical laughter. "So *that's* it! *That's* how it was done! Oh, very clever! Brilliant!" She swung to face Henry. "The perfect frame-up—and she might have got away with it, if I hadn't nearly hit that lorry outside Versailles!"

In a small voice Sylvie said, "What do you mean, Chantal?"

Chantal was still talking to Henry. "I missed the lorry, but there happened to be a gendarme around, and he asked to see my license. I looked in my bag, where I generally keep it—but it wasn't there. Neither was my passport. I know I'm scatterbrained, so I thought I'd simply left it in another handbag. Anyhow, the gendarme told me to bring it to a police station within three days. Well, when I got home that night, after being at Sylvie's apartment, I searched everywhere, but I couldn't find it. And the next day—wonder of wonders!—there it was, with my passport, in my handbag all the time. Well, I didn't give it a thought—just imagined I hadn't looked properly after the accident. But now . . . don't you see, she pinched my passport and my driving license, used them for hiring the car, and slipped them back into my bag during the evening!"

"Don't be ridiculous, Chantal," said Claudet. "Sylvie is more than twice your age. She couldn't have traveled on your passport."

"She didn't, stupid! She traveled on her own—but she produced mine for the car-hire people! The young photograph on the license wouldn't surprise them—I've seen Sylvie's own, and it was taken when she wasn't much older than I am now—and the car people don't look at the passport photo; they just compare signatures! If I hadn't happened to need my license that day . . ."

Henry said, "It would be interesting, Mme. Claudet, to know how you came to know that it was a blue Volkswagen which was hired that day. I don't think the fact had been mentioned."

"Well . . . you implied . . ." Sylvie was thoroughly confused.

"And another thing. As I understand it, when Chantal was here in the winter, Jane packed up her work at half-past four. However, you had been here more recently, and knew that she went on until five. Whoever impersonated Anne-Marie had planned it carefully, to make sure that Jane Weston saw her. So if it had been Chantal, she would have arrived before half-past four. She had plenty of time, after all—the whole day to get here. Whereas you were in the conference till noon."

"That doesn't mean—"

"In any case, Mme. Claudet," Henry went on, "Jane Weston recognized you—in spite of the blue overall and the umbrella."

"You're lying! She swore in court that it was Anne-Marie—"

"Ah, yes. At that time, it never occurred to her that it could have been anybody else. But once I had shown her that it might have been, she thought back—and she remembered. She has known for some time, and she has been very unhappy about it, because you have been so kind to her. Not, perhaps, for entirely altruistic motives."

Suddenly Sylvie became calm. She leaned back in her chair and almost smiled. She said, "Prove it."

Chantal was shouting again. "I don't need to prove it! I've got a better weapon against you, Sylvie. You thought I'd never use it, because I loved you—and I did love you, but I don't any longer, so I'm going straight from here to the dirtiest scandal sheet I can find, and I'm going to tell them the whole story about Frivolités and Pierre Claudet and—"

Sylvie was on her feet, two bright red spots burning on her cheeks, her eyes blazing.

"You little bitch! You wouldn't dare—"

"I wish I'd done it years ago." Chantal was suddenly deadly quiet. "I held my tongue because I loved you and I thought you loved me."

"But I do, Chantal!"

"Your whole life has been one great confidence trick for the last six years, hasn't it? Not a shred of truth in it anywhere. No wonder you had to kill Robert Drivaz—he didn't have any emotional inhibitions. He'd have sold his story to the highest bidder, and good luck to him."

Suddenly a change came over Sylvie's face—a sudden shaft of comprehension, turning to pure hatred. She whispered, "It was *you* who told him! It wasn't Mario or Giselle or Michel. It was *you*. . . ."

Chantal laughed, full in her face. "Of course it was me. I told him! I told him everything!"

"And made me into a murderer! My God, it may have been me who stabbed him, but it was you who killed him! Well, you can take the consequences. They say it's easier the second time—"

Claudet, who was looking utterly dazed, tried to stop her, but he was too late. Sylvie was at Chantal's throat, scratching and clawing. It was unbelievably horrible—not just the obscenity of two women fighting physically, but the terrible transformation of Sylvie from a charming sophisticate to . . . to her real self.

Henry was on his feet at once. He shouted to me, "Emmy! Police!" and launched himself onto the two struggling, kicking bodies. I pulled myself together and ran out of the open door to the telephone in the hall.

The duty officer at the gendarmerie had a slow, deliberate voice with a pronounced regional accent. My idea had been just to report an emergency at Les Sapins, and ask for a police car to be sent at once, but I was not allowed to get away with anything so simple. The name of the chalet had to be spelled out, letter by letter, and a detailed description given of how to get there. Then the officer demanded to know what the emergency was.

What could I say? "There's a fight going on. . . ."

"Ah. Had a bit too much to drink, I expect."

"No. Not that. Please hurry."

"Now, now, not so fast, madame. There are certain formalities—"

"For God's sake, this is a matter of life and death!"

In other circumstances, I would have felt sorry for the gendarme. Apart from the Drivaz affair, which had been handled from Charonne, the most that the local police had to cope with was the regulation of traffic during the high season, the clearing of snow from the roads, and the occasional drunken punch-up at the Café de la Source. Obviously, my call had been pigeonholed among the last category.

"Don't you worry, madame." The officer's voice was infuriatingly unruffled. "We'll be along in no time. They'll soon sober up, I promise you." He laughed ponderously, and rang off.

It was then that I became aware of the curious silence in the sitting room. Whatever had happened, the fight was over. I did not know what to expect when I went back through the open door.

Whatever else, I certainly had not expected to find the scene of apparent normality which confronted me. The two antagonists had been separated, and now sat on opposite sides of the table again. Chantal was flushed, tense, and breathing deeply; but Sylvie had been miraculously transformed back into her usual self. She must have become disheveled in the fight, because she was now studying her face intently in a small mirror from her handbag, combing the odd errant strand of hair back into place. She looked more at ease than either of the men.

Henry glanced up as I came in, and said, "Come and sit down, Emmy. No, leave the door open. Now, Chantal—please go on."

"Well," said Chantal, "when Sylvie first went to work there, she thought it was just an ordinary shop. Or so she says. Actually, I believe her. Most of the *vendeuses* came in all innocence, and some of them even stayed that way. But not Sylvie." Chantal spoke with pulsating excitement, the unburdening of a lifetime of secrets. She took a deep breath and went on. "Sylvie found out what was going on, soon enough. Oh, very fast. And then she found me. She also found out what most people didn't know—the name of the man behind the whole thing. Pierre Claudet."

I had to look at Pierre and Sylvie. They seemed curiously unmoved, like people listening to a familiar gramophone record.

"So what did she do?" Henry prompted.

"Well . . ." Chantal hesitated. "I think perhaps she really was interested in getting the place closed—not for any normal reason, but because of me. To have me to herself, you see. However, she also decided that it would be a good thing to marry Pierre Claudet —his first wife had recently been killed. So she didn't do anything so crude as to confront him with what she knew about Frivolités. Oh, no. She made friends with a young man called Jacques Lamaire, who was Pierre's private secretary. She told him that she had enough evidence to make a big scandal over Frivolités. She advised him to tell Pierre that he might as well cash in and get the credit for exposing the place, because if he didn't, somebody else would. Well, that suited Pierre. He'd only run the racket because he needed money—lots of it—and the first Mme. Claudet kept too close a hold on the purse strings. Now, she was dead and he had inherited. Frivolités was a positive embarrassment—he wanted to be rid of it, and the best way of keeping his own nose clean was to report it to the authorities himself—keeping himself carefully out of it, of course. Creating the mystery man who was never caught."

Pierre Claudet held out his hand to Sylvie, who took it. It was somehow moving to see them, middle-aged and defeated, in the face of Chantal's young hatred.

"Go on," said Henry.

"Well, it's obvious, isn't it?" said Chantal with a sneer. "Pierre Claudet was established as a knight in shining armor. But he had put himself in a position where he could never risk the truth coming out. So Sylvie—whom he had not met before—scraped an introduction and then brought out the blackmail. He must marry her, or else . . ."

"That's not true!" Sylvie burst out.

"Isn't it? How odd. If it's not true, why did you have to kill Robert Drivaz to shut his mouth? He came to you in Paris, didn't he? He threatened to sell the story to a newspaper, unless you paid him. So you agreed to pay, you said you would come down here with the money. But it wasn't the money you came with, was it, Sylvie? It was a neat plan for framing Anne-Marie. And if anything went wrong with that, you had a second line of defense. Me. If Anne-Marie didn't kill Robert, then Chantal Villeneuve did. Go on. Deny it if you can!"

There was a moment of absolute quiet. Then Sylvie said, "I don't deny it. I just say—prove it."

"But—"

Sylvie leaned forward and fixed her eyes on Chantal. "You," she said, "are a poor, perverted, warped child. Not your fault, of course. Forced into prostitution . . . oh, I have ample proof. You are also a habitual drug addict. Here, this afternoon, you lost control of yourself completely. You began by threatening us all with a loaded gun. You then attacked me physically. The police had to be called." Sylvie nodded briefly at me. "You made wild accusations against me which Henry and Emmy overheard—but of course I shall deny that there was any truth in them. Perhaps I made a few injudicious remarks in the heat of the moment. Henry and Emmy may repeat them. Do you think that your word and theirs would stand up against the testimony of Pierre Claudet, against the documentary evidence that it was you who hired the car? The word of a drug addict against the word of a cabinet minister? My poor, silly Chantal. I can hardly wait for the police to arrive."

I sat there as though mesmerized, listening to Sylvie's quiet, measured voice. It was like a nightmare, because everything she said was true. Against the immense weight of Claudet's position and influence, against the documentary proof against Chantal, against the fact that I had telephoned the police, babbling about a fight—against all this, whoever was going to quash the case against Anne-Marie and open proceedings against Sylvie Claudet? I heard the screech of brakes as the police car drew up melodramatically outside the chalet, and my heart sank, in anticipation of the humiliation to come.

Through the window, I saw the two local gendarmes plodding noisily up the path to the chalet in their solid black boots. And then there were quiet voices in the hall—and I sat there goggling, because not two but three men came into the room. The pair of police officers from Montarraz—and a third man. Inspector Colliet of the Geneva police. He nodded briefly at Henry.

"Afternoon, Tibbett. Nice to see you again."

"You got it all?"

"Every word." He laughed. "You may be too much of a gentleman to use a tape recorder, as Veron remarked, but he never thought of anything so simple as a live policeman taking notes through the open door of the spare bedroom." He grinned at Henry, and then turned to Claudet. "M. Claudet, I shall have to ask your wife and yourself to accompany me to the police station. There are certain matters which require further investigation. . . ."

The Claudets went to the police station, protesting loudly about calling their own lawyers and the French consul in Geneva. Chantal, dry-eyed after a bout of hysterical weeping, was collected by Giselle—who was strangely gentle with her—and driven back to the unhappy splendors of the Chalet Perce-neige. The September evening grew chilly, and Henry fetched wood and coal, and lit Herbert. Then he came back to the sitting room and opened a bottle of Jane's wine.

"I don't think Jane would mind," he said. "I think we deserve a drink."

"So it was Colliet you telephoned from the airport," I said.

"That's right. I had to have an independent witness. Luckily I caught him at home, and he agreed to drive up right away. He got the key from Lucia and installed himself in the spare bedroom while we were still at the Chalet Perce-neige."

"You might have told me," I said.

"I didn't dare." Henry grinned at me. "You're too honest, you might have given the game away. I told him on the telephone to make himself known to Jane, and to explain that you didn't know he was there and mustn't be told."

"Hence your mysterious remarks to Jane about unexpected visitors."

"That's right."

"So he was here all the time we were having our lunch—and when I tried to telephone Jane from Perce-neige."

"Of course. But he obviously couldn't answer the phone."

"And what will happen now?" I asked.

Henry sighed. "The wretched part," he said. "Colliet certainly has enough against Sylvie Claudet to get a conviction—but . . . well, influence is influence. We can but see. The important thing is that the case against Anne-Marie can't possibly stand, in view of what has happened today. What's more, Pierre Claudet has settled a handsome sum of money on her."

"And Chantal—what will happen to her?"

"Don't ask me—I've no idea."

"How much of what she said was true?"

"I suppose we'll never know," Henry said. "My personal view is that it was all true—with the exception of the bit about Sylvie having blackmailed Claudet into marrying her. I think she did . . . all that she did . . . in order to protect him. And herself, of course. Let's not get sentimental. But I think she really did want to shield him. I'm afraid his career's finished now."

"I'm not sorry," I said.

"He's an able man," said Henry. "There aren't so many about, you know."

I felt a great weight of depression on my shoulders. I said, "Henry . . . why is it that we always seem to be destroying people's lives? Everybody here was perfectly happy until we came along, and now look what we've done! Sylvie and Pierre and Chantal and—"

I was interrupted by the ringing of the telephone. I glanced at Henry.

"You take it," he said.

"Emmy? This is Jane. I'm speaking from the hospital. The baby's arrived. It's a boy—the most beautiful baby you ever saw. Yes, Anne-Marie's fine . . . well, as far as her health is concerned. But when I think that they're going to take the baby away from her . . . that she has to go back to that ghastly convent . . ." Jane's voice trailed away.

I said, "It's all right, Jane. Jane, are you listening to me? Go and tell Anne-Marie that it's all right. Henry's done it. He's cleared her name, and she'll have enough money and be able to keep the baby and leave the convent. . . . Oh, Jane, go quickly and tell her that it's all right. . . ."

I admit I was near tears when I put down the telephone. Then I was aware of Henry beside me, and his arm around my shoulders. He said, "You see? We don't always make people miserable, do we? What did Jane say?"

"Nothing." I could hear the wonder in my own voice. "She didn't ask any questions at all. She couldn't wait to get back to Anne-Marie and the baby. . . ."

"Jane," said Henry, "has her priorities right, don't you think?"

JANE

EPILOGUE ♛

Well, it's all over. The last packing case has been nailed down and roped, the last suitcase packed. Anne-Marie has scrubbed out the kitchen of Les Sapins for the last time, and she and I are waiting in the empty sitting room for the removal van to come for the furniture, and the taxi for us. Little Henri is sleeping in his carry-cot, as good as gold and as plump and pink as a rosebud.

I shall miss Montarraz. I shall miss the Bertrands, and M. Bienne, and Mlle. Simonet, and my other good friends in the village. To be honest, I shall also miss the occasional slap-up evening at the Chalet Perce-neige. But obviously Anne-Marie could not stay here, and she begged me to go with her. I couldn't have refused, even if I had wanted to.

The Claudets' apartment has new tenants now—a fat, jolly banker from Brussels and his small, vivacious wife. Pierre Claudet resigned his government post, of course—you must have read about it; but Sylvie will never stand trial. I don't pretend to understand exactly how it was managed, but money and influence are extraordinarily powerful.

As far as I could make out from Giselle, Sylvie made a full confession but claimed that her mind was unhinged at the time. She even produced a private diary which she kept during the Tibbetts' last visit, which her lawyers claimed proved that she was hysterical, out of touch with reality, and crazily trying to pin the murder on Chantal. Crazily? I wonder. Anyhow, she was backed up by a battery of high-powered psychiatrists, who pronounced her mentally unfit to stand trial, and she has entered an extremely expensive private nursing home for psychiatric treatment. As long as she stays there, the law will take no further action. On the other hand, if she leaves the clinic . . . Well, it sounds like a life sentence to me.

I finished Giselle's head a few weeks ago, and she seems pleased with it. I'm not. I know it could have been much better, if I had tackled it in a more tranquil frame of mind. I refused to take any money for it, so Giselle insisted on sending a big check to Anne-Marie instead.

Anne-Marie. She and little Henri are the really important people in this story. As soon as Sylvie had made her formal confession, Anne-Marie was granted a free pardon, and told that she could keep her baby and leave the convent whenever she wanted to. Of course, the poor girl had no place to go—so, equally of course, I brought her to Les Sapins.

The baby was baptized Henri, after Henry Tibbett, and I am his godmother. Michel Veron and Henry Tibbett are the godfathers—but Henry could not get over here for the ceremony, so M. Bertrand stood proxy for him. The widow Drivaz not only refused to come to the church service, but wouldn't as much as set eyes on her grandson. Confession or no confession, she will never forgive Anne-Marie, or believe in her innocence.

After the christening, Anne-Marie and I sat down to talk about the future. Our roles were curiously reversed from those at our first meeting. Pierre Claudet had settled a handsome sum of money on Anne-Marie, and she also had Giselle's check. She was now the person with the money, and I could only promise to contribute my small pension and whatever I could make from my work.

Fortunately, Anne-Marie was never in any doubt about what she wanted to do. Apparently, ever since her spell of work at the Café de la Source, she had dreamed of owning a small restaurant of her own one day. Now, she had enough money for the initial capital investment—but she also had the baby, she was young and inexperienced and no businesswoman. She needed somebody older to help her.

So that's how it is that Anne-Marie and I are leaving Montarraz today to open up our establishment in the village of Mallières on the other side of the valley. Mallières is still a tiny place—we were able to buy a pretty little café with good living accommodation at quite a reasonable price—but big things are in the air. Next year, the new *télécabine* will be open, and there are plans for two new hotels and a development of private chalets. We think we are very lucky to be getting in on the ground floor of what promises to become a fashionable new ski resort.

We've had the café completely redecorated and modernized, of course, but we've tried to keep its cozy alpine atmosphere. Anne-Marie will be the *patronne,* naturally, but she will wait on the clients herself—at least until we get onto our feet. I will have a studio alongside the restaurant, but of course I'll help in the bar as well as looking after the business side of things and being a more or less permanent baby-sitter. We've engaged a professional chef, and we are looking for a girl to help in the kitchen. Perhaps the good Sisters from the convent will be able to send us somebody.

So, if you plan to spend a winter holiday in Mallières, do come to us for a meal. Oh, I nearly forgot to tell you the name of the restaurant. Chez Henry. I protested at first that it should have been Chez Henri, but Anne-Marie smiled and said very firmly that it was to be Henry with a *y.* And I think she is right.